# ONE TRUE WORD

'A fabulous premise and a dark female protagonist... A lovely slice of icy winter chill'

SERVER

'A strange haunting tale'

LY MAIL

'As the narrative delves into the history of the couple's relationship, fascinating psychological portraits of them both emerge... Original and intriguing'

*LITERARY REVIEW*

'So gripping I simply couldn't put it down. An atmospheric and original story with an ending I did not see coming'

EVA BJÖRG ÆGISDÓTTIR,
AUTHOR OF *THE CREAK ON THE STAIRS*

'A truly unusual crime novel which kept me reading until the very end. Highly enjoyable'

KATRÍN JAKOBSDÓTTIR, FORMER ICELANDIC PRIME MINISTER
AND AUTHOR OF *REYKJAVIK: A CRIME STORY*

'Well-crafted, very intriguing, and the end is a brilliant surprise'

★★★★ OF 5, *MORGUNBLAÐIÐ*

'A psychological thriller that delves into the soul and mind of the protagonist'

*THRILLERNORD*

'Hypnotic and disturbing'

*SOLOLIBRI*

'Brilliant, compelling and breathtaking'

*CONVENTIONALE*

SNÆBJÖRN ARNGRÍMSSON is an Icelandic author, translator and publisher. After penning three mystery stories for children, which won multiple awards, he turned his hand to writing for adults. *One True Word* is his first thriller and was inspired by a terrifying night spent trapped on an uninhabited island during a storm. It became a No.1 bestseller in Iceland.

LARISSA KYZER is a writer and prizewinning Icelandic to English literary translator whose work has been supported by cultural institutions in Iceland, the US, and Europe. For more: www.larissakyzer.com

Snæbjörn Arngrimsson

# ONE TRUE WORD

TRANSLATED FROM THE ICELANDIC
BY LARISSA KYZER

Pushkin Press
Somerset House, Strand
London WC2R 1LA

EITT SATT ORÐ


Published by agreement with Copenhagen Literary Agency ApS, Copenhagen



*One True Word* was first published as *Eitt satt orð* by Bjartur in Reykjavík, 2022

First published by Pushkin Press in 2025
This edition published in 2025

ISBN 13: 978-1-80533-504-7



This book has been translated with financial support from:

A CIP catalogue record for this title is available from the British Library

The authorised representative in the EEA is
eucomply OÜ, Pärnu mnt. 139b-14, 11317, Tallinn, Estonia,
hello@eucompliancepartner.com, +33757690241

Designed and typeset by Tetragon, London
Printed and bound in the United Kingdom by Clays Ltd, Elcograf S.p.A.

Pushkin Press is committed to a sustainable future for our business, our readers and our planet. This book is made from paper from forests that support responsible forestry.

www.pushkinpress.com

1 3 5 7 9 8 6 4 2

# ONE TRUE WORD

# 1

Is this what it's like to be dead?

That was my first thought when I opened my eyes that morning.

Everything was black.

No light, no sound, no smell.

Just a dark and odourless silence.

I was pretty sure I'd opened my eyes, but it didn't make any difference. I was still enveloped in the same deep darkness as before. I closed my eyes again. Lay still for a moment and then opened them wide. The same darkness. I was completely disoriented. It wasn't just that I didn't know whether I was still alive, I also had no idea where—or who—I was.

My name had forsaken me.

At first, this filled me with more fear than distress—I wasn't sure how I was supposed to react to such a state of mind. And what could an imagined death be called, if not a state of mind? The fear felt like a powerful electrical current had sliced right through the middle of my body, paralysed me, left me breathless.

It wasn't until I pulled myself together, sat up in bed and shook myself out of my drowsy stupor that the light went on in my mind and my name returned to me.

I sighed, relieved.

Júlía, I said to myself. My name is Júlía.

I reached behind me, and my hand smacked into the soft headboard. I pictured it in my mind—grey upholstery with grey buttons that had been sewn onto it in orderly, diagonal lines.

I was hot.

With my other hand, I flung off the thick duvet, fumbled on the nightstand for the remote control for the blinds and pushed the button.

The motor buzzed softly in the morning stillness and snatches of light trickled through the floor-to-ceiling windows as the blinds drew up at a sedate pace.

Outside, it was quiet. The day had not yet begun.

That's how I woke up that morning: a bit dazed and—hard as it may be for me to admit it now—pretty anxious, too.

My head was pounding.

I hadn't slept well.

# 2

This is a fateful morning, I thought.

It came to me suddenly, the idea that's always slumbering in my subconscious and pops up whenever I discover just how unpredictable this world is: everything can change in an instant. The thing that shouldn't have been able to happen, happened. The world had turned upside down and I wasn't prepared for it.

Gíó—my husband—was not in bed beside me. This fact had followed me into my restless sleep, woven itself into my dreams, and filled me with a terrified foreboding because I realized he could be alive, or dead, or somewhere in between.

Alive or dead?

Was this my new reality?

Strange how shocking it can be when the unexpected occurs. We know that our lives stand on shaky ground, depend on caprice, luck, misfortune and strange coincidences. And still, we're caught unawares.

I threw myself out of bed. The minute I stood up, I could feel how bad a night I'd spent. My head was splitting, and I stumbled into the bathroom to splash cold water on my face. A weary-looking woman gazed at me from the mirror over the sink, her eyes filled with resignation and hopelessness. 'Stop feeling sorry for yourself,' I said out loud to my reflection.

I grabbed my grey robe from its hook on the bedroom door, wrapped it around me and padded out of the bedroom.

Although it was still dark, I didn't turn on any lights, just slowly made my way down the stairs in the dim morning light.

I looked out the living room window. Outside, an autumnal tree stood in the garden. The birds were singing with the voices of autumn. I could hear a car honking on the street. The driver was probably blocked in, because he was laying on the horn. Soon, it would be winter.

A scrap of paper was lying on the windowsill. I picked it up and saw that at some point, long ago, I'd written a single sentence on it. The letters were faint, faded from the sun, and I could hardly make them out. I'd used a pencil, written lightly, like I wanted to be sure I could erase the words. 'Together they went to sow the same field.'

There was comfort in the line.

An empty wine bottle stood in the middle of the coffee table and next to it, a glass with dregs of red wine in the bottom. The light from the living room window was shining through the green glass of the bottle. I gawped, walked over to the table and lifted it up to the light, trying to convince myself it really was empty.

Did I drink the entire bottle when I came home yesterday?

No, I couldn't have.

There was no way I'd had more than one glass.

There was no way I'd had the whole bottle without realizing it. But it was empty, that much was certain. I couldn't make sense of it.

I ran through the events of the previous day as I went to make coffee. I'd opened the bottle of red wine in the kitchen when I got home from my trip down to the harbour. It had been late, and I was exhausted.

# 3

I was exhausted.

That much I remembered.

I was shaking with anxiety, and in my haste, I almost destroyed the cork with the corkscrew. Then I'd taken the bottle into the living room, poured myself a glass and put it on the table… Yes, I'd only had one glass before going to bed.

I didn't remember anything else.

I shook my head at myself.

How could the bottle be empty?

Gíó and I had taken a trip to Hvalfjörður earlier that afternoon. I'd accepted a commission from a textbook publisher to write about a few female heroes in the Icelandic sagas. Among these remarkable women was Helga Haraldsdóttir, the daughter of a jarl, who'd swum the 1,600 metres from Geirshólmur, an islet deep at the base of Hvalfjörður, to a place on the shoreline called Helguvík. This act of heroism not only saved her own life but also those of her two young sons.

I'd more or less forced Gíó to come with me. I wanted to sail out to Geirshólmur and had made the necessary arrangements.

A farmer with whom I was friendly had lent me an inflatable boat—a ramshackle dinghy with a feeble outboard motor. I'd borrowed it from him once before. But I don't have much experience sailing, so I'd asked Gíó to come with. He clearly wanted nothing to do with the expedition, though, and said, among any number of other excuses, that he didn't have the time.

In the end, he'd decided to join me, but he dragged his feet for the better part of the day. I'd started to wonder if we should postpone the outing because it was already so late. Night would be falling soon—I'd seen that sunset would be around six—and I didn't want to sail out into the middle of a fjord in pitch darkness. There'd be no point.

'Shouldn't we get a move on before it gets too dark?' I'd asked.

Gíó hummed and hawed and sat a bit longer in his office, tapping away at his computer before getting to his feet and starting to put on his outdoor gear and shoes.

'All right then, shall we?' he said tiredly. He was standing in the front hall, ready to go out with his black hair tucked behind his ears and an aggrieved look on his face.

Gíó was an attractive man: tall, straight-backed, broad-shouldered and muscular. He was an aikidoka.

Something had clearly been weighing on Gíó, and he was surly because I'd been so pushy about him coming. Maybe he thought the project was boring and that there was no reason for me to mix him up in this fool's errand. I was having a hard time reading him.

'What's the point of sailing out to some rock in the middle of a fjord, just because you're writing about this woman?' he asked, failing to hide the displeasure in his voice. 'What are you going to do, exactly? Repeat her swim?'

'No, Gíó, I'm not going to swim. Relax, would you? I just think it will give my writing more heft if I visit the island in person. I get a better feel for what I'm writing about if I can see the setting with my own eyes. It'll make the piece more vibrant, more interesting.'

'Then you ought to swim, too,' said Gíó. 'C'mon, get in there—be a real journalist.'

'Ugh, Gíó, stop sulking like a child. I'm no journalist. I just thought we could go on a nice Sunday drive. I didn't realize it was going to be such a big deal for you to spend a few hours of your weekend helping me out. Do you have somewhere better to be?'

'I think you're blowing this project out of proportion… There's no reason to spend so much time on it. The pay isn't that great, especially not if you've got to wrangle assistants to get it done. The farmer with the boat called me this morning. Me! Why'd you give him my number?'

So it went that chilly October day when we started out for Geirshólmur.

I was having a hard time making my peace with Gíó's behaviour. He was usually fun, a straight talker. He could turn the most mundane events into an interesting anecdote. He eventually turned everything into a story, although not necessarily a funny one. Rather, he was able to build an engrossing world around everyday incidents. Gíó was a born storyteller.

I'd felt on edge around him the past few days. I wasn't sure what was going on with him, and I had good reason to suspect he had some mysterious secret hanging over him. I'd grown suspicious of his every action and explanation.

Gíó had always been guarded in his manner—what you might call closed off—without ever giving the impression that he was hiding something. He'd played it close to his chest for as long as I'd known him.

# 4

The farmer told me the boat would be beached right next to the Miðsandur pier. I could just take it out and bring it back to the same place when I was done. He'd come and get it later. No problem.

Gíó and I drove along the fjord in silence, him behind the wheel and me in the passenger seat. He'd been jumpy the whole drive. Flipped the windscreen wipers on and off, even though we hadn't had a single drop of rain. Turned on the radio, switched stations, switched stations, switched stations, then turned it off again.

At one point, in the middle of the drive, he stopped the car—pulled over to the side of the road and laid his head on the steering wheel. His shaggy hair fell forward, covering his face. I looked at him, not saying a word.

'What's wrong?' I asked finally.

'Nothing,' he said.

'Nothing? That's obviously not true. You can't just suddenly pull over, bury your face, and say that everything's fine. Something's the matter, Gíó. Can't you just tell me what's…' But I didn't manage to finish the sentence because he interrupted me.

'Everything's just so awful,' he said softly. He was talking more to himself than me. 'Reality is exhausting, it's utterly unbearable… and then you come to find out that reality is exhausted by *you*, too—and has been, for a very long time,' he said, smiling a strange, grim smile that I'd never seen on his face before.

It scared me.

'Seriously, Gíó—what is wrong?'

He put his head back down on the steering wheel and made no move to answer.

I tried to understand what he was getting at. He never talked like this. I had a feeling it had something to do with the unsettling discovery I'd made last weekend. I tried to quash the lurid images that suddenly popped into my head, but they burst through all the same. I'd been agonizing over it, and I knew I had to talk to him. I had to have an explanation, or I'd lose my mind.

'If there's something on your mind, just tell me,' I said simply.

But Gíó didn't answer. After another moment, he sat up, scratched his head and stared thoughtfully out the window. For a second, I thought he was going to make some sort of confession, but he just glanced in the wing mirror, flicked on the indicator and pulled away onto the road without a word.

He grabbed a half-full bottle of Coke from between the seats, unscrewed the cap and took a sip. Then he wedged the bottle between his legs.

We drove the rest of the way to Miðsandur in silence. There, he turned onto a gravel road right before the old oil pier that stretches into the fjord.

Pebbles from the road clacked against the undercarriage as Gíó sped along the loose gravel at full speed, pulling off when we reached the shoreline.

The orange rubber boat was moored to a heavy boulder, exactly where the farmer said it would be.

Looking at the sad little vessel, I was suddenly of two minds about our expedition. It was a lot flimsier than I remembered.

'It's not exactly a yacht, is it?' said Gíó as we inspected it. He kicked half-heartedly at the bulging rubber and gave a rueful sigh. 'We're taking this old tub over to the island?'

'It's only a few minutes' sail. It's a bit choppy, but not too bad. There's nothing to worry about,' I said, trying to sound upbeat. 'Let's just get going before it's dark.'

We had no trouble getting the boat into the water, as it was extremely light and the motor very small. We sailed out into the fjord, towards the islet of Geirshólmur. The sea was a metallic grey and looked heavy as liquid lead.

It was a calm day. The ominous black clouds dozing over the surrounding mountains could have easily struck fear into the heart of any inexperienced seafarer, but the easterly wind was so light I wasn't particularly concerned by the gathering storm. It would only be a short trip.

On our approach, we sailed all the way around Geirshólmur, a grassy scarp rising abruptly out of the fjord, to find the best place to land and make our ascent.

We tethered the boat to a jagged outcrop with a thin rope.

'Let's keep the motor running,' I said to Gíó before jumping ashore. 'Just let it idle while we're on the island. We won't be long. It can be such a pain to get it started.'

We climbed the path leading up the steep slope and I was surprised to find that the island was practically furry—covered in tall, green grass even though it was late autumn. Gíó walked ahead with one hand in his trouser pocket and the other holding the Coke. He took a seat on a grassy bank and looked around without interest.

'You need to be a little more independent, gutsier,' he said out of nowhere, without looking at me. As if he'd just come to this conclusion. He fiddled with the bottle cap, screwing and unscrewing it in turn.

'What do you mean?'

'You can't fend for yourself. You need help with everything. Even these little, nothing projects.'

'Must you keep going on about this? That's not true. I don't need help. At all. I fend for myself all the time. And I make my own decisions about what projects I'm going to take on, regardless of how mundane they might seem to you. Seriously, what is wrong with you? I just thought it would be nice for you to get out into the countryside for a little while, take a break from all the pseudonature of the city, spend some time with me.'

Gíó didn't answer, rather lay down and closed his eyes. 'Pseudonature?' he scoffed.

I shook my head and started picking my way down the slope, thinking about a trip we'd taken to a different island off the coast of Italy just before we'd moved to Iceland.

When I turned and looked towards the whaling station tucked at the base of Mount Þyrill, I saw that Gíó was still lying on his back. His eyes were still closed. I walked over to him, stood looking down as the wind rustled his hair so that now it hid part of his face, now it didn't. He was lying with his mouth half open, and I could see his nostril hair. He pretended not to notice me. That was the spark. Anger flared inside me, and I made a snap decision. Let *him* fend for himself for once.

I strode purposefully down the sloping path, clambered into the boat, unknotted the rope and motored away.

I'd sailed about twenty metres when I looked back and saw that Gíó had got to his feet. He was standing at the highest point of the island, his back ramrod straight and muscular after years of training. He watched in silence as I sailed towards the shore.

# 5

Gíó's always thought of himself as a man who understands the secrets that hide deep in other people's psyches. That's one of the stories he tells about himself.

And maybe he was right about that, but probably not.

Who can truly comprehend another person's psyche?

Who can even comprehend their own?

I, for one, lacked the insight to penetrate all the creases, crumples and tangles of my own psyche and discern the enormous turmoil that had been seething inside me all week. I hardly registered anything beyond the faintest vibrations within me, an unsettledness that I didn't give a second thought to. I acted like everything was fine. But eventually, the embers became so incandescent they ignited, with these disastrous consequences.

I didn't look back again, rather sailed the straightest line back to land. Dragged the boat ashore, got in the car and drove towards home.

I was furious. Boiling over. I burned. A devastating fire raged inside me.

The sky was darkening, the road was empty, and I didn't encounter any other cars as I raced along, not until I reached the crossroad where Hvalfjarðarvegur met Route 1, the Ring Road.

I didn't hesitate as I turned towards Reykjavík. My mind swirled with thoughts of Gíó, of me and Gíó.

Was I really going to leave him out there to fend for himself, to rescue himself from that barren rock?

No one on the road would see him out there, and certainly not now that it'd started getting dark.

How long could he survive in this cold, with no food and no water?

He didn't even have his phone—it was lying in the console between the seats. Without thinking, I grabbed it and put it in my bag. The car hurtled along, and I'd gone down into Hvalfjörður tunnel and up out of it again before I shook myself out of my reverie and realized where I was.

I pulled over and killed the engine. He *should* have to huddle out there on that rock until it got good and dark. He *deserved* to be a little scared, to have to deal with the reality he hated so much.

I sat there for a few minutes, felt my anger well up inside me. But little by little, as the fire within me subsided, doubts took over and I started to worry.

What if he tried to swim to land like the jarl's daughter? He wasn't a particularly keen swimmer. Could he manage it? He was probably no worse a swimmer than Helga Haraldsdóttir, and he was stronger. But did he have her grit?

In an instant, I decided to turn around. There was no time to lose.

The headlights illuminated the Ring Road, but the surrounding mountains were shrouded in darkness. I sped up, but the traffic on the narrow, single-lane road was unusually heavy and slow. I was getting nowhere fast, and trying to overtake was hopeless, because the oncoming traffic was just as bad.

My anxiety was getting worse by the second; suddenly, I was out of my mind with despair. I pictured Gíó trying to paddle to shore, fighting to keep his head above water in the choppy sea. There was no way he'd make it.

But no. He wouldn't resort to swimming. He probably didn't have the guts.

What had I done? What was I thinking, leaving my husband alone on a deserted island for so long?

I had to get back to him before he did something stupid.

It wasn't until I turned off the Ring Road and back onto Hvalfjarðarvegur that I could put my foot down and drive at full tilt along the little-travelled country road. I accelerated, driving so fast I was afraid I wouldn't be able to keep the car on the road.

It started to rain. Leaden drops fell from the heavens.

I white-knuckled the steering wheel and leant closer to the windscreen.

The high beams created a cone of light, tunnelling through the darkness that was rapidly descending, settling its full weight on the land. There wasn't a soul to be seen. If it hadn't been for the flickering lights in the windows of the few farms dotting the mountainside, you could easily have thought the area deserted.

I could feel the seconds ticking by, the minutes, but it was still so far to Miðsandur. Hvalfjörður is such a long fjord.

Onwards I raced, the car careening over uneven patches of road, and when I finally made it to the pier, I could make out the shape of the boat in the darkness. The rubber boat was still tied up where I'd left it.

I got out of the car. The wind was sharp now and it was raining steadily. I squared my shoulders and strode into the wind, towards the dark mass of the boat on the shore. It was impossible to see the island, no matter how hard I peered into the darkness. I rushed to push off the boat and sailed back towards Geirshólmur, which the night seemed to have swallowed whole. But after a short sail across turbulent waters, I saw it cresting out of the sea like a black shadow. The little motor shrieked as I pushed it as hard as it would go. The boat hopped on the waves, and it was a struggle to keep from falling out.

I approached the island from the north, slowed down and strained to see through the darkness and rain. There was no sign of life—nothing moved, nothing stirred at all except for the grass bending in the wind.

Gíó was nowhere to be seen.

Maybe he was lying down. Maybe he was hidden by the grass. I called out for him.

'Gíó!'

No answer. I could feel my voice being snatched away by the wind, swept across the barren landscape. No one could hear me. I shouted again at the top of my lungs.

'Gíó! Hey!… Gíó!'

But still, there was no answer. I sailed around to where we'd moored earlier in the day. I tied the boat to a crag, walked up the path, onto the grassy mound, and looked around.

I was completely alone.

I ran down the slope to the eastern side of the island, but there was no Gíó; he was nowhere to be seen.

He couldn't be hiding from me, could he? There was nowhere to hide on this little island, no shelter. And why would he hide?

What on earth could have become of him?

I scrambled up a hillock and looked all around. No two ways about it—there was no one here. There was no one on this little island but me.

'Gíó!' I screamed. 'Gíó!'

Again, my cry was carried away by the wind.

I looked towards the shore. I saw nothing.

There wasn't much water traffic in the area, as the fjord is sparsely populated, and the only place to dock is along the whalers' pier or the oil pier. Few people pleasure sail in Hvalfjörður, and it was very unlikely that someone had rescued him by boat. Wasn't it?

I'd heard tell of shadow ships gliding back and forth along the fjord at dusk or in the dead of night. The farmer said he'd often seen the comings and goings of the shadow ships in the moonlight. I had no idea what a shadow ship was. Could you hitch a ride on one? Was Gíó aboard one now? Where did they come from, these ships, and where were they going? But no, shadow ships were just an old folk tale. Weren't they?

He wouldn't have risked swimming, would he?

No, he wouldn't have. Not unless he was certain he'd reach the shore. Right?

It didn't matter how long I stood on that island, turning the situation over in my mind. Gíó obviously wasn't there any more. That was the reality and I found myself heartily agreeing with what he'd said earlier: reality can be utterly unbearable.

There was no one on this island but me. Gíó wasn't here. He'd vanished.

# 6

There was no question that I was alone, but I still ran a few despairing circuits around Geirshólmur before getting back in the boat and sailing swiftly towards land. I scanned all around for Gíó, zigged and zagged, circled back and hopped across the waves in the direction I thought he might have gone if he tried to swim. Even though the waves were neither high nor particularly powerful, I myself would have never even considered swimming across those murky, agitated depths. Surrounded by all that darkness.

It was well into evening now and it had been completely dark for some time. The rain had dissipated and was now hanging over the fjord like a filmy veil. There was almost zero visibility, but I sailed back and forth, over and over, my eyes boring into the pitch-black sea. I didn't see anyone in the water. No shadow ship on its night-time sail.

In the end, I gave up, pulled the boat ashore and tied it to the same boulder it had been tethered to before.

Then I walked along the beach towards the whaling station, shouting as loudly as I could: 'Gíó!'

No answer.

Not a sound other than the heavy waves and wailing wind.

I knew there was a cluster of old Nissen huts on the other side of the road. Tidy, corrugated-iron structures with arched frames and a scattering of little windows along the sides. There was definitely no one living there now, but I knew the huts had been built as barracks for the Allied soldiers who were stationed on the fjord during the Second World War. I had no idea what they were used for now—maybe bunks for the whaling station employees or workshops to repair old whaling gear. But if Gíó actually had swum across the fjord and come ashore soaking wet, that was the most likely place for him to go in search of shelter and help.

It took me close to ten minutes to tramp down the shore, across the road and up to the barracks. I jogged up the wide gravel road that ran between them, panting and calling for Gíó.

Some of the huts had lamps above the doors, and the weak shafts of light cast a ghostly glow on their windowless facades. There was all sorts of junk piled next to the buildings: barrels, pallets and stacks of timber that cast long shadows and lent an even eerier feel to the silence.

It was so dark between the huts that I could hardly see more than five steps on either side, and it took all my courage to keep inching deeper into the blackness. I felt like I was completely alone in the world. It was a ghost town.

I fumbled between the huts in the dark, opening doors and knocking on each one I found locked. There was no one there. The silence was heavy, oppressive. I was afraid of attracting the attention of anyone who might be hiding out here in the middle of nowhere.

I was suddenly afraid that something would leap from the darkness, clasp me tightly in its sharp claws, bite my neck and suck my blood. Maybe that's exactly what I deserved after the terrible thing I had done.

But I pushed aside my fears, braced myself against a wall where a hanging lamp cast a faint smudge of light and shouted over and over for Gíó as loud as I possibly could.

But it was the same as before.

My cries dissolved in the wind. I held my breath, listened. At first, the only thing I could hear was the hum of silence, but then, a sound in the distance, an answer to my call. I yelled again, shouted as loud as I could, and again, I heard a strange noise from the darkness. Was it a cry of distress?

Not daring to breathe, I went towards the sound. Again, the same pitiful howl. The shadows cast by a jumble of tall, dusty machinery reminded me of a creature in a sci-fi novel.

I'd taken a few steps along the row of huts when I saw some movement ahead of me. My heart skipped a beat, and I leant back against the wall. After a moment's hesitation, I decided to chase whatever had just rounded the corner.

I could still hear the wretched keening, and I had no doubt about where it was coming from now. It was a deep sound, a sort of moaning. I ventured into the shadow cast by the huts, peeked around the corner. There, in a dark recess, stood a fat and woolly black sheep with savage horns. It gave me a cockeyed stare, an evil gleam in its eyes.

Sheltered behind its big, fleecy belly were two snow-white lambs, both ready to bolt.

I backed away, worried the belligerent mother would attack and stab me with her menacing horns. I retreated to the gravel path.

I continued my search around the rest of the huts, calling out and knocking on doors until I was drained, hopeless and exhausted.

It was pointless, I admitted to myself before heading back the way I'd come. Every so often, I stopped to look over my shoulder in the hope I'd see some movement or sign of life.

There was no one here but a bedraggled family of sheep that was no longer bleating.

I'd made my way back to the gravel road when I saw a car driving at some speed down the path between two of the huts, headed in the direction of Hvalfjarðarvegur. I ran after it, waving my arms in a frenzy. But the car drove on, and it was clear the driver either hadn't seen me or had decided to ignore me and continue on their way.

# 7

So that's why Gíó wasn't lying next to me that morning. He'd vanished and I didn't know if he was alive or dead.

We are born, we grow and evolve, we accumulate what we can in this life—knowledge, talent, joy, food, time, affection, grudges—and then we go. Vanish. And when the people you love vanish, life seems pretty meaningless.

Alive or dead? And if Gíó was alive, what did he intend to do? Start a new life? Avenge himself, make me pay for my malice? Isn't that what love—that is, unrequited love—calls for? Malice, lies and rampant hatred? Yes: alive or dead?

I once thought I'd seen Elvis Presley, the King of Rock and Roll.

I was young and living in southern Italy, in a little town just north of Bari called Molfetta.

The summers there are scorching.

Elvis was thought to be dead when we met, was said to have died decades before.

I put it like that because not everyone believes Elvis really died when they said he did. A rather large number of people, in fact, think that he's still among the living. That he has a new life, maybe a better life—a life where he's no longer the King of Rock and Roll, but rather footloose and fancy free, far away from the spotlight of fame.

And yet.

I found myself thinking about those who are still alive though they've been declared dead, and those who are dead, though people think they're alive.

Wandering restlessly around the house that fateful morning, I stopped to look out the living room window again.

I was surprised it was still morning. Would it never end?

I took the brisk progress of the rain clouds across the sky as confirmation that time was not standing still. Seconds ticked by, a dark grey cloud obscured the sun, a shadow fell across my face.

An autumnal tree stood in the garden.

Blood rushed through my veins with a deep roar, and my small, delicate heart was beating in my breast like a frightened baby bird's.

He wasn't coming back.

Gíó? The sea must be cold in the autumn, mustn't it, or does it still hold summer's warmth?

Gíó, you'll die if you try to do as Helga, the jarl's daughter, did.

Gíó, you'll drown and die.

Don't drown, don't die.

# 8

I mentioned that I woke alone in my bed after a restless night. For years—I no longer remember how many—Gíó has almost invariably been lying on my right every morning I've woken up in the bedroom of the little house we share.

But not that morning.

Gíó's often told me that I overrate my own strength, that I miscalculate the consequences of my actions, that I don't learn from my mistakes and thereby both make my life harder than it needs to be and get myself—and him—into unnecessary trouble.

When he says this, I always act like he's right.

But I'll admit I couldn't sleep when I realized that he wouldn't be coming home that night.

I regretted what I'd done. Sorely regretted it.

I'd thought about calling the police, but I was afraid they'd charge me with a crime, and I couldn't see what good that would do Gíó. So I decided to wait. Maybe that was stupid.

I'd abandoned my husband on a deserted island. That in itself could hardly be a crime, could it?

After much thought, I concluded that I could get the police to help me figure out what happened to Gíó and to look into his disappearance without casting suspicion on myself. I could probably steer their investigation the direction I wanted it to go.

But it was still much too early to get the police involved; I was tired.

I kept pacing. Now and again, I paused in my rambling, stood by the window, closed my eyes, and let time pass. I tried to focus on figuring out what would be the best thing to do, the right thing to do in this moment.

What was right?

What was expected of me in this situation?

Finally, I reached a conclusion: I'd call Gíó.

I reached for my phone, called his number, and listened to the ringtone.

Beep… beep… beep… beep… beep… beep…

No answer.

I let a few minutes pass and called again.

Still no answer.

I did this several times. It would have surprised me to hear Gíó's voice on the other end of the line. It would have made my heart flip-flop, because I knew for a fact that his phone was lying on the bottom of the ocean. Where the only ones to wonder at its ringing would be the fish who'd strayed from the depths of the open sea to an unsightly wharf in the south-western corner of Iceland.

# 9

See, the previous night, after it all happened, I'd sneaked out under cover of darkness. It was just before midnight on Sunday.

Gíó had vanished, and if he was gone for good, I didn't intend to bear the blame for his disappearance.

You get what you want, just not in the way you think, my mum always said.

It gradually dawned on me that this turn of events on Geirshólmur wasn't particularly fortuitous—not for me, certainly, and even less so for Gíó—and so I began to take steps to avoid being suspected of attempted murder or gross negligence. I had to be careful about phones—I'd read that phones are the criminal's greatest enemy. Which is not to say that I'm some kind of criminal. But I wanted to get rid of Gíó's phone, which I'd put in my bag on my way out of Hvalfjörður.

After I was pretty sure that most of my neighbours had gone to bed, I crept out to my car with Gíó's phone in my handbag. My own phone I left in our bed, hidden under my pillow. That seemed like a good idea.

Outside, it was pouring.

The rain fell in sheets from the coal-black night sky. There were deep puddles everywhere—on the pavement, the road—and the air was cold and humid. The streets appeared to be deserted, not a living soul to be seen and no lights in any of the windows.

People go to bed early around here.

I was sure I was being totally silent and that the drumming rain would drown out any noise I happened to make. I was positive no one would see me; I was practically invisible as I crept stealthily towards my car.

The banger I drive was parked towards the end of the street and cowering like a kicked dog.

Raindrops on the car roof glinted in the light from the lamp post on the corner, but other than that, the old rust bucket was cloaked in darkness.

I got in and closed the door softly behind me. The cold from the driver's seat seeped through my rain-soaked trousers and coursed through me. I'd managed to get soaked and frozen through on the short walk from my door to the car. The interior was clammy and unpleasant. I sighed. My breath came out in a cloud and mist curled from my wet clothes.

I was a human steam engine.

It's in wretched moments like this—because it truly was a wretched moment—that I often find myself beset by a kind of helplessness, something akin to paralysis—so I sat there for a long time, watching as fog clouded the windows of the car.

I knew I needed to get going, but I wasn't capable of doing anything but sitting and staring, yawning and shuddering. My thoughts were as foggy as my breath, the condensation on the windows getting thicker by the moment. Gradually, the world outside disappeared, and I found myself tucked away inside a cottony cloud.

Just as I'd managed to gather my thoughts and was about to start the car, I heard footsteps approaching and a man and woman bickering.

I heard the voice of an older man speaking softly: 'Is someone in that car?'

No answer.

The footsteps fell silent, and I could feel four eyes—at least—staring at the car.

I held my breath and sat completely still, careful not to move a muscle. I sat like a statue and pricked up my ears. Would they yank the door open to see if anyone was sleeping in the old wreck?

'I can't see in. There's so much dew on the windows,' said a woman's voice. She sounded old.

'Dew?' snorted the man. 'That isn't dew, you can't call that *dew* on the windows. That's condensation...'

'All right, *condensation*, then, if it makes so much of a difference... Let's go, why don't we? I'm dissolving in this rain. I'm soaked to the bone,' said the old woman.

'Pfft,' said the man faintly and then whispered: 'Someone might be in there... There's either someone in that car, maybe asleep, or else someone just got out.' There was an obstinacy in the man's voice.

'And what exactly does it have to do with you, even if there is a person in that car? Let's go, come on... It's none of your business. There's not the slightest reason for you to stick your nose in,' she scolded.

I heard their footsteps fading in the distance, and I rolled down the side window a crack, the better to see the cantankerous couple. I watched them walk down the street, still nattering as they skirted deep mud puddles, dragging a rain-drenched dog behind them. The man, who was wearing a waterlogged cap on his head, was holding an umbrella over them both.

Their soppy hound padded after them.

# 10

It wasn't until the old couple with the dog had rounded the corner and I'd wiped clean the windscreen with the arm of my jacket that I turned the key in the ignition and started the car.

I felt my whole body tense as the engine rumbled to life with an ear-splitting squeal.

'God, what a racket this wreck makes,' I muttered as I shifted into gear and pulled into the street.

There was no question in my mind as to where I should go. It was a twenty-minute drive south to the town of Hafnarfjörður and I set off quickly.

Traffic was light. Rain continued cascading from the heavens and the wipers struggled to sweep the deluge from the windscreen long enough for me to see the road.

Suðurgata.

Miklabraut.

Kringlumýrarbraut.

Hafnarfjarðarvegur.

Strandgata.

And then I turned onto Óseyrarbraut, into the industrial neighbourhood around Suðurhöfn, the South Harbour.

No one had any business being here in the middle of the night.

A few cars drove by on Strandgata, but no one took the same route as me. No other driver turned onto Óseyrarbraut.

The wind moaned. Lighting on the street was minimal, just the occasional lamp dotting the walls of the tumbledown buildings and casting their dim yellow glow on the slovenly surroundings. I reduced my speed. There were warehouses along the road, giant industrial buildings, rows of tall, steel tanks, and all sorts of rusty machinery languishing in the most unlikely places—in a dyke, upside down in an old shipping container… Some of the industrial buildings looked abandoned—dilapidated, their windows smashed out, of no use to anyone.

It was what you'd call a real wasteland.

It gave me the creeps.

There wasn't a soul to be seen, no cars nor late-night pedestrians, and the wind howled like a wounded wolf.

I had to get out of there as quickly as possible. But first, there was something I needed to do.

Óseyri Harbour, where misery moors, I thought, and drove on.

I had decided to survive. And it was for that exact reason that I'd come to this sinister place all by myself in the middle of the night. My excursion to this abject quay was part of my own, personal rescue mission, an attempt to save my own life.

# 11

There must have been something tentative or inept about my driving, because suddenly a flashing blue light illuminated the darkness behind me. I looked in the rear-view mirror to see a police motorcycle racing towards me.

It was as if the motorcycle and its rider had just sprouted from the earth. Only seconds before, this place had been entirely devoid of human life—nothing but pouring rain, howling wind, tumble-down buildings and rusting junk. But now, I had this supercharged, bike-riding policeman on my heels.

I slowed down even more and a dozen thoughts flitted through my head before I pulled over and stopped the car.

I brushed my fringe out of my eyes and tried put on a genial expression. But I was sure nothing could fully hide the frustration and anxiety that I knew was written all over my face.

The motorcycle pulled up alongside me. The glow of the flashing blue light lent an even more mournful ambiance to the surroundings. Long shadows and flickers of blue.

The uniformed man took his sweet time dismounting. He carefully removed his gloves and laid them on the seat of the bike with great precision, as if trying to protect it from the rain.

He walked around to the front of my car and then behind it. I watched in the rear-view mirror as he used a tiny pencil to write down the registration number in a black pocket notebook that he hunched over to shield from the downpour. A thought: is this my fall? Rather poetically worded, I thought. As if I were a statue atop a high pedestal poised to topple to the ground.

The policeman milled around the car some more as if inspecting its condition and then stopped next to the driver's-side door. He was wearing a ring with a black stone on his ring finger, and he used it like a knocker on my window.

'Open the window. All the way,' he commanded.

I obeyed. A head in a dripping wet white helmet thrust itself through the aperture.

The policeman's red, rain-spattered face was far from friendly. Maybe he was peeved about being sent out to patrol in this godforsaken part of town in the middle of the night in this lunatic weather. He was quite chubby-cheeked, the policeman, and his cheeks bulged like a chipmunk's. His eyes were small and malicious.

He shoved his whole helmeted head through the window and peered behind me to see if anyone else was with me. I looked over my shoulder, too, to check what was in the back seat. Nothing. Then he looked me dead in the eye, his whole head still in the car. If I didn't know better, I'd say he was sniffing me. I saw his nostrils flaring slightly.

'Are you... smelling me?' I asked. Maybe that was unduly hostile.

The policeman shot me an angry look but didn't answer. It seemed like years passed before he finally said something.

This guardian of the peace also knew the power of silence, I thought.

'Is this your car?' he finally asked. His voice was unusually thick and came from deep in his throat. It was like he hadn't managed to swallow his last bite of food. Maybe he had something lodged down there?

'My car...? Yeah, um...' I cleared my throat on his behalf.

I suddenly remembered that the vehicle was registered in Gíó's name. I felt my heart hammering in my chest. What rotten luck to have crossed paths with this buffoon. But nervous as I was, I still managed a convincing response: 'Yes, you could say it's mine. That is, when does a person own a car and when don't they?'

I was on the verge of adding: 'Mister Officer.' It somehow felt right in this place, far removed from other people. I felt like a courteous and solemn form of address would act as a counterbalance to the decaying wasteland around us. 'Yes, this is my vehicle, Mister Officer,' had a nice ring to it.

'Where are you coming from?' he asked drily—before I'd even finished answering his last question. I hadn't got the chance to tack on the 'Mister Officer' bit.

'From home…' I started.

'From home?' he interrupted. 'You drove all the way from home?' He didn't attempt to conceal the sarcasm in his voice.

'Yes, well… I came from Reykjavík…' I'd expected him to parrot my words back at me, but he was silent. I didn't know if I was supposed to finish the sentence, so I just said the first thing that occurred to me: '… our fine metropolis, Mister Officer.'

He gave me a quizzical look, unsure if I was mocking him.

'Your licence, please?' He held out the hand with the ring on it.

It was like this man was incapable of listening—the police academy hadn't done its duty in that respect. No, the police academy hadn't successfully trained this dull and scowling officer of the law. Knowing how to listen is an important part of a policeman's job. But this policeman wasn't paying the slightest attention to what I was saying. Instead, he just dug words from the depths of his throat, flung them from the gap between his lips, and interrupted me.

The beady-eyed man's mouth was so close to my cheek that when he spoke, I could feel the sound waves on my face, or maybe not precisely sound waves, but rather the air that had squeezed out of his lungs and through his vibrating vocal cords such that I could make out minute barometric changes on his jowls.

I found his proximity downright loathsome and was suddenly afraid he'd stick out his meaty, rain-sodden tongue and lick my cheek. I squirmed in my seat and tried to inch away from him.

Again, he hurled his next question before I'd managed to fully answer the preceding one.

'You do have a valid driver's licence, don't you?'

I fumbled for my wallet and pawed through it. Instead of watching to see if I'd produce a valid licence, he withdrew from the window and put his policeman gloves back on. Maybe his hands were cold.

# 12

I fished my old licence out of my wallet.

I looked at the photo of myself for a moment, at that bright, young face. My expression was all lightness and joy. My eyes were shining and full of life, my mouth wide, and there was a shy smile playing at my lips.

Or no, a defiant smile.

The face in the photograph was spirited.

The face was full of self-confidence.

I was young and happy.

One thing's for sure: I know myself less well now than I did when that picture was taken. Maybe I'd never really matured, I thought. Or rather, maybe I'd got less mature as I'd got older. I did some mental maths. Fifteen years.

I speak fewer and fewer words.

I understand less and less.

These were the thoughts that darted through my head before I placed my pink licence on the black glove that was now extended in front of my nose. I smelt wet leather.

Now, to be clear: This policeman gave me the creeps. And while he was freeing the flashlight from his belt and pointing the light at my licence, I buried my face in my hands. I was breathing rapidly, and I tried to calm down. Slow my heart rate by gulping down air and exhaling slowly.

At first, the policeman didn't notice this new posture of mine because it took him quite a long time to locate the necessary information on my licence. He seemed reluctant. I didn't see if he jotted anything down with his little pencil.

But he seemed shocked when he looked back into the car and saw me covering my face like that, slumped over the steering wheel.

'Are you okay, ma'am?' he said with some alarm. 'Don't cry, this is just routine stop. Driving in an industrial area at night is both unusual and ill-advised...'

'Yes, yes, it's fine... I'm fine, I mean... I'm not crying. I'm just so tired of all this.' I let the last sentence sound as snappish as I felt.

He hesitated for a moment before turning on his heel, reaching over to the handlebars of his bike, grabbing the radio and saying something quietly into the mic.

It was almost a murmur, from deep in his throat again, and I couldn't make out what he was saying. He looked thoughtfully up at the sky while he waited for a response from the other end.

I also looked up but didn't see anything of note. Just a black sky and that heavy rain still falling from it. My mind was a shambles, and I stopped trying to hear what he was saying on the radio.

'Listen, ma'am...' I suddenly heard at quite close range. I looked up and saw that the policeman's chubby face was on its way back through the window.

'Where are you headed?'

'Nowhere in particular. I just wanted to get some sea air.'

'Are you okay?'

'Yes, I'm fine,' I answered immediately.

'Are you feeling poorly or...?'

I paused. Truth be told, I felt dreadful, but I had no need to confess that to this unnerving policeman and much less in these circumstances, with his helmeted head jammed through my window on the side of the road in the bleakest place I'd been in a long time. I'd never gone to confession, although there were many times it would have done me good, but this wasn't the sort of confessional I'd have chosen to unburden my heart. Nor was this policeman a desirable confessor. So, in the end, I just stammered:

'Listen, I… I just wanted to smell the sea air… I wasn't planning on drowning myself, if that's what you're worried about.'

'Yes, well now, uh…' He started scratching his throat, stretching his neck out and clawing at the skin, as if he had suddenly been hit by a terrible eczema flare-up.

When he finally stopped scratching himself, he looked back at me. If I didn't know better, I'd have said he looked almost tearful. 'You've no business here. This isn't a place for a woman in the middle of the night. I'm surprised you're here all alone.'

'Oh?'

'You live in Reykjavík?'

'Yes.'

'Do you have somewhere to sleep?'

The question caught me completely off guard, and at first, I thought he was laying a trap for me.

'Why do you ask?'

'You're not planning to drive around all night, are you?'

'No.'

He gave a smarmy smile, and I could see that he had an unusually large gap between his front teeth. Those beady little eyes in that big red face were extremely off-putting. 'I'd be very interested to know if you have a decent place to sleep.'

A chill went through me. Was he trying to scare me, or was that supposed to be some kind of joke? What did he want? I glanced at the policeman, and he gave me a look that spoke volumes. An inscrutable smirk twitched on his lips. I had no intention of sparring with this halfwit and pretended not to notice his suggestive glance. Instead, I gazed back at him quizzically.

'Well, I have a house with a bed and a pillow and a blanket, and that's where I'm going to sleep. No worries, Mister Officer,' I answered, giving him a jaunty salute.

He laughed.

'I want you to turn your car around and go back to Reykjavík. Find somewhere else to smell the sea air. This is no place for you, and by that, I mean a woman of your age. Perhaps you should stick to *our fine metropolis*, as you call it.'

I hastened to thank him for the tip and said I'd bear that in mind. I wanted to be free of this lawman as quickly as possible. I shifted into my best ready-to-drive pose.

He slowly withdrew his helmeted head from the window and stepped back.

I drove at a snail's pace, indicated, first to the right and then to the left, and made a show of turning the car around.

I watched in the rear-view mirror as the policeman got back on his motorcycle and sped down the road in the opposite direction, back the way he came.

The wharf was at the end of the road, and when I was sure the policeman was gone, I drove purposefully towards it and didn't stop until I reached the very edge.

I opened the door and leapt out of the car.

There was a sailboat docked at the wharf. It was swanky—clearly didn't belong in this hideous harbour. Its towering mast stood out against the sky. Everything sang and whistled in the gale and the piercing cold wind tore at me, buffeted me around, seeped into the very marrow of my bones.

I walked behind the car, digging for the phone I'd brought with me. The waves slopped loudly at the pilings. I stepped onto the edge of the wooden pier and looked briefly out at the ocean, sniffed the air and fished Gíó's phone out of my trouser pocket, pulled up the contacts and scrolled to the entry for STRONZO.

I typed out a quick text: BE THERE IN 30.

After a moment, I called the same number.

Beep… beep… beep.

It rang for a minute or so and then a brisk woman's voice sounded at the other end of the line: '*Haaaalló*… this is…'

I took the phone from my ear and looked at the screen in my palm for a moment. STRONZO was written right there in capital letters. I shuddered and flung the phone as far as I could, out into the ocean. It flew through the air and disappeared in the darkness.

# 13

Such were the previous night's adventures. I'm not ever going back to Óseyri Harbour in the dark—not so long as I have any say in the matter.

Standing by the living room window and staring at that lonely tree, that autumnal tree, I was dogged by memories of my night-time outing—the atmosphere, the darkness, the police officer, the space between his front teeth, the rusty machinery, the biting wind. And then another thought that overpowered all the others: What happened to Gíó?

It probably wouldn't be unnatural for me to call Gíó's office and check whether he'd come into work. I grabbed my phone, found the number and waited for someone to pick up.

I recognized the voice of the young girl who answered.

'Hi,' I said. 'This is Júlía, Gíó's wife. I can't seem to reach him on his phone. Can you tell me if he's happened to come in yet?'

'Gíó? Yes, hm, I haven't seen him… but… one moment,' she said. She set down the phone. In the background, I could hear music playing quietly and people talking. Then she came back on the line:

'So, Gíó's not actually coming in today. He called in sick.'

'Huh? He's not coming in, you say? He called in sick?'

'Yes… yes, I can't say for sure. But that's what someone wrote here on the notice board. Um, yes, it says: Gíó, out of office today.'

'Today? You mean, *today* today?'

'Yes.'

'And you're sure that was written today?'

'Positive. All the old messages are erased at night. And even if they weren't erased on Friday, the cleaning crew would have wiped it off over the weekend. Clean slate. *Tabula rasa.*'

'Right… who writes… uh, who writes the messages on the board?'

'It's usually me, but I'm not sure who wrote that exact message. Shall I check?'

'Yes, if it isn't too much trouble…'

'Just a moment, I'll ask.'

I could hear surprise in the girl's voice but could tell she didn't dare ask what was going on.

A long time passed before she came back to the phone.

'Listen, Júlia, uh… I don't know who wrote that message on the board. No one here seems to have taken it, but I can't ask everyone, and some people haven't come in yet and some are out… gone to meetings or something, you know. But should I… um… is something wrong?'

'No, no… it's fine. I just needed to ask him something, nothing major, but his phone's off… out of the service area, or something.'

'Okay… Should I tell him to call you if I… or… oh, no, right, he's not coming in today,' she said haltingly.

'Don't worry, I'll get hold of him somehow… bye now,' I said blithely.

I hung up, gobsmacked. Should I call the police? If not, when exactly should I get the authorities involved? It hadn't been that long since he disappeared, and after brief consideration, I decided to wait until I'd finished my morning project. I squared my shoulders and brushed aside the anxiety that was nipping at the edges of my consciousness.

I'd not lost hope that Gió was alive. Nor had I lost hope he'd come back to me. The hope blossomed within me but then vanished all too quickly again, a tiny sprout that peeked through the soil only to wither again.

# 14

The silence in the apartment was palpable. Nothing broke it: no clock ticking, no water dripping from the kitchen tap, no car barrelling by with a faulty exhaust pipe. I considered turning on the radio, but I couldn't imagine listening to all that empty chatter. I'd rather the silence. I opened the kitchen window to let in some fresh air and hoped the street noise would cut through the oppressive quiet.

I had an appointment at 10 a.m. on the dot that morning. It was time to buck up and pluck up.

I was glad I had something pressing to do and went back up to the bedroom to dress for my interview. I didn't do much in the way of primping, but I made an effort to look presentable.

I haven't had a real job in years. I've been working freelance instead. I mainly write articles and conduct interviews for daily papers and magazines, but I also work as an editor and proofreader for publishers. The projects have been fewer and farther between of late, as Gíó's pointed out to me. But thankfully, as far as I'm concerned, I've still got plenty to keep me busy.

I'd arranged to interview an author who was just about to publish a book of 'titillating tales', as she'd put it to me.

It was called *The Laboratory*—a good title for a collection of erotic stories, I thought. I'd been mulling over the title, and it had kindled all sorts of associations for me, both positive and negative. It had, at the very least, raised enough questions to build a conversation around.

The interview was going to be published in a popular new arts and culture magazine that I'd worked for before, and the author suggested we meet at her publisher's on the west side of town. There'd be a room there, she said, where we'd be able to chat.

# 15

I arrived at the office of a respected publisher in Vesturbær, on the west side of town, well ahead of the appointed time. I'd got so restless that I'd been orbiting from the living room to the kitchen and back again, unable to focus on anything. So I'd decided to walk instead of biding my time at home. But I'd expected the walk to take longer than it did, and I got there even earlier than I'd meant to.

A tall woman with conspicuous red acne all over her forehead greeted me when I entered, but she was altogether dubious when I told her I had an appointment with the author in question.

'Here?' she said, dumbfounded, as if never before, in the entire history of the company, had one of their authors ever conducted a meeting at their office. She glanced about her, as if looking for a co-worker to rescue her from the situation, which, as far as I was concerned, was innocuous enough. But we obviously saw the world through different eyes.

'Yes, here. At ten. I'm a bit early, perhaps,' I said, looking at my watch. It was ten to ten. I tried to relieve some of the tension by giving the girl an encouraging smile, but she was just as flustered as before. Her eyes wavered, and she didn't even have the nerve to look at me. I was suddenly positive I'd misunderstood my arrangement with the author. The meeting was probably supposed to take place somewhere else. Maybe at a different publisher altogether. At the very least, this girl didn't have the faintest clue what I was talking about.

'Maybe there's been a misunderstanding... um...' I started to apologize, but the young woman interrupted me.

'Wait here a moment,' she said and went through the door that separated the reception area from the offices.

All of the walls were lined with shelves filled with books, both old and new releases. In the gaps between titles, there were photographs of some of the publisher's authors. They gazed down at me with severe, mirthless expressions. Being an author was clearly a serious business.

'Books don't have to be *about* anything, they just have to lead their own lives,' read a placard hanging in the window.

I hadn't been waiting long when the door opened again and a middle-aged man entered the reception area, the acned young woman on his heels. He was wearing round, gold-rimmed glasses and had a goatee and yellowish hair that looked as dry and dead as Saharan sand. He had an unusual haircut, the sole purpose of which seemed to be to hide his ears.

He regarded me suspiciously, his expression just as severe as that of his authors.

'Good morning,' he said brusquely, as if he was anticipating trouble and wouldn't brook any objections from me. He clearly wanted me to explain myself, post-haste. 'What's your business here exactly?'

'I'm sorry, what kind of a welcome is this?' I asked pettishly.

'Wha—?' That took him by surprise.

I'd just launched into an explanation with no small amount of irritation when the front door swung open and a woman with a mass of curly blond hair attempted to shoulder her way in with great deal of fuss and groaning. She was carrying at least three chock-full, bulging, multicoloured cloth bags and was struggling to squeeze through the door with all her burdens.

She looked up and saw the three of us.

'Oh, hello, my dears, are you all here, then? Is everything all right?' She paused on the threshold and looked at us inquiringly, as if she were trying to read the situation she'd stumbled into. 'I'm not that late, am I?' She scanned the faces of her sullen welcoming committee. 'Hasn't it just gone ten?' she asked after a moment's pause.

None of us answered, just stood there open-mouthed and ineffectual, gaping at the woman's attempts to squeeze through the door. Eventually, she managed to kick it open a crack with a boot-clad foot and tumbled in. She set down her bags with sighs and oaths aplenty before giving us a sunny smile and combing aside the locks of hair that were hanging across her eyes like curly curtains with a swift and practised sweep of the hand.

I hurried over and introduced myself.

'Hello, I'm Júlía.'

'Delightful, lovely,' she answered breathlessly. 'I've been so looking forward to our chat. I've been preparing as if I were… hm, how should I say? As if I were about to take an important exam.'

She gazed at me like a besotted teenager, eagerly looking me up and down.

Her face was all aglow, and she clasped her hands in front of her as though she was about to recite a prayer, but instead, she turned to the publishing contingent, who were watching the proceedings open-mouthed and plainly baffled.

'Hiya,' she said amiably to the goateed man. 'How gorgeous you are, all come to welcome me, how lovely… Now: where can we two gals make ourselves comfortable and have a confab? As you know, there's going to be a big interview with me in that new arts and culture magazine… you know, oh what's-it-called… and our friend here,' she pointed at me, 'is going to write it. Isn't that just terrific?'

The billy goat with the gold-rimmed glasses looked at us uncomprehendingly. He'd yet to respond. It was clear he didn't recognize the author, and he had no idea who I was, and it took him a strangely long time to get a handle on the situation. But when it finally dawned on him who the curly-haired woman with all the luggage was, his eyes lit up and he leapt to her side.

'Welcome… Edda! Wonderful to see you… wonderful, wonderful. Are you moving house, dear?' he said with a smile, pointing to her bags on the floor.

'Ahh… ha ha ha, goodness me,' the author laughed liltingly. 'You might well think so. But no, this is all for the interview. One must be prepared. I've all sorts of data, source material… ha ha… Yes, I have a tactic, you see, an interview tactic.' She cast us another sunny smile as we looked at her expectantly. 'I'm going to dig into stuff that *no one* wants to talk about. The dark side of things. I'm going to talk about disease, death throes, disfigurement. I'm going to talk about dying and oblivion. About jealousy, indifference, disillusionment and lovelessness. Which is all to say that I'm going to disgust people—because that's when you know you're really telling the truth.'

We gaped at her, and I think the publisher must have broken out in a cold sweat because he stammered something about watching what you say around journalists, but then Edda interrupted him.

'Don't fret, now, I'm just joking. Of course I'm not going to talk about anything of the sort. I'm going to be charm personified. I'm going to talk about love and lust, about pricks and pussies… ha ha! But where can we get settled? We need a place where we can have total privacy, my loves. Total privacy. And I mean that: total and complete privacy,' she said and smiled at me, the receptionist and the publisher in turn.

'Come along with me, I've got just the place,' said the billy goat, clapping his hands as though he were suddenly brimming with energy and enthusiasm. He led us through a maze of narrow hallways, past little cubicles where people were busy at work, and into a spacious office that was almost entirely taken up by a giant circular and visibly flimsy conference table. The table was mounted on four feeble white aluminium legs that seemed on the verge of collapsing under the weight of the uncommonly large tabletop.

'You'll have plenty of space in here and no one will bother you. Make yourselves comfortable,' said the publisher, gesturing towards the table. Then he backed to the door, paused on the threshold and took his leave with a deep bow and ceremonial sweep of the hand, as though departing the company of royals.

# 16

'He's a bit of a ninny, but a good man,' whispered Edda as soon as the publisher had closed the door behind him. She moved as though to put her bags on the table, but after a brief consideration—I noticed her eyes flitting down to the table's spindly legs—placed her bags on the floor instead.

'Thank you for inviting me to do this interview. Lovely. I'm so pleased—honoured, as they say—ha ha ha. I've so much to tell you… We're going to have loads of fun.'

She rooted through her bags. Pulled out a book and laid it on the table.

*Anna Karenina* by Leo Tolstoy.

'*Anna Karenina*,' I said. 'Is it good?'

'A masterwork.'

I wrote 'Anna Karenina' on a piece of paper on the table in front of me. Then I circled it.

Though the novelist was interesting and spoke with great gusto, I realized early in our conversation that my mind was elsewhere. As such, I had trouble immersing myself in her protracted trains of thought about gender relations, storytelling and authorship. In the end, I had to cut her off.

'I'm so sorry, but I have to make a call before we continue. I'll be very quick, is that okay?' I said in the middle of her lecture about the soundscape of what she called 'crazy sex'.

I didn't wait for her response but took my phone out of my bag and walked over to a window that faced the street. I scrolled to Gíó's number and called it.

No one answered.

I noticed that one of the authors who was pictured in the reception area was running down the pavement across the street. She had rather poor form as a runner—bent at the waist, lopsided and knock-kneed—and the movement of her arms was completely out of sync with that of the rest of her body and her stride. I watched as she hurried through the door of the publisher. She was no athlete, that author, and she probably was no great shakes as a dancer, either. Looking at her photograph, I'd noticed that she had nice eyes, but who'd have thought her physical movements could be so asynchronous?

I thought about calling again but decided that one attempt to get in touch over the phone would do and returned to the interview.

I double-checked the recording device on the table in front of us to be absolutely sure it was working. Everything seemed to be in order. Then I looked up at the author of titillating tales to signal that I was once again ready to listen to her reflections on the auditory world of ecstatic lovers.

'Sorry for the interruption. Shall we continue? Is there anything you'd like to add to what you were talking about, or would you perhaps like to tell me a bit about where the book's title comes from?' I could feel that my heart wasn't really in this conversation of ours and congratulated myself internally for having brought the recorder. I'd never have been able to write anything of sense or remember a word she'd said.

'Why yes, I certainly would like to speak to how the title of the book came to be. *The Laboratory*...' She trailed off and then reached over the table and tapped on my notebook. 'Funny... or extraordinary, really... You've got a rather unusual notebook there... but... look...' She picked up one of her bags, laid it in her lap, and rifled through it before holding up a black notebook that looked just like the one I had in front of me.

'They are identical... i-den-ti-cal, look! Identical!' she said breathlessly as she placed her own notebook next to mine. There was so much enthusiasm and conviction twinkling in her eyes that she could have ignited a bonfire.

'Yes, they're exactly alike,' I said, looking at the notebooks in front of me. And indeed, they were the same size and were bound in the same black plastic material.

'Where did you get yours? These aren't your run-of-the-mill notebooks.'

I considered the book on the table in front of me, stroked it lightly with my fingertips and said, 'I don't remember where it came from, no... this... uh...'

I was having trouble focusing on what she was saying. It was as if my body was simultaneously numb and running all its systems at top speed. But all the while, I was trying to act like there was nothing wrong.

In my mind's eye, I pictured my outing in the rubber boat, remembered how the sea spluttered up into the bilge, how soaking wet I got, how cold, heard my shouts for Gíó through the keening wind and saw that wild-eyed sheep.

Could it be that Gíó had come home and was now tucked up under the duvet, warming away his chills?

It was like I had no control over my thoughts. I tried yet again to focus on what the author was saying but could not banish the events of the previous day from my mind.

'Sorry, I'm all over the place. My apologies, dear. I get like this sometimes, I can't help myself, but I'm a notebook junkie. So okay: I'm going to tell you something amusing—or intriguing, if you will.'

She fell silent for a moment and sat regarding me, as if to draw out the suspense. She made herself comfortable in her chair as though settling in for a long story.

'The inspiration for *The Laboratory*—my book, you know—was actually just such a notebook...' She fell silent once again and looked at me intently. '...A notebook I found unexpectedly on a bookshelf at home.'

'Oh, right,' I said, without really understanding where she was going with this.

She gave me a mischievous look and then said theatrically: 'I'll remind you that I specialize in erotica... spicy stories.'

She laughed merrily. She was so cheerful, this woman. Was she always so cheerful?

'Yes, right. Exciting,' I managed to reply.

'So—now we get to the meat of the matter—I found just such a *notisbok*,' and here she used the Danish word and made air quotes around it with both hands, 'on the shelf where I keep all my notebooks. It was like new, seemed entirely unused. At first, I thought it was mine, that I'd bought it somewhere and just stuck it, untouched, on the shelf. I love buying notebooks, I've got so many, and I always believe that if I have a notebook to hand—and a writing implement, of course (she giggled)—that I'll be able to put my life in better order. That life will become somehow more linear. I don't actually know why that's supposed to be preferable, but there's something calming about the thought of an orderly life. You know?'

'Ummhmm,' I hurried to mumble, although I still didn't really get where she was going.

'My life's about as orderly as a car graveyard... you know? It's just total chaos, everything upside down or on its side, as if a tornado's just blown through. But this notebook was large, unusually large, and wouldn't fit in my pocket or my handbag. Which… it surprised me, you know, just oh my God… because why would I have chosen to buy such a big notebook, it wasn't like me at all. But then when I opened it—because, you see, I'd decided to make a go of using it, even though it was terribly oversized—bigger is better, they say, ha ha—I saw it wasn't my notebook at all. Someone had written in it. Not on the first page, but rather on several pages in the very middle of the book. Yes, right in the very middle—a strange place to christen a new notebook. Yes, someone had written in the very middle with a pink ink pen. The handwriting wasn't mine, it didn't look like my handwriting at all, but I thought it had a feminine look to it… See? Here, I have the big book with me—the match that started the fire, ha ha ha.'

She gave a hearty laugh as she paged back and forth through the notebook and was quick to find what she was looking for. 'See the handwriting… pink pen… a feminine hand, don't you agree?' Then she turned the book so I could get a good look at the pink lettering. A moment later, she pulled it back to her and said: 'I'll read to you what I found written here. It's so inspiring, I think, especially because I've got no idea where the book came from. It just lit a fire within me, gave me so many ideas.'

She started reading:

> Breakfast at a café. Three men are sitting around a circular table and drinking coffee out of large mugs. One of them orders bacon and eggs.
>
> Hung between the mirrors on the wall are colourful pictures of outdoor cafés and attractive terraced houses.
>
> There's a newspaper on the table. On the front page is a picture of an MP and under the picture is the giant headline: WOULD YOU SLEEP WITH THIS MAN?

The descriptions of the man, who is variously referred to as The Shrimp or The Dwarf, are not flattering. The paper wants to turn it into a little game, put it to a vote. Would you like to sleep with this man? (Photo of the MP.) If yes, text 1234; if no, text 4321.

The next morning, when I sit down in the same café, there's a soggy copy of the paper in the newspaper rack and I can see the headline:

804 ICELANDERS WANT TO BED THE SHRIMP.

She finished her reading and looked up. There was an expression of delight on her face. She glowed as if the two of us had been witness to something truly magnificent.

I gave her a quizzical look.

'Yes, now: isn't that wild?' She tapped her index finger on the notebook a few times and then looked back at me. It was obvious from my face that I didn't understand what she was trying to tell me with this story. I was entirely clueless and wanted nothing more than to go home.

'Sure… that is strange…' I said finally.

'So, this was the inspiration for the first story in the book… you know, about the little, or sorry, the short gentleman with the laboratory… And after I wrote that first one, story after story just came to me, one after the other. I couldn't stop. It was an incredible feeling to just write like that… so unrestrainedly…'

# 17

What followed was a long recitation of how the mysterious entry had unleashed a mighty torrent of writing for the author. I felt myself fading again in the face of this long and detailed account and my mind wandered back to Gíó—what I should do, what I could do. I sat as though paralysed by the author's steady stream of chatter.

I tried to shove aside my seething thoughts and redirect my attention, but it was out of the question. I couldn't help myself. My thoughts fixated on the day that, much like the erotica author, I myself had found a notebook. In my case, however, it was a small notebook that could be stuck in your breast pocket—if you had a breast pocket, that is. It was almost like receiving an electric shock, this discovery, and it had an immeasurable impact on my life.

I found the notebook exactly a week before Gíó disappeared, and after I found it, I could hardly think about anything except what I'd read in its pages.

It was a pale red, ruled notebook, and its heavy cover was bound in a rough, scaly material. The paper was creamy yellow and rather thick. The book had unusually dense ruling—only the tiniest of letters would fit between the lines, which themselves had been printed in such a light shade of grey that I sensed rather than saw them. I'd dug the notebook out from under an ashtray in our kitchen one Sunday morning—that is, exactly one week before Gíó watched me sail away, stranding him on Geirshólmur.

The night before I found it, Saturday, we'd hosted one of the spontaneous gatherings we often had at our house. It was a fun party, most of which we spent in the kitchen. The morning after, I started the day by tidying up: collecting bottles and glasses, washing used cutlery and bowls.

Gíó was still asleep; he'd got very drunk the night before.

And there, in the midst of all the kitchen chaos, was this notebook. I picked it up and opened it to see what it was and figure out who it might belong to so I could return it.

I didn't have the faintest idea which of the guests could have forgotten it under an ashtray in the middle of the forest of bottles and glasses. I hadn't noticed any of our guests reading out from it or jotting anything down in its pages the night before. I turned to the first page, but there was no indication, as there often is in such books, as to who its owner was.

There'd been ten or twelve of us the night before and I knew all the guests fairly well.

Two things immediately jumped out at me as I continued to flip through the pages. Firstly, it was full of all kinds of sexual descriptions, that is, descriptions of intercourse. These were, on one hand, play-by-play outlines of planned sexual escapades between two parties, many-stepped instructions on how the couple should go about their business, and on the other, risqué accounts of recent encounters. Each entry went on at great length and was written in a particularly delicate and neat hand. The letters themselves were minuscule and beautifully drawn with a black, fine-tip ink pen.

What came as an even greater surprise—as is, perhaps, understandable—was that although only one of the two participants was ever named—and then, only by their first name—the author presented them like guest stars on a meticulously rendered stage.

The entries described, in great detail, the couplings of two individuals—never more. The scribe and owner of the book was presumably one of the participants in these rendezvous but again, they were never mentioned by name. Every chapter began by specifying the date and location of the tryst. Sometimes, it was a living room, kitchen, or balcony of a private home. A few times, the couplings took place in a holiday cottage, once in a greenhouse and once in the bed of a truck in a garage. The bedfellows varied from chapter to chapter. A few of the named appeared in more than one episode, but one woman—María—took part in more than ten assignations. I felt like I knew this woman intimately.

Here and there in the book, María was referred to by the nickname Stronzo. It seemed an odd choice to me, for a woman you have such a close relationship with. Stronzo is an Italian insult that means 'arsehole'. There had to be an explanation for it.

I couldn't be sure, of course, who any of the women were, because of the first-name-only policy. However, the first names of most of the female guests at our party the night before were among those used for the women in the notebook. Of course, some of the names didn't match with anyone I knew.

But the entries that evoked the most revulsion in me, and which I found almost unbearable to read, were those that described the couplings between the author and the woman named María.

My sister's name is María.

# 18

I was aware that the author was still talking, but I was preoccupied with my own thoughts about that unhappy notebook discovery. There was naturally no way for me to know if what was written in the red notebook was pure fantasy or accounts of real happenings.

And I tried, of course, to figure out which of the party guests from the night before could have left the book on our kitchen table. Who could have written all those smutty, graphic descriptions?

To my great horror, I immediately recognized something in the handwriting that reminded me of Gíó's, although I'd never seen him write so small or fussily. And regardless of any similarity, there was still something unfamiliar about the script, and nor was there anything that pointed to him in the details of the stories as far as I could tell. I'd never encountered that side of him. I doubted he'd be able to write anything like that, and furthermore, I found it incredibly unlikely that he'd have such a fervent interest in that aspect of gender relations that he'd spend considerable time and effort recording—at great length and in explicit detail—these passionate coital encounters.

There was also no way for me to be sure if the María who frequented the sexual fantasies in the notebook was my sister or some other María. But I couldn't help myself—I feared the worst and couldn't think of the notebook without picturing the two of them, Gíó and María, entwined in bestial lust.

For the last few years we'd been living together, Gíó had shown very little interest in sex. I'd wondered at how quickly he'd flagged, this handsome, strong specimen of a man. But maybe it was just me who'd stopped arousing his interest? Maybe he was brimming with sexual energy and writhing with desire but found the prospect of unleashing that energy with me unexciting. I'd never understood this limpness of his. And he'd never been able to explain it to me. 'Nature,' he said once, and that was a valid explanation.

I know that I myself am peculiar during sex. Namely, I have a tendency to start crying in the heat of the moment. It actually happens every time Gíó and I are together. Suddenly, tears will start running down my cheeks and although I try to stop and think of something happy, the tears keep coming until I'm full-on sobbing. For some reason, intimacy arouses an incomprehensible sorrow in me. I don't know that I can really call it unhappiness. It's a kind of missing. I miss happiness.

Gíó was taken aback by this every time, and I think he'd started to almost fear these sudden fits of weeping. In the beginning, he asked me what was wrong, asked if I was sad or if it was something he'd done, but all I could do was tell him that everything was fine and that he should just keep going. But I can definitely say that these constant tears were a real turn-off. And little by little, Gíó stopped touching me.

That's just how it was.

Still, I couldn't really imagine Gíó having the patience for that kind of handwriting, even if he had the ability to write. I'd never seen him sit down to write anything and I'd never seen the notebook before, either.

But in spite of my doubts, these uncomfortable suspicions about his double life weighed heavily upon me. Truth be told, the book, its contents and its author were never far from my thoughts for the entire week that passed between when I found the notebook and when Gíó disappeared.

I immediately hid the notebook in a good place, where I'd have it to hand if the owner eventually came forward or if I managed to muster the courage to confront Gió with it.

I allowed myself to dream that the notebook and the conversation Gió and I would have about its contents would mark the beginning of a new and exciting chapter in our lives together.

# 19

'You can, in essence, look at life in one of two ways: from the perspective of birth, or from the perspective of death,' I heard the author say without really being able to properly focus on her point. My mind was still on the red notebook, Gíó, and the secret life he was potentially leading. Maybe the incident on the island was the perfect chance for him to start the next chapter of his life. Maybe this was a heaven-sent opportunity to leave behind the mundanity of the everyday and the hassle of so much duplicity.

'From the vantage point of birth, the beginning is what's important. Everything's in a ferment: flowers are blooming, love guides our course, vitality begets new forms. Everything is new, fresh. Sunrises, optimism, hope. New life.

'If you look at life from the vantage point of death, however, the world is shrouded in twilight, everything is in ruins. Withered flowers, infertility, decay, drought, sorrow—all movement is just fleeing from the inevitable end. Life is a tragedy.

'So then what draws me to the sensual, yes, is that erotica is full of life and love, energy and juice, and power, and optimism, and hope. These stories are not only told from the perspective of birth, but rather, their narrators are positioned at the beginning of the birth process—at its very conception. When the egg is fertilized, when new life begins. Everything alight in flames of joy. A succulent new beginning, or actually, the beginning of the beginning…'

I started out of my reverie as Edda gave a cry of satisfaction, delighted by her own eloquence. She looked at me as though she were waiting for me to agree with her, to fawn over her clever way with words, or ask her a related question. I could find nothing to say. I felt exposed. But I had the feeling that speech had been a healthy serving of word salad.

'A new beginning, yes... Sorry, I was distracted for a moment,' I said.

'Is everything okay, my dear? Is there something troubling you?'

I've always been fond of people who pepper their sentences with pretty endearments like *dear, love, hon.* This author was one of those people. She was cheerful and good and I liked the way I felt in her company.

'No... no, no... um,' I stalled. 'Yes, a new beginning... of course... that's a good line of thought... I think I've actually got plenty of material to work with, it's going to be a good interview. You're so well spoken... so many good lines of thought... and interesting, too...' I was going to mention her notebook but stopped short.

I got to my feet and started collecting my things.

'I plan to write up the interview this week, and you should be able to read it over in two or three days. Is that all right?'

'No rush. Just take your time, dear. The most important thing is that it's good—and I haven't the slightest doubt it will be.'

We walked out to the reception area together, but there was no one there to receive us or see us to the door.

Out on the front step, Edda took me by the arms and looked into my eyes with a smile. She found it necessary to embrace me, kiss my cheeks and stroke my hair. I took care to smile in return, to look her in the eye. 'Thanks for today. It was such a pleasure to speak with you,' she said, continuing to stroke my cheek. I took her hand, held it for a moment and said goodbye. Then I hurried up the street. There was a catch in my throat, as if I couldn't handle the author's affection and goodwill.

There was a cold wind blowing off the sea and it whirled up little tornados of street dust that danced along the pavement ahead of me.

Why was this backwater always so cold?

I wrapped my jacket tighter around me and hurried towards home. When I turned onto Túngata, I could see that the doors of the Catholic church were open. I wondered if I should go in. Wasn't it possible to confess, talk about your sins and oversights, and receive absolution from the Catholics? Wasn't that exactly what I needed—to purify my blackened soul?

I stopped and watched an old man who was standing in the door of the church and looked to have no intention of moving any time soon. I didn't feel up to the ordeal of squeezing past the decrepit fellow, and so I continued on my way.

It wasn't a particularly long walk. There were few people out at that time of day, and it was quiet as usual in my neighbourhood. Not a soul to be seen but for a small white cat that trailed after me like it wanted to follow me home. A plane landed at the domestic airport which was located just on the other side of the street, and there was a couple canoodling in a car parked along the kerb.

It was almost noon when I reached my front door. I was about to stick my key in the lock when I heard an elderly voice say something behind me.

# 20

I turned around.

My neighbour Finna was standing on the pavement, broom in hand. She was elderly and spent the better part of each day sweeping her front steps and keeping an eye on the comings and goings of everyone who lived on the street. She was an inquisitive person, always eager to hear how her neighbours were doing and she regularly sought out conversation with them so as to find out the latest news about their families.

Years ago, Finna had owned a little wool shop in the neighbourhood. Working there had allowed her to sate her curiosity and slake her thirst for company, as the shop had been popular among the local residents. The shop had closed a few years ago, as Finna was too old to oversee it with the same zeal she had in her younger years.

But ever since, she'd taken up residence on her front step, broom in hand, and seized every opportunity to chat with those who happened by.

'Good morning!' she said brightly. 'Out for a walk?'

'Well, hello and good morning. I didn't see you there,' I answered with brio. 'Yes, I took a walk. A little morning ramble. I had an errand on the west side.'

'I knew it. I had a feeling no one was home at yours—all the lights off, no movement anywhere. Which is why I was surprised to see a man prowling around your garden this morning. Was he there on your account?' asked Finna, her clouded eyes narrowed.

It was like she was from another world and another time, ancient as she was, her eyes watery and cataracted. She seldom wore anything other than a thick, quilted nylon housecoat with a flower pattern. And as long as I'd known her, she'd worn a delicate brown net on her head that I assumed was meant to hold her hair in place.

'A man prowling… in *our* garden?' My first thought was Gíó, but presumably she would have just said she'd seen my husband. She knew him well.

'Yes… just around back.' She spoke slowly, as if she herself was beginning to doubt it.

'No one you recognized?' I asked.

'No—he was wearing a large woollen hat and carrying a bag on his back. An overstuffed rucksack.'

'Could you tell what he was doing? I mean, he wasn't here at my invitation.'

'No? I don't know who it was. I thought he might be a landscape gardener, doing some sort of work for you, collecting leaves, tree branches or something. He had a big canvas rucksack on his back.'

'How odd. I've no idea who it could have been or what he might have been doing. No idea. Not a burglar, surely?'

'A burglar? I wouldn't want to say. He did have that bag though…' Finna looked at me thoughtfully.

'I didn't ask anyone to do anything in my garden. But thank you for telling me. It's good to know you're keeping an eye on things. I'd better go in and see if anything has been stolen.'

'So, your husband's not at home, then? All the lights are off at yours.'

'Yes—I mean no, he isn't at home. Why do you ask?'

'Well, if he were at home, you could just ask him if he'd seen the man… the man with the rucksack.'

'Right, of course. But, unfortunately, he's not. Thanks so much for letting me know. And as I said, it's good to know that someone's looking out for our home. Take care.'

I turned around, opened the door and walked in without looking back. I could feel the old woman's eyes on me.

For reasons beyond me, I called out after closing the front door.

'Hello—anyone home? Yoo-hoo!'

No answer.

'Gíó, are you here?'

I knew it was an unnecessary performance, of course, but I felt like I needed to take my role seriously, to play my part in this farce that I myself had staged and was starring in, even if the only audience was an old woman who was—I was sure—still keeping vigil on her front steps.

I took my time removing my jacket and shoes, which I arranged tidily on the shoe shelf. I walked into the living room and looked around. There was no sign of any burglar. I went to the window and looked out. Finna had walked across the street and was standing at our garden gate. She was gazing into the garden, as if to check whether the man with the canvas bag was still prowling around the house. Then I watched her turn around and totter back home.

On the windowsill, there was a statuette of cheerful, chubby-cheeked cherubs and a flowerpot with a leafy green plant: *Plectranthus argentatus*. I picked up the flowerpot, held it aloft and dropped it onto the floor.

The clay pot exploded on the floor with a loud smash, shattered to smithereens, potting soil flying up into the air, skittering across the parquet.

I examined my handiwork, knowing as I dusted the dirt from my socks that the time had come. There could be no justification for putting it off any longer. I took out my phone and made the call.

'Reykjavík and Capital-Area Police Department,' answered an authoritative voice on the other end of the line.

'Hello, my name's Júlía. I'm calling to report… uh… a disappearance. My husband has gone missing… or at least, he hasn't come home, he's not answering his phone, hasn't contacted me. I don't know where he is.'

# 21

I'd reported my husband as missing. Now I was waiting for the police to take the matter seriously.

'People disappear and then reappear all the time,' said the officer on the phone. 'And we don't need to be calling out Search and Rescue every time someone gets anxious and notifies us that a fully grown man who can take care of himself has yet to come home.'

'I'm just a bit concerned,' I said after answering some routine questions about Gíó. When I'd last seen him, where—all the other details. I also had to answer questions about myself.

'Is there anything to indicate that he may have been the victim of viol—'

'No...' I hurried to interject. 'It's simply so unlike him not to come home or let anyone know where he is. I've called him over and over, but he isn't answering his phone.'

'He isn't answering his phone... and you've called many times?' the officer repeated.

'Yes, I've called all morning—both his mobile and his work phone. And there was also something strange this morning. When I came downstairs, I noticed that a flowerpot had fallen off the windowsill and broken on the floor. It was almost like someone had crawled through the window and knocked it over.'

'Wait, are you saying there's been a break-in at your home? Are there any other signs that there's been a robbery? Any valuables missing?'

'No, it doesn't look like anything's been stolen, but the flowerpot is in pieces on the floor and the window's open.'

'It could, of course, just have been a cat that jumped in and knocked it over. You know how many cats we've got running loose in this city... Have a good look-around and see if anything is missing—other than your husband, I mean—and then be in touch later today if he doesn't show himself. But I wouldn't be too concerned just yet.'

I could tell that he wanted to end the conversation and didn't want to hear any more of my hysterics.

'Look, it really seems like someone might have come through the window last night. We are... or, I mean, the living room is on the first floor and the window isn't so high up that it would be impossible to climb through. And the window—I mean, just the fact that it was open this morning. That's unusual.'

'Sure, sure... So are you saying that you're worried your husband's been abducted? Are you trying to tell me that someone sneaked into your house in the middle of the night and took your husband?' the policeman asked. I wasn't sure what I should infer from his tone of voice. Was he just tired of me and everyone else who rushed to report their loved ones as missing or was the sarcasm in his voice telling me that he thought I was a stupid sheep of a woman?

'My neighbour saw a man in my garden this morning with an overstuffed rucksack on his back,' I added. This last addition was obviously mischief-making on my part, a response to the officer's impatience and rudeness. He didn't realize that, of course.

'A man with a rucksack, you say? You don't think your husband was in it, do you?' The sarcasm was on full display now.

I didn't answer so he hurried to add:

'We will be more than happy to look into this if you don't hear from your husband today. But let's give it some time… Let's just try to keep our heads and see if he doesn't resurface. That's usually what happens. Some of them even come home with their tail between their legs, if you catch my drift.'

# 22

Any drive I'd had seemed to have stalled. I could neither sit still and do nothing nor find myself something to do. I felt numb. I doubted my brain activity was even measurable. I didn't feel like doing anything outdoorsy, and all the books that were staring at me from the bookshelf and inviting me to read them filled me with nausea. I let my eyes run along the spines. Flaubert, Tove Jansson and Knausgaard, whose books I'd recently devoured. I shook my head and nearly gagged.

The six volumes by Norwegian author Karl Ove Knausgaard had entirely bewitched me. Never before had I been so intensely sucked into a work of literature. I had Knausgaard on the brain. I fell for him, hard, even started googling photos of him on the internet. I'd gaze dreamily at that bearded, long-haired Norwegian, and for a time, thought I'd fallen in love with him. Night after night, as soon as we'd finished dinner, I'd pick up the book of his I was reading and say to Gíó: 'I'm going to bed with Knausgaard.'

He found it funny at first, but after I'd repeated the joke over and over, it seemed to wear thin. He even came into the bedroom a few times to investigate.

'What?' I said when he peeked around the bedroom door.

'You're just reading,' he said, and then went back out.

But that was months ago. Now, I could no more think of reading Knausgaard than anyone else.

What had it said on that poster in the bookstore window?

Something along the lines of books not needing to be *about* anything... Was that the right attitude to have about literature?

Everywhere I looked, there were books. On tables, on the sofa, on the shelves. But regardless of whether they were about something or nothing, reading simply couldn't tempt me in that moment.

I couldn't bear being confined by the walls of my own home. I couldn't focus on anything. So instead, I stalked around like a caged lion, made myself a snack of crispbread and cheese, poured myself a cup of coffee, drank a glass of water, stood up, sat down, flipped through the newspaper, ate some nuts and finally, gave up.

Hope had abandoned me far too quickly. As it was, it almost never came to visit. Whenever I woke in the morning, I could feel fear crashing down on me like a heavy wave. I never thought: maybe today something good will happen. Maybe it was that paralysing fear of mine that smothered any hope I had of Gíó coming back. Any hope that he was okay and I was okay and we were okay.

But that day, I walked to the living room window again and again, hoping that some light would break through, that the sun would draw the clouds from its face and send its warm rays across the blue sky. That didn't happen. It was absurd to think I was going to walk to the kitchen window and see Gíó suddenly appear on the pavement, about to walk through the front door.

I was hopeless and helpless.

I threw on my shoes and a coat and ran out of the house as if escaping from a burning building.

The car was parked on the street out front, and I decided I'd drive somewhere instead of pacing around and around our home sweet home.

The rust bucket spluttered into life and moved off before I'd even decided where I was going. But it was as if the car was dragging me in the direction I most feared—straight out of town. Some terrible force was drawing me towards itself, super magnetized. I drove north in a sort of trance.

Mount Esja appeared before me, strong, broad-shouldered, cold, and white halfway down its slopes.

The sun shone and the sky over the mountain was a brilliant blue on that cold, dry and windy autumn day.

There was a lot of traffic heading out of town, bumper to bumper, and I inched along single-file behind everyone else who was driving the same way through Mosfellsbær—the capital of roundabouts—and then out to Kjalarnes, until suddenly I was at the mouth of Hvalfjörður, driving down into the tunnel that ran deep underneath it. One hundred and sixty-some metres above me, bug-eyed fish and heavily laden freighters sailed on the surface; maybe there was even a whale or two making a quick tour of their namesake fjord—Hvalfjörður, Whale Fjord—their huge, glistening stomachs full of men.

But it wasn't thoughts of fish and freighters that plagued me. Rather, my mind wandered back to the time when I was working at a restaurant abroad and first met Gió.

In Italy, at a bar in Florence.

# 23

I've worked in bars twice in my life. Once was in Florence, in what was essentially a speakeasy that very few people frequented. It was called Winslow & Winslow Old English Pub.

The other time, I worked in a small and far smarter pub in London, right by Selhurst Park. It was, or is, called The Clifton Arms.

I lived in London for almost two years, during which time I had a boyfriend with whom I was head over heels in love for precisely nine days. On day ten, I'd had enough of the young man and left him in the same place I found him, no worse for wear.

I never saw him again.

During those years, I also bought myself a motorcycle. A powerful red Triumph.

For years after I returned to Iceland, many of my sentences began with the words: 'When I was living in London…' or 'When I was living in London and had a motorcycle…' But to be fair, whenever I got any time off from the pub, I'd ride around England on my Triumph. I rode east, I rode west, and I rode south to the coast—John Fowles territory.

I read Fowles's *The Collector*, about a lovesick man, or rather, a man made sick by love. The main character is probably best described as a love-sucking monster, but the book stayed with me, so I wanted to go check out the author's home turf.

I'd always dreamt of moving to England for a time.

Both of my parents had lived in England, and it was their paradise. As far as they were concerned, nowhere was better than

England. Maybe I'd wanted to please them by sharing their interest in the country.

They were delighted, of course.

In my mind, England was grassy hills, narrow and winding rural roads, country pubs and heaths populated by wild horses standing silent and invisible in thick fog.

During my time in Italy, however, England was a snooty little bar in Florence and that was where I met a dashing young man named Gíó.

Everything in the Winslow & Winslow Old English Pub was meant to recall an English gentlemen's club. I was put on the day shift and worked alone because there were so few patrons during the day. I was a terrible bartender. Truth be told, a worse bartender would be hard to find.

When I got the job, I'd never made a cocktail in my life, nor mixed a drink in the correct proportions. I didn't even know what a cocktail was when I started. My main association with the word was the home-made explosive, not an alcoholic beverage. But thanks to my experience at The Clifton Arms, I knew how to pull a pint.

I told the owner all of this right off the bat. He still decided to hire me and schedule me on my own.

In the early part of the day, hardly anyone came into the bar, so I had plenty of time to devote to my favourite activity: curling up with a book and listening to music without any interruption from anyone else.

The bar was furnished with soft English leather chairs intended for English gentlemen or locals longing to ape the lifestyle of the English gentry. They were arranged in foursomes, two facing two. They were roomy, with broad backs and thick arms, which also functioned to limit the number of people who could sit in the bar at any given time.

Small, low tables were arranged between the leather chairs. Each had a typical English lamp on it, which emitted a dim, greenish light and was basically useless—just there for decoration and to create a respectable English club vibe.

A selection of English newspapers hung on the wall by the entrance, each on its own hanger. I'd sit in one of the soft, leather chairs for hours at a time, reading. Not English newspapers, although the selection was outstanding, but rather the books of Italo Calvino (I was in Italy, after all), John Fowles (I read *The Collector* again), as well as Agatha Christie's Miss Marple novels because I wanted to learn how to write murder mysteries.

I'd been working at the pub for several weeks when three young men started coming in every afternoon, much to my dismay.

They were clearly painters with a job in the neighbourhood because they all wore white boiler suits splattered with paint. They'd come in and take a seat on the tall stools at the bar and order Guinness—more than one round every time they came in.

The youngest of them was an Icelander, and it was due to him that the painters had started coming in. He'd heard there was another Icelander in the city (that is, me) who worked at a bar near where he had his painting job, and he wanted to pay a visit to his compatriot.

And Bob's your uncle, the trio made it their habit to come to my pub at lunchtime.

Anyone who's worked in a bar knows there's nothing duller than pulling pints of Guinness. They foam incessantly and it takes an eternity to fill a single glass. These beer-swilling painters were dragging me away from my books and when they were in the bar, I couldn't play the music I wanted to hear.

The owner had put together a long playlist of songs he thought would create a good atmosphere and bring in more customers. I was supposed to play this playlist any time the bar was open and there were patrons present. It was practically the only rule the owner had set for me and I obeyed it unconditionally. Outside of that, I had a free hand.

I think they were painting a church in the neighbourhood. There's no painting job that takes longer than painting a church, and there's no entity that takes a milder view of procrastination, time wasting and sloppiness than the Catholic Church.

But before long—and actually, against my better judgement—I started to enjoy these fellows' visits, found myself laughing at their banter and cheek. I started looking forward to their company—the Icelander's in particular. He wasn't just funny, he was also well spoken and handsome and incredibly charming. He was muscular and radiated energy and vitality. He was perfect, and suddenly, without warning, I realized that I wanted to be around him.

Forever.

That was Gíó.

# 24

Gió only painted churches in the summer. He was finishing his studies in architecture and design at the University of Florence under the guidance of some super-famous guru who'd wangled the job for him.

But aikido was actually Gió's primary passion. Although he was reserved and said very little, he tended to forget himself and launch into long, detailed narratives when he was talking about something he was interested in. He was a natural storyteller, able to create uniquely vivid, arresting and multifaceted anecdotes, no matter what the subject.

Gió became interested in aikido when he was a teenager after someone told him, possibly as a joke, that he had the soul of an aikidoka. Gió had no idea what that meant. But it stuck with him.

'Look, Gió, you're not a strong guy—you don't have a strong character or a strong body,' the person had said, then added, before Gió could protest:

'But you don't need to be strong to be a good aikidoka. Aikido is about using the strength of your opponent—the strength of their body and mind—to your own advantage. If someone attacks you—for instance, if someone tries to punch you—you don't try to punch them back; rather, you grab their fist and use the power that your attacker put into the blow to fling him into a wall. That's the kind of guy you are, Gió. You're not strong, but you know how to use other people's strength to your benefit.'

This assessment lay dormant in Gíó's mind throughout his teenage years and into adulthood. He was taken with this vision of himself as a man with an aikidoka's soul. It wasn't until he moved to Florence, however, that he encountered aikido again. Whenever he walked to the university, he'd often pass a run-down building in the neighbourhood where he lived. The building was tucked away in a dirty passageway next to a slovenly butcher and surrounded by other ugly buildings. It seemed like the passageway doubled as an abattoir, because there were always barrels and large plastic trays of tendons, sinews, tissue and other meat waste stacked against the gables of the building. Some kind of shield hung on the door of the shabby building in the butcher's passage—a thick, red metal plate in relief. On the shield, the words AIKIDO CENTRE were written in big, black letters with a Japanese character just beneath.

Every time Gíó passed through this repellent passage and walked by the entrance to the aikido centre, he thought about the words of the man who'd said he had an aikidoka's soul and considered going in and registering for a class in that venerable martial art. Obviously, he should.

But he did little more than think about it every time he hurried through the putrid alley.

Then, one day in high summer when Gíó was on his way to class, he decided to take a shortcut through the meat-processing passage and there was a man standing in the doorway of the aikido centre. The man was short, probably Japanese, and seemed to be some kind of doorman or bouncer. He held the door so it stood open, as though he were waiting for Gíó to walk in. Gíó slowed his pace and stared at the man, who took a step to the side, bowed, and said, as if nothing could be more natural: 'Come in.'

Gíó didn't know what was going on, but obeyed. He entered a small studio with surprisingly high ceilings. He felt like he was standing on the ground floor of a tower that reached all the way up to heaven. He stood there, head back and gaping and on the point of falling backwards from dizziness, when someone led him into a cramped and unassuming office where three small women, also most likely of Japanese origin, were each sitting at their own desk.

One of them, young and black-haired with super-short bangs and black eye make-up, offered him a seat across from her and without any formalities, took down his name and other personal information as if was a foregone conclusion that he'd be registering at the centre.

He was treated with pure benevolence and courtesy, like he was the prodigal son returned home.

'You are most welcome,' said the women, rising to their feet and bowing. All three, each in their own way. 'We're glad you're here. Your arrival brings much happiness to our ranks.'

'It was all quite unusual,' Gió would generally say at this point in the story. 'It was like I'd stepped into an alternate reality, into another world. Then a short young man in a white gi came in. He bowed and welcomed me and then calmly informed me that I would need to attend four times a week.

'And I thought to myself: what can this little man mean? Four times a week? Does he think I have nothing else to do with my life than to practise martial arts? I took my programme at the university seriously. But somehow, there was no turning back. There was nothing I could do but obey these people who had treated me so warmly. I began training. Truth be told, it only took a couple of weeks for me to become completely obsessed with this exquisite martial art. Four times a week wasn't nearly enough for me.'

Typically, this story—I knew it backwards and forwards because I'd heard it so many times—was followed by descriptions of adult men rolling about on the floor in all kinds of positions. After which, he'd talk about the time he found himself pinned, bathed in sweat, under a 100-kilo man who was trying to both crush and choke him and how he'd managed to shift their centres of gravity just enough to reposition the man's weight and flip the circumstances to his advantage.

'It's not a sport you can practise alone. You have to have contact with another person,' he said before zealously throwing himself into a long lecture about the cultural history of aikido, about clandestine practice sessions held by Japanese youths in the nineteenth century, about the difference between aikido and taekwondo, a similar martial art from Korea, and then the narrative moved on to boxing and MMA. That's the kind of storyteller Gió was. The narration was smooth, seamless and sonorous as a babbling brook, free of any hesitations or filler, the whole of it flowing so naturally.

His passion for aikido and his years-long training explained how muscular Gió was, how well he carried himself.

# 25

It did not escape me that Gió had taken an obvious interest in me, right from that first day when I'd bustled incompetently around the bar while he sat straight-backed on a bar stool with his friends who made fun of me and each other while guzzling their Guinnesses.

I was unmoved in the beginning, as I've said, but after a few weeks, I felt my interest in the guy in the paint-splattered boiler suit growing from day to day.

I'd sneak a glance at him while I filled one glass of Guinness after another, covertly check him out when he was looking the other way. I'd sneakily sniff him, breathe in the irresistible scent of his body, and touch him as if by accident when collecting glasses from the bar.

When I set his beer in front of him and looked at his long, delicate fingers picking up the glass, I could tell what colour he'd been working with. If the paint on his hands was midnight blue, I pictured him painting the night sky behind the Virgin Mary, cradling the holy infant in her arms. If it was a dark red, I imagined him painting the wound in the side of Jesus on the cross.

I dreamt of him at night, and I dreamt of him during the day.

He'd sparked a terrible, wonderful sort of neurosis in me. I was floating around in sweet bliss, while at the same time, I felt flustered and agitated, heart pounding as if always on the verge of a heart attack.

One day, when I walked outside after finishing my shift, a leather-clad man was waiting for me at the entrance—although actually, the pub itself was on the first floor, like every other pretentious bar. He was sitting on a red Vespa. I didn't recognize him right away because I'd never seen Gíó dressed in anything but his white boiler suit.

I thought about Clegg, the lovesick collector, lying in wait for Miranda outside her school.

Gíó was lying in wait for me.

'Hi,' he said, grinning broadly.

'Hi,' I said, surprised by the greeting because I still didn't know who he was.

'I got off work early. C'mon, hop on,' he said, patting the seat behind him. 'Let me show you some of the countryside.'

A light bulb went on and I recognized him finally, his familiar outline—broad shoulders, dark hair peeking out from under his helmet, his deep voice. I should add here—and repeat often—that I've often thought, even after knowing him for years, that Gíó is still, in some respects, a complete mystery to me and always has been. I genuinely never really figured him out, though I loved what I did know of him. He rarely spoke about himself, avoided talking about anything too personal. It was like he was afraid to give out any personal information. Maybe he was afraid of revealing himself and whatever secrets he had. I certainly don't know all of them.

People are so quick to judge and don't want to see others as the complex phenomena they are, full of quirks and contradictions. Instead, we have a tendency to pick either a glossy, airbrushed version of someone, or a crude sketch of them, all of their blemishes unfiltered, before cramming them into a preformed mould. But people are complicated and have many sides.

But in that moment, on that autumn day outside the Winslow & Winslow Old English Pub, I was glad to see Gíó. I was sure that with time I'd solve the riddle of this man and find the key to his locked and mysterious soul.

I was just about to get on the Vespa behind him when he grabbed my arm in an iron grip and pulled me to him. He held me so tight that my arm flared in pain, and gave me a soft, sweet kiss on the mouth.

I yanked myself free and shrieked, 'Stop!'

He froze.

'I'm sorry, I just…' he stammered.

I could see the fear in his eyes.

I could feel the anger welling up inside me. I tried to calm down.

'You can't just grab someone like that… What's wrong with you?' I said. 'Don't ever do that—grab me like that,' I repeated, fighting to regain my composure and speak calmly.

'I'm sorry.'

'You hurt me,' I said, a little quieter.

'I'm sorry.'

I wiped my mouth with the back of my hand.

I didn't move for a moment, just stood there thinking.

I could feel him looking at me, rattled.

That kiss was a sort of monument in our relationship, like a cairn built to mark an unfortunate beginning, to which we returned regularly over the years that followed.

It wasn't just how severely I'd reacted to the kiss that Gíó never forgot, but also his sense that from the very beginning, he'd been misunderstood and treated unfairly.

I don't know if I'm unfair. I don't think I am, but he does sometimes.

After a moment's hesitation, during which I shuffled my feet around his spiffy red Vespa, unsure of what I should do (stay or go) and Gíó apologized some more, I got on behind him. We drove out of the city, up into the hills where trattorias with red-checked tablecloths served cold prosecco and other afternoon refreshments.

We didn't say a word all the way up the hillside, the road winding and bending sharply and the engine too loud for conversation anyway.

But I couldn't have uttered a single word even if I'd wanted to. My stomach was in knots.

Gíó had prepared everything. He'd booked a table and planned out what he should offer the lady, and I think he'd probably organized something for after the trip up into the hills too, but nothing came of that.

We sat across from one another at the trattoria, which looked out over houses and trees. The afternoon was warm, and colourful butterflies flitted around the flowers along the restaurant terrace. Between us on the table was a chilled silver bucket, a bottle of prosecco peeking out of it. Bubbles streamed upwards in our glasses.

The date wasn't living up to all the beauty, the light and the bubbles, and neither was it as Gíó had dreamt or expected it would be. We did, however, put the kiss behind us that afternoon, chatted and tried to forget the embarrassing start to this surprise expedition up into the hills.

# 26

Our glasses fizzed and the prosecco bottle was empty.

It was our first and only Vespa trip that autumn. Gíó tried a few times afterwards to pick me up after work and invite me on another trip through the hills, but I always had some excuse prepared.

He continued to lie in wait for me.

He didn't give up, but he did tread more lightly. He approached me with caution and was always offering to help me and surprising me with gifts. Naturally, I appreciated this and I found it difficult to maintain such stubbornness. But there was something in me that resisted his advances.

I wasn't going to give in so easily, even if I did want his love.

Gíó came to the bar every day with his friends. Sometimes with blue paint on his fingers, and sometimes his hands were smeared with red, like blood.

I could always feel his eyes on me, but whenever I glanced in his direction, he looked away.

He was guarded and didn't speak without carefully considering his words.

One Saturday, a few weeks after the kiss, I had the day off, and he invited me out for a meal. Lunch. I accepted, and it was clear that he was happy and relieved that I was finally giving in.

I'd been meaning to tell him that I felt bad about the incident with the kiss and that he shouldn't worry about it any more. I'd forgiven him a long time ago. I was just generally over men lusting after me. I was uncomfortable with the way they stared at my thin body, I felt nauseous listening to them go on about my big blue eyes and the shape of my lips and everything they found 'irresistible' about me and thought would somehow guarantee their eternal happiness—and possibly mine as well if I'd only succumb to their charms.

'I think I deserve something else, something more than stealth attacks built on romantic clichés,' I said. He blushed and looked down before answering.

'Could we just forget the whole thing?' he said. 'I've apologized and I think I've shown you how sorry I am. I feel terrible about it. I thought you'd be charmed by my spontaneity. I miscalculated.'

'I don't think that kind of spontaneity was acceptable when you didn't know my heart,' I said. I was young and I felt it was the right thing to say at the time.

Gíó looked at me like he was receiving a message and carefully fixing it in his mind.

'You're right,' he said then.

'I like you, and I like you taking it nice and slow with me. Can we just keep going like this, see where it goes?'

'Of course.'

'I need you to give me time and space. You can't come on so fast, crowd me. Don't try to tie me down.'

I scolded myself for being so hard on him, and sometimes even mean.

The days went by. Gíó danced gingerly and gently around me. He didn't crowd me; he didn't come on too fast. He took me at my word.

And he continued to invite me out to lunch. Until the spring day when he arrived again on his Vespa and silently gestured for me to get on behind him. We drove out of the city and up into the hills.

The sun was shining and everything was in bloom. The leaves on the trees were fresh and cast their patchy shadows over the paved country road. The grass on the verge was lush and green. We rumbled around sharp turns and up slopes until we were sitting back at the same trattoria he'd first invited me to.

We sat at a table with a red-checked tablecloth, and before the waiter had even come over to take our order, Gíó said in a calm voice: 'I'm sure you're aware, Júlía, how—how can I put this—how I feel about you. Aren't you? And I know what stands between us, too. But if you're ever ready… at any time, I don't care when… to be… uh… to be my girlfriend… then you take the first step. It would help me…' He looked at me and I could see the shyness in his eyes and maybe also kindness.

I wasn't sure if I was ready. I felt this strong physical resistance—I was wary about this kind of thing—but in spite of that uncertainty, I still took both his hands, lifted them to my lips, and kissed them. First the right and then the left, with my eyes closed.

I'd grown afraid that he'd soon give up on me, on this endless and difficult trek through the desert. In spite of everything, I felt for him, deeply.

That was back before I knew about aikido tactics.

'I'm ready,' I said.

It was a terribly romantic scene, and, in that moment, I didn't regret a thing.

# 27

I drove as though in some kind of trance in the column of cars wending its way along the base of Mount Esja like a long, slender snake. The image of the outdoor trattoria with the red-checked tablecloths up in the hills outside of Florence was still clear in my mind's eye. I was still seeing bubbles in prosecco glasses.

When I finally stopped daydreaming, I'd long since come up out of the dusty Hvalfjörður Tunnel and could see the Grundartangi aluminium smelter in the distance.

I looked around, getting my bearings, and felt despair taking hold of me again. I pulled out of the line of cars, onto the side of the road, and braked hard. The car skidded on the gravel.

After it came to a stop, I sat for a moment with my eyes closed and my hands in my lap before switching off the ignition.

I couldn't continue like this.

I pictured Gíó standing at the highest point of Geirshólmur, watching me sail away in the dinghy. Straight-backed and broad-shouldered. His long, black hair whipping in the wind. His expression one of shock and disbelief, as if he didn't really understand what was happening, but feared the worst. Trying to see from my face if this was all a joke. And then gradually, shock turned to fear. But he said nothing and didn't call out to me, just grimly watched me sail to shore.

Then I looked away and I hadn't seen him since.

I had to drive back to the fjord to look for him again. I cursed my impetuousness. Why didn't I think about the consequences of my actions? I was beside myself.

I pulled back onto the roadway and sped all the way back to the Miðsandur pier. I jumped out of the car and rushed down to the shore to where the dinghy had been. The farmer had obviously come to get it. There was no boat, but there were deep tyre tracks in the black sand around where the rubber wreck had lain, presumably from the trailer he'd used to transport it. I peered out to Geirshólmur to see if there were any signs of life there. I'd already checked; he wasn't there. And yet I kept looking.

What had I been thinking, leaving Gíó out there?

Although visibility was good, it was impossible to make out if there was any movement on the islet. I had to get closer—it was too far away. I thought I might walk out to the end of the long oil pier that reached into the fjord, but a tall fence was blocking the way. A posted sign forbade all unauthorized entry.

Examining the obstacle before me, I saw that someone had cut a big hole in the wire fence. I squeezed through the gap and hurried along the pier. Someone might come running after me at any moment (though that seemed unlikely, given how few people lived on the fjord) but I didn't care.

Thick metal pipes ran along and under the pier. All of the oil in the country was pumped from here, I thought. I've crossed a line now.

If I'd had a cigarette, I'd have smoked it.

At the end of the pier, I stopped and squinted, staring out at the island, focusing so I wouldn't miss the slightest movement. I stood absolutely still and didn't take my eyes off it for what seemed like an age.

I wouldn't be getting any closer to Geirshólmur than the end of this pier.

I'd ruled out the possibility that there'd been anyone on the island the day before—that wasn't even a question. No one could hide out there. It was beyond the shadow of a doubt. I couldn't know how long Gíó had stayed on that spit of land yesterday, but however long it had been, he wasn't there now.

He must have attempted to swim. I imagined him making his way from the island to the shore. I pictured him as a middling swimmer, doggy-paddling. I actually had nothing to go on as far as that was concerned. I'd never seen him swim. But when I estimated the distance from Geirshólmur to land, it seemed way too far to swim. *Way* too far.

I stood there, unsure what to do next, just staring out at the fjord.

To my great surprise, I suddenly longed to talk to María.

María had been on my mind a lot in recent days. Her spectre had been hanging over all my conjectures about Gíó and his life. The image of the two of them passionately making love popped into my head again and I felt a sort of paralysis taking hold of me—like sinking into a deep pool. I took a deep breath and decided to call her.

She answered on the first ring.

'María speaking,' barked a sharp voice on the other end of the line.

'Hi, it's me,' I said. 'Your sister.'

We look alike, María and I. We both have curly, black hair, are tall and slender, big-eyed and small-nosed, and our voices sound alike, too. We're sharp and curt in our communications, as if perpetually sullen or angry or just in a bad mood. It seems to be in our genes. People are afraid of my sister. She seems smart and strong; her expression is so focused and her eyes so piercing that it's like she can see through people. People stand naked before her; she tolerates no bullshit, and she coddles no one. I'm either a milder version of my sister or she's a harsher version of me. But either way, she's not the buffoon I am.

'So I hear,' she said and sighed tiredly. Then she added: 'What's wrong?'

'What's wrong? Why are you asking that?… Why is the first thing you say when I call "what's wrong?" Why would you think something's wrong?' I was immediately on my guard.

I was the defender in our relationship, while she was the goal-hungry striker who never stopped trying to evade me and score, no matter what. She got a lot of goals, but I was a strong defender, a wall.

'Just… What do you want?'

'Have you heard anything? I mean…?' I felt taut, like a string stretched to its breaking point. Like I was holding my breath, even as I spoke.

'Heard? What are you talking about? What am I supposed to have heard? Calm down, woman. Breathe,' she commanded. After a short pause, she added: 'It's obvious something's wrong. Getting a call from you is enough in itself for me to know that something's off.'

'That's not fair. But I need to see you. Are you home? Can I come over?'

'Yes.'

'Now?'

'Yeah, just come… really. I'm home.' I heard her sigh again.

'I'll be there in an hour. I'm… in Hvalfjörður.'

'Hvalfjörður? What are you doing there?' She snorted impatiently.

'No, not Hvalfjörður, sorry. I mean, I'm in Mosfellsbær… sorry, I don't know which way's up. All those roundabouts, you know…

Puts your brain through a blender… Mosfellsbær-Hvalfjörður, potato-potahto, same general area…'

'Okay. Whatever. Let's just talk when you get here. Drive safe. Bye.'

# 28

My sister was standing in the doorway when I drove up to her beautiful house. She was wearing a solemn expression—severe, even—and her arms were crossed over her chest. I could clearly make out the shape of her strong, well-defined biceps through her thin sweater. She was elegant, thin, and wiry. Dressed in black from top to toe, her long black hair draping perfectly over one shoulder. A wide gold bracelet had slipped out from under her black sweater and glinted on her left wrist. Her back was ramrod-straight, like a soldier's.

Her forehead was high and handsome, a lofty vault for all her high-flown ideas. She conveyed prosperity, sangfroid and strength. I'd long idolized this sister of mine. I could hardly have admired her more. She was a born conqueror. In my younger years, I never suspected, in my adoration of her, that she experienced emotions as banal as loneliness or could show such weak-willed feelings as jealousy. In my mind, she was too tough for that kind of thing. So it was strangely refreshing for me to eventually discover, much later in life, that she could suffer from these like anyone else.

I got out of the car and walked up the steps. She didn't say anything, just gave me a searching look as I shambled slowly towards her. I faltered with every step, probably out of an abundance of self-pity, as if I were losing my balance and about to sink to the ground every time I lifted a foot. I stopped on the deck, and she stood aside to let me in.

'You're walking like you're drunk. You're not drunk, are you?' she asked drily.

I didn't answer.

María lived alone. I think, in her mind, there had never been any question of doing otherwise. Not because she lacked for suitors or lovers—plenty of men dreamt of cuddling up to her—rather, I think she didn't want to have anyone else in her home for too long at a time. Her house smelt like her. She didn't like other people's smells.

I took off my shoes. Her eyes rested on my back as if she were trying to tell from my posture what was bothering me, as if she could tell from the way I moved and untied my laces what was weighing on me.

She was good at reading people. Not just because she was educated in that very skill—she was a psychologist—but also because she had the ability to discern a million little details in the blink of an eye and interpret them judiciously. People call this talent emotional intelligence, and rightly so. She also had the inborn ability to see through people. She had the upper hand in any interaction, and she knew it; that was just the way she liked it.

'Something up with you and Gíó?' she finally said, after I'd flung myself into a chair in her kitchen.

She stood over me, waiting to take a seat herself.

She'd sussed out my state of mind, and the conclusion she'd drawn was, in some respects, correct. I don't know why I say, 'in some respects'. I probably believed there was something else harrying me besides my relationship with Gíó.

I didn't answer right away but looked searchingly in front of me, and she started talking again when she grew tired of waiting for me to answer. Patience and forbearance have never been her strongest suits.

'Are you mute now, too…? Where is Gíó?' she asked sharply, putting her hands on her hips as though getting ready to kick me into gear. There was neither accusation in her voice nor concern, just a demand to get the requested information immediately.

Yes, where was Gíó? That was a very good and important question, of course, and one that my clever sister had thrown out not two minutes after I'd come through her door without me even having opened my mouth. She'd diagnosed the situation correctly.

'I don't know where he is,' I said with a heavy sigh. 'He's missing and I've notified the police,' I added resignedly and looked her directly in the eyes, as if allowing her to gaze into my mind and get an unobstructed glimpse of my soul. 'I don't know where he is. No idea. He's disappeared,' I said, my voice sombre.

'Disappeared? What do you mean "disappeared"? You just don't know where he is. Why are you saying that? Did someone see him disappear? Did someone disappear him?'

Her sarcasm was palpable.

'No, no one saw him disappear. But I still have no idea where he is or where he's gone. He's missing and I've notified the police… but the police don't want to do anything yet.'

'Are you being unnecessarily dramatic? Just tell me what happened,' she said, finally taking a seat across from me and looking at me intently. Now, she looked concerned.

'I haven't seen him since yesterday.'

'Where were you two yesterday?'

'Home… Then we went out to Hvalfjörður… I needed to look around a bit for a piece I'm writing.'

I fell silent. She watched me and waited for me to continue to reel off the details she believed she had a right to.

'You haven't heard from him?' I asked, giving her a wide-eyed look.

'Me?' She wrinkled her nose in contempt.

'Yes, you.'

'No,' said my sister, and judging from the tone of her voice, she was both offended and confused. 'No, I haven't heard from him.'

'The officer said… The officer I spoke to said I should ask everyone close to us.'

'What happened—when did you last see him? This is insane… Can you just try to speak plainly? I can't possibly understand what's happened—whether this is something serious or just some bullshit. When did you actually see him last? Let's try to get this out in an orderly manner.'

I stared blankly into the air and didn't answer.

'What?' said María, now as abrupt as a drill sergeant talking to some idiot new recruit.

'I saw him last night. We were at home, and we got into an argument, and he stormed out. He said he was going to your place. No… or yes, he said: "I'm going to María's." I figured he meant you. I don't know any other Marías and I don't think he knows any Marías other than you, my sister.'

'To María's?'

'Yeah, that's what he said.'

'To my place? What horseshit,' she said sharply. 'What kind of nonsense is this? What is wrong with you two? Why—?'

'It surprised me, too. He hasn't visited you… come over? He didn't come and see you last night?'

María hesitated for a moment, and I could see in her eyes that there was something bothering her.

'No… of course not… I mean… Why would he come to my house all of a sudden? He's always welcome, of course… It's not that. But why should he visit me? Now. He couldn't have meant me. It must have been some other María that he… I mean… Gíó and I hardly know each other.'

# 29

I have a habit of lying. Generally speaking, I see saying something that isn't *entirely* true as a harmless amusement, and I expect the people I'm speaking to get as much a kick out of it as I do. I'm persuaded that my carefree relationship with the truth makes me more fun to be around and my life more interesting.

But that's maybe not the main reason I take such a flexible approach to the truth.

I seldom lie for selfish reasons; the happiness and pleasure of others is my foremost concern whenever I tell an untruth. I believe it's a way for me to make the lives of those around me better—pleasanter, more enjoyable.

It's not honourable to lie. I've learnt that much. But when the truth brings destruction in its wake, it's forgivable to be dishonourable and say something that sounds better than the truth.

I sometimes lie to embellish reality, to make the world more mysterious and interesting. As you get older, you slowly begin to realize that not much happens in people's lives from day to day. Life tootles along, and usually there's not much that excites, tickles or surprises amid the drudgery of the everyday.

# 30

I think I developed this tendency to lie as a young child because I was assigned the delicate responsibility of cheering up my mother, who struggled her entire life with listlessness and despondency. She was the classic dissatisfied housewife who'd go days without leaving the house, much to her own—and others'—distress. Don't get me wrong, my mum was kind and a lot of fun, but this was her cross to bear; lethargy and depression could take over her life for days and weeks at a time.

When I came home after playing outside with my friends and encountered my careworn mother busying herself with something in the kitchen, I'd often make up something amusing to tell her to drive her gloom away, to perk her up and make her happy for a moment. I was quick to learn that the stories my mum liked best were about our neighbours, and the neighbour women most of all. She was most interested in hearing stories about how their houses were furnished and decorated. How our neighbours' families behaved behind closed doors, sheltered from the outside world, while we children played at their houses.

We lived in the city, in a townhouse—one in a terrace of identical homes. If you stood at the front gate, or the back, you'd see eight identical houses side by side, white with brown doors, brown windowsills and grey, corrugated-iron roofs. The differences between them weren't visible from the outside but had to do with how the interiors were done up—what furniture was in the living room, what colour the kitchen was, what kind of flooring they'd chosen, what they hung on the walls. Did they have pictures and bookshelves, or were the walls bare? All of this was enormously interesting for my mother. And so I always made sure to have something new to tell her about my friends' houses when I came home.

Although my mum knew all the women in the houses around and adjoining ours, she didn't know much about them. But she was fascinated by their lives.

Mum was a shy woman and reserved. It would have never even occurred to her to knock on one of her neighbours' doors for a chat or to stop by for a coffee and use the opportunity to check out what they'd done with the place.

I was an inexhaustible well of information; I went into these homes and didn't skimp on reports about these people's lives. If I didn't have any new titbit to share when I came home from a visit and could see that Mum was down and needed a dose of gossip, I'd just make up something interesting about our neighbours.

It could be as simple as saying 'Snúlla got her hair done' and Mum would immediately brighten.

'Oh, she got a new haircut, did she? Is it very short? Where does she get her hair done? Does she colour her hair? Does it look good on her?'

I made up stories about the Turkish ambassador to Iceland—*such a charmer,* he'd come on an unexpected visit to the house next door and gifted my friend's mum a giant, gilded crystal vase that cost more than a good month's pay. He obviously must be wildly in love with her. Her husband hadn't known how to eject the strutting rooster, shamelessly circling his wife, from his house, so he'd had to just stand there while the ambassador romanced her.

I could also invent innocent tales about a new sofa that someone got, new rugs, chairs or lamps. This sort of stuff was like vitamins for my mother's sombre soul.

These stories were also key to me being able to thrive within my own home. I'd always found it impossible to deal with sluggishness, ennui and bad moods. I'd get agitated and wouldn't feel any peace until I'd managed to bring my family together into one harmonious, happy unit. I put all my energy—and probably still do—into making sure the family ambiance was good so I could actually relax. I was my family's greatest defender.

# 31

My father the watchmaker—or 'Master of the Clockworks' as he liked to call himself—was quick to notice this tendency of mine. I was only knee-high to a grasshopper when he gave me the job, consciously or not, of maintaining a positive atmosphere in the house. Whenever my mother or sister were 'out of sorts', as he called being depressed, he'd call me over and say: 'Go talk to your mother, would you? She's a bit out of sorts and you're so good at getting her back into a good mood. Go on, now. Make her happy again.'

He got just as agitated as I did when he sensed some sort of melancholy or disquiet in the house and, having sent me off to divert the depressed, he'd disappear into his office, light a cigar and listen to organ music and hymns in his easy chair behind closed doors.

But in spite of my talent for improving the mood within my family—bringing light to the darkness, overseeing the entertainment and sparking my parents' and sister's imaginations—my sister was somehow still our brightest star. My parents practically worshipped her as if she were the sun itself.

My little sister María had, without a doubt, an unusual abundance of good qualities, but it was first and foremost her superior intelligence that paved her way and escaped the notice of no one.

My sister had an unusually good head on her shoulders.

And my parents were proud. They veritably burst with pride over their youngest child—so intelligent, precocious, so beautiful.

They heaped praise on her, her wisdom and drive, and nothing could cast a pall over their adoration.

I did not inspire the same devotion. This sounds sad and dramatic, but it wasn't.

My parents were affectionate with me and tried not to let their admiration for my little sister impact on me, though there was never a question that she was their favourite. I could well understand that.

My sister, however, was the kind of person who went out of her way to keep me in her shadow, who did everything she could to ensure that our parents' affection was directed first and foremost—and preferably only—at her. She was two years younger than me, but she acted like she was two years older. She played the part of big sister to me, scolded me whenever I misstepped (which was frequently, as far as she was concerned), and lectured me on how I should arrange my life so that my existence wouldn't be an abject disappointment to myself and my loved ones. She acted like she was the one who had the extra years and experience behind her.

She made every effort to maintain her privilege at home. She was the bearer of a bright future, our family's greatest hope. She was told that there were no limits to what she could dream because there were no limits to what her abilities and intelligence could achieve. On top of which, she was beautiful in her own special way. My parents really dreamt big for her.

I never thought much about this imbalance between the two of us sisters and I didn't take my parents' unconditional adoration of María to heart. I adored my sister, too, because María was special, and you couldn't help but be enchanted by her. I did my best to ensure that she could flourish. I worshipped her, I told everyone how much I admired her abilities and her intelligence. I was sincere about that; I felt like I was telling the truth.

# 32

After we grew up and our parents had passed away, my sister's egotism, her unflagging competitiveness and what I saw as her arrogance gradually started to get on my nerves. Of course I found her attempts to make me feel small while simultaneously aggrandizing herself upsetting, especially when it happened in front of Gíó.

I had the creeping suspicion that she wanted to win him away from me; maybe, in her eyes, Gíó was prey that *she*, not I, should have caught: handsome, strong, fun, and—I now hasten to add, in light of new circumstances—sexy, too. Although she never said anything to this effect.

What she would do was say to other people within my hearing: 'Yeah, my sister maybe isn't the type who understands how things work right off the bat, bless her...' or 'Gíó, dear, how can you expect to pull yourself out of penury and misery if one of you is earning next to nothing from their eternally underpaid idealism?'

She was talking about me, her big sister; she meant I didn't earn my keep. Gíó worked full-time at some sort of marketing company in a job I didn't understand the first thing about, but from which he earned a very tidy salary. I didn't know precisely what his job entailed—it was all really vague and nebulous. It was easier when he was an architect at a design studio, as he was for a few years after we came home from Italy. The lines there were clear. But as time went on, his interest shifted from drawing houses, load-bearing structures and roof slopes to creating castles in the air and mares' nests. He got a job in advertising and, before long, he was all in at a marketing firm formerly known as an ad agency. Gíó said they gave companies and people new lives, or else gave their lives a story or some kind of meaning. He'd become an imagination specialist, as he jokingly called his job.

His job was to make people imagine that other people led remarkable lives. To give humdrum, sad and pitiful existences the appearance of happiness of and joy. He made stupidity look clever, unloveliness lovely and swindlers saints.

'I get people to believe that horses are more than just horses.'

I think in recent years, he'd started to hate his job and all those fake lives he'd created, but he never said anything. He kept mum about work.

What María had been talking about when she mentioned 'eternal idealism' was probably my dalliance with literature. I was always writing. I always wanted to be part of some sort of literary circle without ever doing anything to merit that inclusion. I was always orbiting literary types without being one of their number.

But I did write.

I wrote words. Sentences. I wrote stories I'd been told. I wrote conversations I'd overheard. I eavesdropped on people talking on their phones or to each other. I sat in coffee houses with books I pretended to be reading and a notebook. I jotted down things I heard—not always, but when all the seats were close together and there wasn't much space between people, I sometimes found myself witness to something that seemed worth writing down. Why, I don't know. But I collected conversations. Sometimes, just half-conversations if the person I was listening in on was on the phone.

I'd just recorded a brand-new conversation in my notebook when Gíó disappeared. It was only a day old. I'd sat down at a café, turned towards the window and pricked up my ears. Next to me sat a woman on her phone. Her car had been broken into while her mother was being buried. The car had been in the cemetery car park. She must have told this story many times because there was no break in the flow of her words. She'd polished the narrative into one seamless, continuous line from beginning to end. She was no longer angry or shocked over the broken windscreen or the lost valuables. And her mother's death was no longer coloured by sorrow or loss. She was telling the story to move someone, get sympathy and attention, and I listened, and when she finished speaking and left the coffee house, I wrote the story down. Word for word.

Writing down stories like this is the closest I've come to any sort of literary occupation—what my sister called my idealism.

That's just how María was. She wanted to conquer everything she undertook and ensure that there could never be any question of which of us sisters had the upper hand. It was important to her to win this ongoing competition with me.

But that day, I sat in my sister's handsome home at the table in the kitchen where she cooked her delectable meals and lied to her about Gíó and the circumstances leading up to his disappearance.

I shamelessly told her that Gíó had been planning to visit her when he stormed out, although in reality, Gíó had never—then or ever before—mentioned anything of the sort. Truth be told, he never mentioned María or talked about my sister at all. In my mind, there was a reason for that.

I enjoyed the way lying tasted, the dishonourable flavour of it on my tongue. It's forgivable to tell a lie when the truth will bring destruction and misery in its wake.

I had decided to survive.

# 33

I didn't stay at María's for long. She brought me no peace or comfort. She was clearly upset and having trouble sitting still and focusing on our conversation. She wouldn't believe anything but that Gíó would be back soon. She said as much. I decided to go home, call the police again and then waste no more time in starting to search for my husband. I felt like it had been long enough since he'd disappeared. The wait had become unbearable, and it was only going to get worse with each passing day, regardless of whether the police got involved or not.

I practically fled from my sister's home. Sped away in my beat-up car after a short and distracted goodbye. María herself, I couldn't escape. I understood the difference between running away and getting away.

When I got back home, there was a man standing on my front steps. It seemed like he'd rung the doorbell and was waiting for someone to answer.

I couldn't tell who it was; I didn't recognize him from behind.

'Hello,' I called as I stepped out of the car.

The man turned on his heel. He had a thick black moustache that looked like a shoe brush. He watched me come up the steps with interest and didn't say anything until I was almost right in front of him.

'Good afternoon…' he said, giving me a searching look. There was something sly about this man, something scheming and sleazy. I caught sight of a white stain on the crotch of his trousers.

'Good afternoon,' I responded.

'You'll have to forgive me for stopping by without warning… or warning that I'd be stopping by, that is. I just got the crazy idea to come by and say hello. I've seen you walking around the neighbourhood, past my house… I live there,' (he pointed to a house on the other side of the street, although I couldn't tell which one) 'and I've always meant to come over. You're Júlía, is that right?'

'I'm Júlía, yes.'

'Hi, my name's Jed.' (Or at least, I heard him say *Jed*, but that was probably a mistake because no one is actually called Jed. At least not in Iceland. Maybe he said Jafet.)

'As I said, I've often seen you walking from my window,' he continued. 'So I wanted to introduce myself.'

'Oh?'

'I just moved, you see. Here to the neighbourhood, I mean.'

'Oh?'

He hesitated and faltered. He rubbed the stubble under his chin as if checking whether he needed to shave.

'Yeah, it just occurred to me… or, I just wanted to say hello… since we're neighbours and all…'

'Hello. But I don't have time right now,' I said and moved to slip past the man and open the door to my house.

'You're Júlía M.' Now there was intensity in his voice, as though he had no intention of letting me go. As if he didn't want this meeting to be our last. He wanted to salvage this failed introduction.

'Yes, I'm Júlía M. And?'

I gave the man a sidelong glance as I stepped past him, opened the door and went inside. I stopped in the doorway, as if giving him one final opportunity to say something that would stop me from closing the door in his face.

'Maybe we could grab a coffee together… when you have more time. I know your husband a little and I'd like to get to know you as well.'

I closed the door.

I didn't have the energy to think about this Jed—where he lived, his craving for coffee, that he'd met Gíó and had seen me walking.

I had no interest in getting to know this man and no interest in his laughable attempt to try and create a connection between residents on the street. It wasn't the first time someone had tried to rope me into this kind of conversation.

It was entirely uninteresting.

As soon as I'd closed the door and taken off my shoes and jacket, I strode into the living room, where I intended to make my call.

The clay shards from the flowerpot were still all over the floor and the green plant lay upside down in its tragic pile of dirt. I'd decided not to clean up the soil because I knew the mess would assuredly make Gíó's disappearance more interesting to the police. It would give them a focal point in the house, something that suggested a struggle or an uninvited guest. I stood at the living room window. I liked to be looking at something that was in motion when I was on the phone. It was enough to see the tree branches blowing in the wind or a cat calmly padding its way across a patch of grass.

During my earlier conversation with the sarcastic police officer, he'd given me a phone number I could call directly if I was getting desperate.

I was getting desperate.

This time, I was met with more interest than I'd been the first time. The policeman on the phone was purposeful and invested and seemed to understand the seriousness of the matter.

'I'll send over two detectives. You're home now?' he said, all business, after I'd sketched out the situation for him.

'Yes, I'm at home.'

'We'll be there shortly. Ten minutes or so.'

# 34

That ended up being a spot-on estimate because almost exactly ten minutes later, I looked out the kitchen window and saw a white police car cruising slowly down the street before pulling to a stop in front of my house. The driver killed the engine and the headlights turned off.

Then: nothing.

One minute passed into the next.

The car just sat there and, for a long time, it looked like the occupants were just going to sit there, too. Maybe they'd stopped for a coffee on the way and wanted to finish it before they got down to their actual job.

I noticed that Finna had stopped sweeping the pavement when she realized the police were coming to call. She stared at their car with undisguised interest.

A considerable amount of time passed, and the detectives showed no signs of having any particular business beyond the confines of their car. So there I stood, waiting impatiently for them to get out and get going.

I could see the outline of the driver through the side window of the police car. From the kitchen window, it was hard to tell what he was doing in there because it was getting dark outside. But I determined that he must be finishing a cigarette because his face was illuminated at regular intervals by an orange glow.

*What is wrong with them?* I thought. *Are they staking the place out or something?*

I caught sight of a woman who lived at the other end of my street walking in our direction in a black rain poncho with her dog on a leash. When she saw the police car, she slowed down, but kept walking with some uncertainty until she suddenly turned on her heel and went back the way she came. What does she have on her conscience? I wondered.

I was relieved when two men finally tumbled out of the car. One of them was a large and had a big belly, probably around sixty. He was accompanied by a younger, long-legged man who was moving with visible stiffness. Both of them were in plain clothes and bareheaded.

The older man, who'd been in the driver's seat, flicked away his cigarette stub before crushing it with his heel, twisting his foot twice to snuff it out. They stopped in front of my front door and turned around, scanning the houses and gardens up and down the street. They exchanged a few words, the one with the belly pointing at the house across the street, and there they stood for a long time, deep in conversation, though I couldn't see what it was that had caught their interest. I was leaning forward to get a better view when suddenly they turned around and came up the steps. I retreated slightly from the window so they wouldn't catch me peeping.

The detectives appeared uncertain, looking up at the windows of the house. They spoke calmly, in no apparent hurry, and then stopped abruptly once again. Then the younger one turned around, ran down to the car and came back with a rather large leather satchel. I didn't move from where I was standing a step or two back from kitchen window, careful not to let them see me. Every now and then I'd take a sneaky peek, resting my head on the window frame and waiting for them to ring the bell.

Another eternity passed before they finally got around to pressing the button on the doorbell, as though the decision had required some consideration.

Both men had their backs to the door and were looking at the street, but as soon as I opened, they calmly turned around in one fluid, synchronized movement, as though this was something they'd practised many times.

'Hi, thank you for coming,' I said. 'Please come in.'

'Happy to do so, thank you. This here is Sigurður Jón,' said the older one, pointing at his gangly colleague. 'And I'm…' A noisy car drove by right as he said his name and so I didn't hear what the paunchy detective was called. *Foreigner*, it sounded like? What kind of name was that?

'We're with the police, as you've no doubt worked out. Am I right in saying that you're concerned about your husband? You've reported him missing, is that correct?'

'Yes, that's correct,' I answered, without being sure he'd got the correct information about what I'd actually reported.

They came in and took off their shoes—the older man was wearing thick grey sheep's wool socks—and then stood placidly in the hall, politely waiting for me to lead them into the house.

'I called because of my husband. He's missing, I reported to the police that he was missing, or at least, that I don't know where he is and he's not answering his phone… I'm worried. He went out last night, he didn't come home and I haven't heard from him since.'

'You haven't heard from him since… Has he ever disappeared like this before?' asked the older detective, Foreigner or whatever his name was, who was looking at me attentively.

'No, he's never disappeared before. This isn't some sort of everyday occurrence for us,' I said drily. I immediately regretted the tone I'd taken with this gentleman in his woollen socks.

'No, no, of course not. I didn't mean—'

'This isn't like him. But… I… I'll admit that we had an argument yesterday and he left the house angry.'

'Let's sit down, why don't we?' said the pot-bellied detective, laying a meaty hand on my shoulder as though he wanted to calm me down and show me around in my own home. I felt the heat from his hand flowing down my back. 'Let's just take a seat in the kitchen and you can tell us what happened.'

The scent of cigarettes wafted off him.

'First I want you to take a look at something I find peculiar—here, in the living room,' I said, walking ahead of them.

'Peculiar?' said Sigurður Jón, the younger detective.

'Look. The window was open in here this morning, this flowerpot had been on the windowsill.' I pointed at the plant and the heap of dirt on the floor. 'This is how I found it this morning—the pot broken and dirt all over the floor.'

'But your husband went out the front door…' said Sigurður Jón.

'Yes, he went out the front door—obviously. I'm not saying he went out the window. I'm just pointing out the evidence. I don't know what happened. I can't figure it out.'

I lied easily, unaffectedly. I don't think I'd told them one true word about Gíó's disappearance. It was all fabrication. And the plant on the floor was a sorry testimony to all my lies.

I had decided to survive.

# 35

'You haven't moved anything?' asked Sigurður Jón, his shrill, thin voice taking me out of my wool-gathering.

We stood there in a bunch, hunched over the plant, the downy, succulent *Plectranthus argentatus* that was almost impossible to kill, a plant that could survive drought, sunlessness and total neglect. Although in my living room window, it had received nourishment, water, sun and affection.

'No, I've avoided coming in here, I was careful not to get near it. There's dirt everywhere but I haven't stepped in it.'

'No,' said Sigurður Jón, seeming to be very interested in the plant and the clumps of dirt.

'My neighbour told me she saw a man in my garden this morning. Someone she'd never seen before. And she said he was wearing a rucksack. A bulky, canvas rucksack.'

'That's quite interesting,' said Foreigner, pulling a notebook out of his breast pocket and scribbling something in it.

'Sorry,' I said. 'What did you say your name was?' I directed my words at the corpulent detective.

'Oh, apologies. Did I forget to introduce myself? My name is Haraldur.'

'Haraldur. Right.'

'And this is Sigurður Jón,' he said, gesturing at the lanky man. 'We call him Victory John—bit funnier in English, eh?'

Sigurður Jón looked up at me and waved cheerfully, like a

football player being introduced on the loudspeaker before an important match waving to his fans.

'Who did you say saw this man in your garden?' asked Haraldur.

'My neighbour. She lives in number twelve. Her name's Finna. Or she's always called Finna—I'm pretty sure that's her name. Maybe it's Finnbjörg or something. She's an old woman and lives diagonally across the street from me. House number twelve. She thought he was a gardener.'

I watched as Sigurður Jón walked up to the window and seemed to be checking out the distance from there to the ground. Then he crouched down on his heels so he could take a closer look at the evidence.

'But nothing's been stolen?' I heard Haraldur ask.

'No, as far as I can tell, nothing's been stolen. My computer was here in the living room, and it wasn't touched. There was a bottle of red wine on the coffee table, but it was empty this morning, that is—*emptied*. But I'd only poured one glass from it.'

'Wait, what? Someone came in through the window to polish off your wine?' said Haraldur, a note of doubt creeping into his voice.

'There are no footsteps in the dirt… No one came through the window after the pot landed on the floor, that is,' said Sigurður Jón. 'There are no signs of forced entry. There are no footprints on the windowsill, either. It could have been some *fokking* cat that just jumped up…'

'Stop right there,' I said sharply. 'You will not use the word *fokk* or any derivation thereof in my home. I cannot stand that word. Hate it. Why in *fokking hell*' (and here I made air quotes) 'have Icelanders started aping the vernacular of self-indulgent, materialistic American rappers? They can't utter a single sentence without using that word. It smacks of poverty… by which I mean a *fokking* poverty of intellect.'

Both detectives were staring at me, open-mouthed.

'No, no, go on. I just needed to say my piece before you repeated that word…' I nodded in Sigurður Jón's direction and gestured for him to continue.

He hesitated and it took him a good while to get going again, as if it were costing him some effort to string together sentences that didn't include that blasted word.

'Well, uh, I just meant to say that it could have been a neighbourhood pussycat, er, feline—' he shot me a quick look as if expecting me to scold him for his less high-flown word choice. 'Yes, a cat that jumped up onto the windowsill, inadvertently knocked over the flowerpot, and then got scared and jumped back out when the pot smashed to the floor. Or else someone could have knocked it over on the way out.'

'Yes, that's fine, Siggi,' interrupted Haraldur. Sigurður Jón was still sitting on his heels and had been looking up at us while he talked, his words coming out in an unrelenting stream without even a moment to draw breath between sentences. I was worried he couldn't stop himself, that he would just keep rambling about the window and the plant and who- or whatever had slipped in or out, be that man or beast or whatever other species might have conceivably broken the pot. I was relieved when Haraldur interjected and stemmed the tide of his words.

'We'll determine… or rather, Siggi: you determine if we need to get forensics in here to check out the windowsill and the wine bottle—have you touched that?'

'I picked it up when I saw it was empty. I was really surprised.'

'But I doubt any full-grown man climbed through the window…' said Haraldur with certainty, giving Sigurður Jón a thoughtful look for a moment before looking back at me. 'There's no signs suggesting that.'

'No signs—' began Sigurður Jón again but Haraldur cut him off.

'You didn't wake up to any noise—I mean when the pot fell on the floor and broke?'

'No, I sleep upstairs.'

'Yes, of course. Upstairs. Maybe you slept deeply? Because of the wine?'

'Not because of the wine, no, not at all,' I started but I could see that the detective was entirely uninterested in what I had to say about that.

Haraldur continued. 'You say you and your husband had an argument yesterday? Marital troubles?'

'We're not technically married, it's just easier to call him my husband.'

'Was there a scuffle? Did you come to blows?'

'No, no, nothing like that… but… there was something.' I searched for words and felt myself touching my face, a gesture that Haraldur interpreted as sign of frailty because he said with exaggerated concern: 'Take it easy now. Deep breath.'

Haraldur was imperturbable and something akin to compassion flickered in his eyes. 'Just take it one thing at a time, we're not in a rush. It's just useful for us coppers to get the full picture from the get-go, you understand. Let's just take a seat in the kitchen and you can tell us about it. Take your time. There's no hurry. I know this is a terribly uncomfortable position to be in.'

Haraldur and I walked into the kitchen while Sigurður Jón tottered to his feet like a giraffe and stood quietly at the window. It was clearly hard for him to stop thinking about how the flowerpot could have ended up on the floor. He looked around for a moment before trailing after us.

'Would either of you like some coffee?' I asked perfunctorily. I didn't have the wherewithal to brew a pot for these clods; all I wanted was to sit down and close my eyes.

I felt like giving up.

Suddenly, a shock wave went through me. What on God's green earth was happening? Why was I standing in my kitchen with two police detectives asking questions about what had become of my husband? There was something wrong about the whole thing. This was not my life. This aberration had to have some straightforward explanation. I must have misremembered; I must have got confused somewhere along the line. Got out of the wrong side of the bed. I just needed to start this day again. All of it would vanish: Sorry, I had my days mixed up, the missing man is no longer missing, and the incomprehensible is suddenly comprehensible again.

'No, no – no coffee for me. Just some water if you have it—tap water's fine,' answered Haraldur, flopping into one of the kitchen chairs. Sigurður Jón sat down beside him.

'Same for me. Just water, thanks—tap water, if you have it,' he said in his thin voice.

I put two glasses of water on the table. Tap water, I could manage. Then I took a seat across from the two detectives.

# 36

'So: you haven't heard from your husband since yesterday… and he hasn't come home today,' Haraldur began.

He'd placed a notebook on the table in front of him. He was holding a fountain pen between his index finger and thumb. Now and then he tapped the pen on the notebook thoughtfully and rotated it in a semicircle.

'No, he stormed out and slammed the door behind him right before midnight yesterday. He was worked up and angry.'

'But… things didn't get physical? Siggi, be a good fellow and take a quick look around the house, if you would? Take the bag with you.'

I looked at the detectives in surprise, but didn't say anything.

'Are you angry with him?' asked Haraldur without looking at me. He was staring down at his notes, still tapping his pen on the table.

Sigurður Jón paused in the doorway, giving me a curious look as he awaited my answer.

'Me? No. Do you mean *was* I angry?'

'*Are* you angry?'

'Now? No, I'm not angry… I'm just afraid that he… I'm worried. But I'm not… or… no. I'm not angry.'

'Did you have a falling-out with your husband?'

I couldn't help myself—my mind went straight to the notebook I'd hidden in the bookcase. That blasted notebook was haunting me. All those women, all that weird sex. And Gíó…

Suddenly, I was furious.

'A falling-out! Do you think I killed him or something?' I said angrily.

'Something eating you?' asked Haraldur calmly, not letting my outburst disturb his composure. He set his pen on top of his notebook, leant forward and placed both hands palms-down on the table as if that would help him pick up on the tremors my nervous system was emitting. As if he believed he could perceive the vibrations through the tabletop, using nothing but his palms and fingertips. Then he looked up and gave me an inquiring look, as if he was hoping I wanted to tell him something that would help him understand what happened. As if he was waiting for me to reveal my secrets, let the cat out of the bag. He wanted to solve this thing right now.

'Eating... what? No.'

'Is there something on your conscience, I mean. Just nibbling away?'

'I can't say that there is. Nothing to do with this... thing... with Gíó. I mean, I've got plenty I feel guilty about... my entire upbringing was about instilling me with a perpetual sense of guilt, letting my conscience "nibble away at me". But I don't imagine that's what you're asking about.' I fell silent for a moment and took a deep breath. 'Perhaps you think I shot him or just turned round and stabbed him or something...'

I'd started babbling, so I decided to shut up before I got myself into trouble.

'Okay, I need you to listen to me now, hear what I'm saying. According to the law of the land, everyone is free to come and go as they please. Which is to say, it's not illegal to abandon your family. If the police find your husband on the street or at someone else's house, we can't force him to come home to you. It actually has nothing to do with us where your husband is unless—and let me repeat this—*unless* we have reason to believe a crime has been committed. If we think he was the victim of a crime, we have to determine what that crime was, who committed it, and then it's up to the judicial system to decide what right and fitting punishment should be meted out to the perpetrator. And then it comes back to the police to carry out the punishment, which most often involves putting the perpetrator—once convicted—behind bars or extracting money from him. That is, a fine. Or else if, say, your husband has been in an accident or been injured and is incapacitated, then it's our duty as police officers to come to his assistance… to rescue him, if he's in distress.'

'I understand…'

'That's good to hear,' said Haraldur. He was quiet for a moment and pulled a pack of Viceroys out of his breast pocket before shaking out a cigarette and placing it gently on the table. Then he put the pack on the table, too. Cigarette and cigarette pack side by side on the tabletop—a tidy little still life. Haraldur considered his handiwork and then fumbled in his pocket for a yellow lighter, which he placed on the table so that it, the cigarette and the pack all formed an orderly row. Pack. Cigarette. Lighter.

'Nice,' I said, gesturing at the array.

He flashed me a smile.

'Mmmhmm,' he said, and there was a trace of pleasure in his voice. 'I just like to have everything ready when the opportunity presents itself. The call of the nicotine, you know?'

Sigurður Jón came back from his sightseeing tour of my house. He put down the bag and gave Haraldur a look that I could tell had special meaning for them. But Haraldur just nodded, absorbed in his own thoughts.

Then both of them said nothing and it was clear that they were waiting for me to say something else. There was a stilted lull in conversation; I could think of nothing else to say. Sigurður Jón sat down at the kitchen table, crossing his arms over his chest as if to make it clear that he wouldn't be the one to break the silence this time. It was my turn to talk.

I regarded these two mute policemen sitting across from me. Haraldur with his pot belly. The zipper on his sweater reminded me of train tracks on a hilltop. I looked into his eyes, and he looked into mine, and I could see that he pitied me. He found me pitiable. I was pitiable.

Sigurður Jón was sitting straight as an arrow in his seat. His eyes showed neither pity nor anything else I could interpret one way or the other because they always seemed to flee ahead of my own. Was he scared of something?

We sat in silence until finally, almost involuntarily, I said: 'He told me he was going to María's... just before he slammed the door. Like it was some kind of threat.'

'Oh? To María's? I'm glad you're telling us this... Maybe you meant to say something before. And who is María? Do you know?' Haraldur leant across the kitchen table towards me. His voice was placid and paternal. This was too much.

'He just said he was going to María's. My sister's named María, but I don't know if he meant her or some other María.'

'Have you spoken to your sister?'

'Yes, she said she didn't know anything about it.'

'He didn't go to her house yesterday?'

'No, she said she didn't see him yesterday.'

'Can you think of any other María he might have meant?'

'No, I don't think he knows any other María. But I'm afraid that... I'm not sure... but I suspect he's in a relationship... I mean, that he's in a sexual relationship with my sister.'

Haraldur looked at me with concern. 'Ah. Well, uh, yes...' He sighed as though particularly regretful that the matter should have taken this turn. 'Wellll… these are serious accusations to make against your partner. Is this just a feeling or have you anything concrete that you're basing this suspicion on? He said he was going to her house, you say? Your sister's?' Haraldur repeated knowingly.

'Yes—as I said, he told me he was going to María's, and her name is María. My sister, that is. I called her this morning and then went over to her house, but she said she hadn't seen Gíó nor heard from him… She said she didn't know anything about any of this.'

'Then it's some other María your partner was referring to?' said Sigurður Jón, nodding eagerly. I acted like I hadn't heard him.

'Give me your sister's full name,' said Haraldur. He also ignored his colleague and opened his notebook, pen at the ready. He gave me an encouraging look, letting me know he was ready.

'My sister's name is María—just María, no middle name. I can write her number down for you,' I said, reaching for his notebook.

'Write down her address as well.' He watched me writing on the graph paper of his notebook. 'And the two of you are full sisters? Same parents?'

'Yes, she's my little sister, two years younger than me.'

'You say that they—your husband and your sister—have been having a love affair… Was that perhaps the reason for your argument yesterday?'

'Love affair…? I didn't say anything about a love affair… I highly doubt that their relationship could be characterized as anything to do with love,' I harrumphed. 'I doubt… but I suspect… I'm not positive, of course… but I think they're sleeping together… having unorthodox sex… with one another… and have been for some time… They've covered their tracks well.'

It did not escape me that Haraldur and Sigurður Jón exchanged a glance at this.

'What do you mean by unorthodox?' Sigurður Jón asked, leaning towards me as if to ensure that he didn't miss a word I uttered.

'Let me ask again,' interrupted Haraldur, 'as you seem to be in possession of sensitive information. Why do you suspect that your husband is having a love affair—or, as you put it, "unorthodox sex"—with your sister?'

'It was pure chance that I discovered it. I read a written account of their trysts.'

'A statement?' asked Sigurður Jón.

I didn't answer, as I didn't understand what he even meant by that. There was a long silence and I saw both detectives pause to reflect for a moment before Haraldur ventured his next question.

'Might I ask you to go further into this… discovery? That is, this "written account" you mentioned?'

'I found a *fokking* notebook!' I half shouted. Both detectives looked at me in shock but before Sigurður Jón could point out my infelicitous word choice, I added: 'Yes, I said *fokking*. Because if there was ever an appropriate usage of that word, it's in reference to that notebook.'

I could tell from their expressions that the detectives were pondering my overreaction, and I understood immediately that I'd made a pretty poor impression on them both.

'I really don't want to say anything else about the notebook—it's personal. But the fact remains that there are detailed, written descriptions of their copulations. You can, if you so desire, imagine what those descriptions might entail and ask yourselves if any of this is important to finding Gíó or solving a potential crime. But I'm not going to let you have the… accounts.'

'We can set the notebook and its descriptions of intercourse aside for now. Was your husband's mental state such that you have any reason to fear for his life? Anything like that? Was he driving?' asked Haraldur.

I hurried to interject. 'I have absolutely no reason to believe that he's done himself harm. That's unlikely in the extreme, I think. It would never occur to him to commit suicide—it's not the kind of person he is. He wants to live, that much I can be relatively sure of. He's too… No, I'm just worried that he got into some kind of accident, that he's lying helpless somewhere and waiting for help.'

'We've at least eliminated the possibility, as of a few hours ago, that he was in hospital—we did that before we came over. So that much we can be sure of. No accidents reported within the last twenty-four hours involved your husband and neither did any hospital admissions. We're doing our best to find him. Then there's also the possibility that he scarpered, took off to start a new life. You'll forgive the bluntness, but…'

'Scarpered?'

'Sure. It's not unheard for people to just take off, for whatever reason. Often because of financial problems or trouble in their personal lives.'

'Are you implying that he's hiding somewhere? That he just walked out without saying goodbye?'

'No, I'm not implying anything of the sort. I just want to consider all the possibilities.'

'He'd have to be a real monster to deliberately vanish without a trace, no explanation, just leave me thinking that he was in trouble somewhere, injured or dead… like some sort of punishment or revenge… to let me agonize for the rest of time. He thinks I'm unfair sometimes, unsympathetic. He may have been angry with me… but to disappear like that… That borders on evil. I think that's a bridge too far. The only likely explanation is that he got into an accident. But he wasn't driving, to answer your earlier question. He didn't take the car. He was angry…'

'Don't take what I'm saying personally. I just want to consider all the possibilities. But if he did take off, it isn't necessarily to make you feel bad or to punish you. People who decide to disappear aren't thinking along generally accepted or rational lines. You know that many people go missing every year. Maybe it isn't so common in Iceland, but it still happens now and again. In Europe, there are thousands of cases where someone abandons their family without warning, just goes off to start a new life. Sometimes on the other side of the planet, sometimes on the other side of the city. These are often people who couldn't seem happier in their home until they disappear, and it turns out they've been planning their escape for ages, that they were willing to sacrifice everything and everyone just so they could say goodbye to their humdrum old life and start from scratch with no baggage.'

I understood what the detective was trying to say, and his speculations were obviously not that off the wall. Of course, Gió, like anyone, might dream of a new life. The only problem with this theory was that Gió was probably a washed-up corpse somewhere on the shore of Hvalfjörður. Actually, what happened to the bodies people drowned? Did they sink to the bottom? Or did they get gobbled up by whales as they sunk through the depths? There was precedent for that.

'I think he was ashamed when he left. He was agitated. He hadn't planned on my finding out about him and my sister. But the accounts I mentioned also revealed that he'd been having relations with many other women in recent months or years… I found that out, too… yesterday.'

The detectives shot each other another glance.

'And was it yesterday, after you told him about your discovery, that you knew he'd been cheating on you, that he stormed out?'

'Yes, I told him that I knew he was sleeping with my sister.'

'Can you tell us more about the circumstances—the lead-up?' asked Sigurður Jón, leaning forward on the table. Haraldur smiled at him. 'Great question, Siggi.'

'As I've told you, I found that…' here I mouthed the word *fokking*, but didn't say it, 'notebook in which he'd written down graphic descriptions of sex… sex acts… with women who I thought I knew. Each chapter began with the names of the participants. Now, I can't be sure who owns the notebook. It was a challenge to confront Gíó with what I'd found. But yesterday, we were a bit at odds with one another and I showed him the notebook and read aloud from it.'

I was astonished with myself the moment I blurted out this impassioned declaration regarding a notebook I'd never actually confronted Gíó about.

'And—' started Sigurður Jón, but I interrupted.

'He said he said no idea what I was talking about and that it wasn't his notebook, even though the handwriting was similar to his… I insisted it was his handwriting, but he flatly denied it. The descriptions of my husband's fornications with my sister María are in the dead centre of the notebook. Or, rather—most of the descriptions in it are about sex acts involving a woman and the author, he writes in first-person singular—'

'You mean, "I"?' It was Sigurður Jón who spoke again with a glance at Haraldur.

'You? What?' said Haraldur, looking at his colleague in confusion.

'No, not me. She said the author writes in first-person singular. So: *I*,' said Sigurður Jón looking back at me. 'I just want to be sure I'm understanding the grammatical concepts correctly. Don't want any confusion… We want everything to be clear… no misunderstandings… So, first-person singular, that means…'

'All right, now, Siggi. Very good. I understand.'

'Most of the entries in the book are about the author and a woman named María and I'm almost certain it's my sister. Gíó pretended not to know anything about it, said he'd never written anything of the sort. But with those words, he stormed out and said he was going to María's.'

I was relentless, mesmerized by my own lies.

'Do you have the notebook to hand?' asked Sigurður Jón cautiously. Haraldur gave me a curious look.

'No, he took it with him yesterday,' I said without blinking.

'Of course, yes,' said Haraldur.

'So he has the notebook?' asked Sigurður Jón.

'Yes, he took it with him.'

'This is good for now, Júlía. We won't issue a missing persons bulletin for him until tomorrow morning. Let's hope that he shows himself before it comes to that… But we'll need a good photograph of him in the event that we do need to go public with this. We'll also need a description of him: facial features, hair colour, the clothes he was last seen wearing and so on. We'll disseminate that information to the officers who are on patrol around town. They'll have both Gíó's photo and his description. And then, as I said, we'll just have to hope that he makes contact soon, so we don't have to call out Search and Rescue.'

# 37

I showed the men to the door.

'We'll do our best to track your partner down. I don't know if this is any comfort to you, but most cases of this sort are solved quickly. In most instances, the person in question reappears within thirty-six hours,' said Haraldur on his way out.

'So I've been told. I hope that turns out to be the case this time.'

'Take care, and you just give us a call if you have any questions or if there's any other information you want to share.'

'Haraldur?'

'Yes?'

'Could you perhaps give me a call if there are any developments? There's nothing for me to do but wait.'

'I'll do that, Júlía.'

I watched them walk to the car. Haraldur stuck the cigarette he'd been palming between his lips and lit it before getting in.

I went back into the house. Although I was longing for something to keep my busy, and knew I had to write up my interview with the erotica author, I couldn't motivate myself. Instead of sitting down at my computer, I went over to the bookshelf where I'd hidden the notebook. I opened it and was confronted by one of those farcical descriptions of trysts the author had planned and clearly took great pleasure in documenting.

There was a date and location at the top, below which it read:

PARTICIPANTS
NUMBER: Two
WHO: Myself and María
WHERE: Dining Room

I couldn't bring myself to reread the detailed description of how María was supposed to have worn a thick fur and a fur hat, but otherwise, been stark naked. According to the entry, she'd taken her time smearing green mint oil onto his genitals—Gíó's, that is, or the author's, I suppose—as he lay on his back, completely naked except for a pair of black socks. Then he described how he'd let María wrap a leather cord around his oil-slicked penis so she could lead him around the apartment 'by my cock' like a dog on a leash. I got the reference to the Chekhov story: she was The Lady with the Dog. Sex as literature or literature as sex.

I shook my head, closed the notebook, and tucked it back in its hiding place.

It particularly bothered me that Gíó—or whoever the author was—said he never wore underwear, but went around pants-less all day, a state he found particularly invigorating when in a big crowd.

I'd never noticed that Gíó didn't wear pants.

It took me a few moments to redirect my thoughts away from the blasted notebook, but then I forced myself to sit down at my computer and write up the interview. Truth be told, I focused surprisingly well, and the time passed quickly. It was a break from all the recent distress, and I was deeply engrossed in the text when the phone rang. It was my sister.

'Hi,' I said.

'What the hell is wrong with you?' I heard her nearly shouting on the other end of the line. 'What were you thinking, telling the police that I had anything to do with Gíó's disappearance, or that he was with me? Some cop—Sigurður Jón, he called himself—called me up and said he'd spoken to you. And now he's on the way over here. They think I'm Gíó's mistress! And who are the most likely perpetrators of a crime? Oh, right: mistresses and blind-drunk husbands! You've landed me up to my eyeballs in trouble. Do you get that? I will not be dragged into your bullshit. What is wrong with you? Have you completely… Look, I'm going to say this one more time: don't you dare get me mixed up in your and Gíó's messes. Are you completely out of your mind?' She'd lost control of her voice, which was alternating between a shout and a hoarse whisper that seemed to come from deep in her throat. She was well and truly hysterical.

'All I told him was what Gíó told me—that he was going to your house. That was the last I heard from him… his last words.' I immediately regretted that turn of phrase, afraid that it would become a self-fulfilling prophecy.

'And that we were having a secret love affair. What are you thinking? We—'

'I never said you were having a secret love affair.'

'Oh? Is that so?'

'I said that you were secretly sleeping together.'

'Oh, forgive me, that's right. The cop said you'd told him about some wild sexual relationship. Why are you telling the police this crap? You know very well that it's total nonsense. Just something you've invented to suit the situation, something you're imagining. You can be so… so ridiculously insane.'

'I found Gíó's notebook. He describes your lurid sex life in great detail.'

There was a sudden silence on the other end of the line.

'What are you talking about? A notebook with descriptions of our sex life?' she said in her husky voice after a moment. She seemed calmer now, or perhaps she was just bewildered.

'Yes, as I said. I found Gíó's notebook, and I'm not lying, dear sister, when I say that the descriptions are lurid, racy, raunchy...'

'If this notebook exists anywhere other than in your imagination, any such descriptions are pure fabrication and have no place in reality. It could well be that your sex-starved partner has allowed himself to fantasize and that he was stupid enough to write those fantasies down. THAT... IS... NOT... MY... RESPONSIBILITY.' (She was yelling again.) 'I DEMAND you fix this IMMEDIATELY and tell the police that this is UTTER HORSESHIT. I don't know what's been going on with you two, but I'm NOT YOUR MAN'S MISTRESS AND I NEVER HAVE BEEN! You will make that entirely clear to the police. You will clear my name immediately and tell them you are a SICK LIAR!'

Then she hung up on me.

# 38

The day passed and then the night.

A new day. Every day has its own life. The day before, Sting played a sold-out concert in Zurich. And the day before that, Gíó went missing. No one was any closer to knowing where he could be and the police were finally ready to issue a missing persons bulletin for him in the papers and on the radio, maybe some other places, too.

I'm not quite sure how María's conversation with the police went, how they liked her or what they thought about her part in Gíó's disappearance. The police didn't have much to say about it, although I'd spoken with Detective Haraldur several times. (I couldn't seem to leave him alone.) He said he'd spoken to my sister, who'd categorically denied having any idea what had happened to Gíó and firmly dismissed the idea that they'd ever had any sort of 'physical' relationship. I took note of the wording he used there: 'a physical relationship'.

'She said it was out of the question that she and Gíó had ever had a physical relationship and that anything along those lines was pure fabrication on your part,' said Haraldur in his sedate voice.

Haraldur had been authorized to examine Gíó's bank accounts, monitor his credit and debit cards and track his phone. He said he'd be in touch with any new developments.

It came as a genuine a shock when I saw Gíó's photo published on the state broadcaster's website. His expression in the photo was serious and he was looking directly at the camera. I knew that photo well. It was a recent one that I took of him in front of our new house. We'd moved in that same day. We were happy, and you could tell from Gíó's expression. The house we'd bought was a small, two-storey, corrugated-iron-clad house out in Skerjafjörður, a colourful old seaside neighbourhood not far from the city centre. A little doll's house that suited us perfectly.

At first, I'd given the police a photo I'd taken of him after his graduation from the University of Florence. He was perched happily on a bench in the university grounds when I told him we had to take a graduation picture.

'You should be in the picture, too,' he'd said.

'I haven't graduated. If I'm ever to graduate, it'll be from the nuthouse,' I'd said, and we both laughed. Then I snapped the photo.

The police told me the graduation photo was too old. Which is why I pulled out the one from moving-in day.

Under the photo was the police bulletin.

# Icelandic National Broadcasting Service (RÚV) | ruv.is | 10.10.22 – 10:55

Reykjavík and Capital-Area Police are seeking information on the whereabouts of Gíó Ísaksson.

Gíó is thirty-four years old, of muscular build and 187 centimetres tall. He has dark, medium-long hair and blue eyes.

When he was last seen, he was wearing an olive-green trench coat, black trousers and black leather shoes.

Gíó left his home just before midnight on Sunday, 9 October, and his last known location was Óseyri Harbour in Hafnarfjörður around 1 a.m. on Monday morning.

Anyone with any information about Gíó or his whereabouts is asked to contact police immediately by calling 112.

# 39

My heart was pounding in my chest.

Everything was still so unreal.

I was always so surprised by the unexpected, and yet life was a series of endless coincidences.

The police, or Haraldur at least, hadn't told me anything about Gíó being spotted around Óseyri Harbour, but I figured they'd traced his phone to the wharf where I'd sent a text from it before throwing it into the sea.

I grabbed my phone and found Haraldur's number.

'This is Haraldur.'

It never ceased to surprise me that he always seemed to be just sitting there, waiting to pick up. He was from another time, this policeman. He was probably speaking into a black rotary telephone.

'Yes, hello. I saw the bulletin has been published in the papers, or online…'

'Who's speaking?' There was impatience in his voice.

'I'm sorry, it's me. Júlía.' I'd have expected him to recognize my voice after all the calls.

'Oh, hello, Júlía,' said the detective, his tone changing completely.

'I hadn't heard that Gíó had been sighted near Óseyri Harbour. You promised me you'd let me know about any new developments.'

'Yes, forgive me, I'd not managed to call you yet. I got the information about Óseyri Harbour from the phone company not long ago, just before that was published, actually. He made a call while he was out there. But since then, there's been nothing—no signal from his phone whatsoever.'

'He made a call? Who to?'

'Yes, one very short call. Just a few seconds. The phone company should be able to tell us shortly who he rang.'

'All right.'

'Tell me one thing. Did the two of you go out to Hvalfjörður the day he went missing?'

'Yes… Yes, we took a drive to the fjord on Sunday afternoon. Why do you ask?'

'I'm just painting a picture. Establishing the sequence of events, as we say. Did anything unusual happen while you were there?'

'We were just out for a scenic drive…'

'Why Hvalfjörður, if I may ask?'

'I just felt like it…'

'No other reason?'

I thought for a moment. I couldn't very well mention Geirshólmur, nor the fact that we'd sailed out there in the motorboat.

'No. How come?'

'Was there anything that struck you as unusual about Gíó's behaviour on the drive? Did he say anything that might give some insight into what he was thinking about?'

'I've done nothing but go over our conversations word for word since he disappeared, but… no. He was maybe not in the best mood. He was silent for the most part. He didn't say anything that particularly stood out to me… afterwards.'

'Of course, of course. While I have you on the line, though, or the phone, I mean, I do have two things to tell you. We're checking the passenger lists for all flights out of the country. Could he have decided to go abroad, perhaps?'

'Yes, that's possible.'

'Do you think that's very likely?'

'Likely, no. That's… No, I don't think it's very likely. I've said as much before.'

'Can you think of anyone he might seek out to borrow money from, or anything like that?'

I thought for a moment. Truth be told, María was the first person that occurred to me, but I probably just had her on the brain. Gíó's father had been dead for several years. He'd grown up with his father and had little to no contact with his mother. She lived in the US and had been there since Gíó was a child.

Who were his friends?

He had a large circle of acquaintances, but not close friends. Gíó almost never talked about himself and basically never mentioned his family. But I remembered him once telling me that he didn't have close friends because he didn't really know how to be a man around men. He hadn't had a father who could teach him how men behaved. His father was closed off, locked in himself and his own interests, and mostly left Gíó to take care of himself. As a result, Gíó was awkward in the presence of other men and never himself. Or this is what he said at least and maybe he was right, but I never picked up on anything unusual in his relationships with men.

'No, to tell the truth, no such friend springs to mind, not right away, at least. He has no shortage of casual associates, but there's no one I can think of who would, you know, hide him, or walk through fire for him, as the case may be…'

'No, I see. But still, give it some thought.'

'I will.'

'The other thing I wanted to mention is that we've got two tips that Gíó has been spotted at a hotel on Hringbraut. In the old JL

House. We're going to send some guys over to check it out. I'm telling you this because I promised to keep you updated, but I want to warn you not to be too optimistic because there's seldom—if ever—anything useful that comes out of tips like this. But when we get two sightings in the same place at the same time, then it's best that we look into it. And I'll let you know right away if there's any news.'

'Yes, you let me know… keep me updated…'

# 40

I couldn't bear to be at home any longer. I felt I couldn't just sit and wait for the police to get around to checking out the tips and then report back to me. I had to see for myself if it could possibly be true that Gíó had checked into a hotel in the west end of town.

Had he made it off the island alive? Had he been rescued, or had he managed to get to the mainland under his own steam? My thoughts were going round in circles. Someone must have helped him. He couldn't have got back to the city alone while soaked and chilled to the bone. Someone must have seen him. Found him.

That is, if he was still alive.

That is, if he wasn't lifeless on the ocean floor.

What would he do if he'd survived? He'd probably think I'd tried to kill him. Of course, he had no idea that I'd gone back to get him. He didn't know that I'd regretted the whole thing. How would a man react to his partner trying to kill him? Would he report her to the authorities, have her arrested? Or would he take justice into his own hands and mete out a fitting punishment of his own? What would be a 'fitting punishment' in that man's mind?

Monetary damages?

Not a chance.

Would this man just disappear, forget everything about his partner's murderous intentions and his former life, hop on a 747 and flee the country, never to return? Would his disappearance be the punishment itself? So that the guilty party would be dogged by doubt, guilt and misery for the rest of time? Was that a fitting punishment? It seemed like a very severe one to me.

Fine, just go. But let me know you're alive.

I don't want you back. Just go, I muttered to myself, though I knew in my heart I was lying.

# 41

I'd only just got off the phone with the detective when I slipped on my shoes and jacket and headed out. I had to get out of that house. Naturally, the idea of finding my partner at the hotel, washed up from his recent maritime trauma, scared me, but I still hoped he'd be there. He shouldn't get away with his vengeful vanishing act, sentencing me to a life of torment because I'd got the idiotic notion to abandon him on that skerry.

Bodies don't just disappear. People who drown drift ashore. Or do they sink like a stone to the bottom of the sea? I should google it: do corpses sink at sea?

I hoped I'd find Gíó, and I also hoped I wouldn't.

I jumped when I opened the front door and found Finna standing on the doorstep with her broom. She'd probably been about to ring the bell.

'Whoops, hello there. I almost ran you down, I wasn't expecting to find you here on my doorstep,' I said brusquely.

'I heard about your partner. That he ran off on you. Sorry to hear it.'

'Ran off? That's not quite accurate. But I don't know where he is, and the police are searching for him. I'm afraid that he… that's he's been in an accident.'

'Some policeman called me today and then I saw the bulletin in the papers—about his disappearance.'

'The police called you?'

'Yes, they had some questions about the man in your yard.' The old woman regarded me with her cloudy eyes.

'I'm just on my way out, I'm in a bit of a hurry. I'm sorry, I'm actually on my way to assist the police.'

'I just wanted to mention something to you, given the circumstances. I didn't say anything to the police because I didn't think it right to mention anything I couldn't be sure of,' she said mysteriously.

'Oh? What's that?'

The old woman leant forward as if she meant to whisper something in my ear, but then she looked over her shoulder and pointed furtively at the house next to hers on the other side of the street.

'Did you know that there's a new tenant in that house there? Number ten.'

'A new tenant? No. I didn't even know the house was for rent.'

'It's just the apartment on the second floor that they rent out. Not the whole house. I think that you should keep an eye on the new renter. Maybe he has something to do with your husband's disappearance,' said Finna.

'Do you think so? Why?'

I looked at my elderly neighbour, the transparent drop of jelly on the tip of her nose and her eyes always so wet, as if they were brimming with tears that would soon overflow their banks. I knew Finna well, and I knew that her head was full of strange ideas about the daily comings and goings of her neighbours. She was always certain that there was something illegal or unethical going on in the other houses on the street. So her airing a fresh conspiracy theory was not exactly surprising.

'I'm just saying. Be on your guard. Keep an eye on that new tenant. Be alert.'

'Do you know who is living there now? Have you met them?'

'No, I haven't seen anyone, and I haven't met anyone. I just have this feeling that there's something fishy going on over there.' She gestured covertly once again, poking the index finger of her left hand past her right hip and wiggling the tip of her finger towards the house without turning so much as her head.

I looked across the street. There were no lights on in any of the windows of the second-floor apartment, as though whoever lived there was out. Or maybe they hadn't moved in. It was hard for me to imagine what mysterious activities could be going on in the new tenant's apartment. Nice, friendly people generally moved here—it was one of the most sought-after neighbourhoods in the city. Disagreements between neighbours were few and far between, and everything looked to be particularly peaceful on the street that day. Everyone was easy-going except perhaps the Black Widow—the woman in the black rain poncho. She could be trouble, but she was the only resident on the street who didn't fit the mould.

The Black Widow was a middle-aged woman with grey hair that hung all the way down her back. She lived in a house at the far end of the street. She actually wasn't a widow at all, but she caught everyone's attention because she was always, without exception, wearing that big, black raincoat and walking a giant, mean-looking black dog with cocked ears. The woman herself always wore a baleful expression and she wasn't given to exchanging pleasantries. She particularly loathed a young writer-couple who lived in the corner house and took every opportunity to sling all kinds of derision their way. She got as good as she gave from the writers, particularly the young woman.

'I'll be wary of them, the new tenants,' I said and moved to say goodbye.

'It's just one tenant, mind. One tenant, not tenants. One! It's a young man who lives there,' said Finna with a pointed look.

'Just one man, young, that's what I've heard. He moved in, you understand?'

'Yes, yes, I understand. It's just him. I'll be careful about that guy, but for now, I have to hurry. Take care, Finna.'

I'd only just got down the steps when I thought of the man who'd knocked on my door the day before. Jed.

'Actually,' I said.

'Yes?' said the old woman.

'The man, the new tenant. Is his name Jed?'

'No, I don't think so. He's Icelandic.'

# 42

I got in the car and got ready to drive to the hotel Haraldur had named. I was glad to be out of the house. The car was like a sanctuary for me.

My neighbour hobbled across the street, and I watched her make her way back home in the rear-view mirror. She resumed sweeping the front pavement.

It was well past noon, and a coal-black rain cloud was inching its way closer. It was only the middle of the day and already dark. Soon, a blanket of heavy rain and ceaseless wind would settle over the country.

I looked up at Gíó's and my house. I'd forgotten to turn off the kitchen light. On the other side of the street, no one had forgotten to turn out any lights in the new tenant's apartment. Every window was dark.

Suddenly, there was a rap on the glass, and I snapped to attention. A smiling face was looking through the passenger window. There he was, with his big rabbit teeth and bright expression: the postboy. Besides his large, protuberant teeth, he was recognizable by a quiff of hair that made him look like Tintin.

I rolled down the window.

'Heylo,' he said. He always used the same greeting.

'Hi,' I answered shortly.

'I don't have any mail for you today, but I just wanted to say hi. Maybe you'll get some tomorrow. I have to go now, I have a bag full of letters that I need to deliver to the correct recipients right away.'

He cycled away. I noticed that he'd clamped a Coke bottle to his bike rack. A message in a bottle? He waved and smiled brightly. That's just the way he was, the postboy. He liked to say hello to people.

I couldn't seem to shift into gear. I dithered as though afraid that, after all of this, I really would find Gíó at that hotel. He wouldn't be lost any more. It would be an indescribable relief and an indescribable agony.

We'd had good times, Gíó and I.

We'd lived together for a few years in Reykjavík, but we'd lived together for three months in Florence before that. That was the summer before I came back to Iceland from Italy. He'd moved into the little apartment that I rented on Via Giordano Bruno.

That summer, Gíó had finished his studies with the design guru at the University of Florence. He was an imaginative architect and a good designer. He'd swept up many of the prizes that the university gave out at graduation. I knew he'd be in great demand when he got back to Iceland. He was popular at university and went around surrounded by a big group of people who were clearly vying for his company. Gíó was rather taciturn, he wasn't one to hold the floor and he was no leader, but he had a lot of charm and people gravitated towards him. Wherever he was, he was surrounded by life and gaiety.

Gíó was my winning lottery ticket, and that summer, I had no doubt about it.

I kept working at Winslow & Winslow after Gíó graduated and up until we moved back home to Iceland.

Those first few months of living together were our best times together. Blue skies overhead. I felt that I was loved. I felt our love when I sat on the sofa, when I stood in the middle of the living room, when I was lying in bed and when we sat at the kitchen table in the evening. This was our time, there was no rush, we had plenty of time to look into one another's eyes, speak sweet nothings, touch, caress, kiss… We were like two brooks running together to form one glittering river. Two brooks. One river. Our every interaction was sincere, unashamed, heartfelt, open and natural.

At the beginning of our relationship, Gíó was careful and handled me with kid gloves. He knew first-hand what the consequences of a misstep could be. I told him the moment we started talking about him moving in with me that I wouldn't tolerate him trying to control me. He said he understood and would take care not to hold me back or tie me down in any way. I was used to living alone, and I'd had my doubts about us moving in together. In the early days, I did as I pleased, as did he, and so I didn't feel like we were overly bound to one another.

The life we shared brought me a lot of joy. We were deeply focused on one another. Then time passed and it was like the distance between us melted away and we melted into one another. We made the horizon disappear; horizontal lines were no longer horizontal, vertical lines no longer vertical. I was dizzy from morning till night and from night till morning and it was the best kind of dizziness.

Slowly but surely, however, the lines of the outside world started to sharpen. The dizziness faded, and suddenly, I was noticing birdsong, sunlight, the shadows cast by houses, the voices of people walking by my window, the scent of the bar and grill next door.

I could tell that Gíó had also woken up to a different world. I don't know what his world was like, how it appeared to him, but I noticed that he started to interfere in my social life. He wasn't always pleased with the people I hung around with and hinted that he didn't think much of my friends coming over and that he didn't really understand why I'd seek out the company of this person or that. This applied equally to my female and my male friends.

He also started to grumble that we weren't spending enough time together. It was half-hearted at first, but there was enough of an edge to his complaints that I started to feel guilty whenever I went out without him.

After a few months of this, I found myself lying about who I was going out with so as not to upset him. This irritated me and I felt like I'd started to see less of my friends. I even considered breaking things off with Gíó. He'd begun to ask too much. He was getting in the way.

A few weeks before our planned return to Iceland, we went on a trip. Gíó had bought an old car and begged me to come on a two-week vacation with him. We decided to drive around Europe and delay our departure a little longer. And then it was autumn.

# 43

When I think back on Italy and the days we spent together there, the egg seller is always foremost in my memory.

I remember it was on the evening of 11 September, a week before we moved back to Iceland, that we turned onto Via Cuniberti, right by the harbour in the town of Porto Santo Stefano.

It was a street in the old part of town, narrow and poorly lit.

It was raining. A fine, dense drizzle was falling from the ink-black night sky, causing Gíó to drive at a snail's pace along the street as though blindly feeling his way through the dark.

He was tired after a long day of negotiating motorways, exhausted from driving straight through from the Bavarian village of Schwandorf, where we had, for some reason, spent two nights before driving all the way to this seaport town on the west coast of Italy.

Gíó was in a bad mood—an incredibly rare occurrence—because of something I'd said midway through the drive, and since then, he'd barely said a word. I said such awful things sometimes without realizing that they were awful.

But the fact remained that I felt claustrophobic on this trip of ours: driving together, walking together, eating together, sleeping together, driving together, walking together… It's not good for me or the people around me if I start to get bored or feel like I'm being cornered. And the whole trip, I'd felt like he was suffocating me. He wasn't giving me the space I needed. I needed to breathe. He was constantly on me, he needed me to constantly affirm how great he was, needed my adoration and recognition. It made almost no difference what he was doing; he always demanded my approval.

That eternal embrace, those hands that were perpetually reaching for a caress, those kisses that he showered me with. And always because *he* needed comforting.

I don't know what was behind all of Gíó's insecurity. Maybe he found it difficult to be leaving Italy and the student life. Maybe he was afraid of going back to Iceland. Or maybe I just wasn't nice enough to him.

We were, in any case, in a bit of a slump.

I didn't like being colonized. His gluttonous man's hands—yes, I'm being unfair here—quashed all my desire to be close to him, to be touched, to touch him and give him the acknowledgement and the attention he so longed for. We were caught in a vicious circle.

When I explained to him that sometimes I needed a little time away from him, that I needed space, he got horribly offended, didn't want to understand. I'd probably worded this need of mine too bluntly.

Gíó had always been so good at hiding his sensitivity, at acting laid-back and self-assured. But as soon as I let down my defences, I felt him encroaching, overstepping and increasing the pressure on me.

On that trip through Europe, I felt like I was watching long, deep cracks forming in his armour until suddenly, I saw it: this magma—this soft, pink, hypersensitive magma. This unquenchable longing for consolation and appreciation. It didn't appeal to me.

I always had to be careful, had to tiptoe around him and make sure I didn't misstep, had to take care not to carelessly blurt something out.

But I also didn't want to buckle under the duress of his affection—affection that he went so far as to call love.

'Don't call this love, this is just infatuation,' I said.

I could be cold. I could be indifferent. Why did I constantly feel guilty about not wanting to lie submissively in his arms, rejoice at these tender and exalted feelings and give him exactly what he was seeking? The answer is simple. I didn't have the slightest desire to be beholden to anyone or anything. I didn't want to feel forced or compelled to give love, adoration, encouragement or caresses. That wasn't what I wanted or longed for.

To my way of thinking, this constant goading was tantamount to being tortured by a selfish tyrant.

A tyrant of love?

Sometimes, Gíó was my love-sucking monster.

And yet, I wanted to be with him, and I wanted us to share a life together.

So that was the state of our union the night we drove into that little coastal town in Italy, and I kept trying to talk myself down, to calm myself, to soften and find a way to somehow be a better person. I felt like I was starting to play the same role I had in my family, trying to keep everyone happy and humoured to relieve the tension.

I, meanwhile, was about to explode.

# 44

In spite of its southerly locale, just under two hundred kilometres north of Rome, Porto Santo Stefano was rather brisk that autumn evening.

A chilly wind was blowing in off the sea and the rain was cold. We drove slowly, the headlights boring through the mizzle.

A cat scurried across the street. In the murk, it was impossible to see if it was a black, bad-luck cat, but, of course, that was the conclusion I jumped to as I watched the creature squeeze through a gap between two big boulders on the side of the road. Everything about this trip felt jinxed.

There was no one else out on that narrow street, no one paying any attention to the old car inching along between the buildings. This meant there was no one for us to stop to ask directions, as we'd hoped. So we had no choice but to find what we were searching for ourselves—namely, a room for two.

# 45

The two of us, ball and chain, slumped in our rickety car as it crawled along the streets of the village; we'd been in it all day, so we were relieved that the end of our journey was in sight, and eager to be free of the agonizing silence that had reigned in the car.

Gíó and I weren't married, and in my mind, I was never going to be one half of a married couple. But most people who met us assumed that we would wed and grow old and grey together.

'You two are like an old married couple,' was something I heard rather often, and it always gave me the same discomfiting feeling, as though from then on, I'd just be part of someone else and someone else would be an inseparable part of me. And slowly but surely, I'd disappear.

We hadn't booked a room for the night; we didn't even know if there were any free. It was late, the time when most people would be turning in, and all I wanted was to crawl under a blanket and lie down instead of sitting in this wonky, uncomfortable car seat in this rusty old banger that still had French number plates.

There were four hotels offering their hospitality in Porto Santo Stefano that September evening. Hotel Alfiero was one of them, though not the best in terms of comfort.

It was pure coincidence that the town was on our route that evening and it was also total chance that we made Hotel Alfiero on Via Cuniberti our port of call.

Two golden stars hung from rusty iron pegs over the pink-painted entrance. One of the stars gave off a faint glow, but not the other. Judging by the empty pegs sticking out of the hotel facade, it seemed there had once been more stars over the doorway. I mused on these star lights as we approached the hotel. I knew, obviously, that these celestial decorations had nothing to do with the quality of the establishment, but honestly, at that point, nothing would have altered my decision to tell Gíó to stop at that hotel.

We weren't just exhausted—we absolutely *had* to get out of that car.

We parked in an empty spot right in front of the hotel and stepped out into the downpour without a word. The streets were saturated and the dim street lights and glow from the hotel's reception were reflected in the puddles on the pavement.

I looked up the street we'd driven down. Terraces lined both sides. The weak cone of light hanging from a street lamp further up the street was almost blotted out by the darkness and the heavy rain. I listened to the small-town sounds in the quiet of the evening: the clatter of domestic life echoing from the apartments, the voices of women shouting to their families, the clanging of pots and pans.

Windows all around us were illuminated, bare bulbs filling their rooms with a glaring white light; a corpulent man in a white, sleeveless undershirt was leaning out of one of them on his elbows. He had a cigarette dangling from the corner of his mouth and cast a curious eye in our direction. The man's head was unusually large, and I wondered if it was hard work lugging such an oversized head around on your shoulders all day.

'Will you get the bags?' I asked Gíó.

They were the first words we'd exchanged since motoring along the autobahn that morning, or more specifically, since Gíó proclaimed in his biblical fashion that he would talk no more: 'I will be silent. I will not open my mouth. This is your doing.'

I didn't feel like buttering him up, so I just let him sit there in silence. And I was silent, too, in my way, as we crossed half of Europe.

I walked swiftly up the steps to the hotel without waiting for a reply, opened the door and went into the carpeted reception. I was met by a heavy smell that reminded me of wet dog as soon as I entered. I looked down at the carpet, as if to figure out where the smell was coming from. It was bright red, and I could see the outline where the vacuum had ruffled it earlier in the day. The walls were hung with old-fashioned sconces with gold fringe that filled the entrance with a soft, yellow light.

A massive, bow-shaped reception desk stood in one corner but there was no one behind it. The whole place felt abandoned, devoid of all living creatures, because there was a suffocating silence in here, too. I could see the hotel bar through a door at the back of the space, but all the lights were off.

The silence was broken by a stream of groans and clattering coming from the doorway. Gíó wobbled in with two heavy suitcases, one in each hand. He took a few unsteady steps towards me before dropping the luggage right inside the door. Then he sighed quietly, grabbing the small of his back with both hands and grimacing as though in great pain.

I took a few soundless steps across the thick hotel carpet towards the reception desk, scanning around for someone whose job it might be to receive guests.

Gíó stayed where he was, examining the doormat at the entrance. The hotel logo had been sewn into it with gold thread. I was sure he was thinking about back when he'd had a job collecting dirty welcome mats from all the libraries in the capital and replacing them with freshly washed ones. He sometimes told long, funny stories about this simple summer job that he'd genuinely loved. It was rewarding work, as he never tired of mentioning.

There was a convex, silver bell on the reception desk. 'Ring for Assistance' was written in big letters on a sign taped beside it.

I amused myself by banging roughly on the bell, which emitted a shrill, ear-piercing ring. I was in a nasty mood. Caustic.

I looked around and caught sight of myself in a mirror hanging behind the desk. I pushed my curly hair out of my eyes and saw that my features were warped by impatience and exhaustion. I simply couldn't wait any longer.

I turned around, leant against the reception desk and gave a sideways glance to Gíó, who was still standing in the same spot between the suitcases at the entrance, as if he couldn't believe that he'd have to spend more than a few minutes in this hotel and was ready to carry our stuff straight back out to the car.

He didn't return my look, just pulled his phone out of his pocket and hunched over the screen, which cast a faint glow on his face.

He's still in a mood, I thought irritably.

I hit the bell just as vigorously as I had the first time and then leant forward on the desk, resting my head in my hands.

I was exhausted in body and soul.

What a ridiculous trip.

# 46

Then, suddenly and without warning, a smartly dressed older gentleman with a tidy black moustache appeared. It was as though he'd come up through a hatch in the floor or else just been hiding under that unwieldy desk the whole time.

This was Alfiero, the owner of the hotel. He lived in a little apartment on the ground floor. I would soon get to know him better.

'Madame!' he shouted with concern when he saw me slumped on the desk, face in my hands. I looked up in surprise.

'Madame, how can I be of service?' he asked before adding solicitously, 'You look dead on your feet.'

Alfiero was a widower and had been sitting in his parlour, drinking his last cup of coffee of the evening, munching on a slice of cake and listening to a cello composition by Luigi Boccherini, which is why he hadn't heard us ring at first, he explained. There was concern in the widower's voice, a tone he'd adopted in his later years, and which suited him well. This considerate tone of his had made him considerably more popular among the older residents of the town, and these days, they often came to him in moments of crisis. Alfiero enjoyed his pastoral role; it affirmed his importance in this little community and lent him an air of dignity that he very much aspired to.

Alfiero brushed his close-cropped, jet-black moustache hard with both hands and bent peculiarly at the knees while he awaited a response. It was a strange, unthinking motion, but he was obviously worried that crumbs from the crumbly cake he'd been enjoying with his evening coffee were still on his face.

'I'm looking for a room… For us… For two… Do you have any availability? For us?' I said.

I didn't make much of an effort to sound friendly and nodded my head towards Gíó, still rooted to the same spot, to indicate that I was talking about him when I said 'us'. Gíó had stuck his phone into his pocket and had now directed his attention to the proceedings at the reception desk.

'Of course, madame, of course, I can check for you. You haven't made a reservation, or… no?' Alfiero gave me an entreating look and tilted his head to the side while he waited for my answer. His eyes were bright, brown and gentle.

'No, we haven't booked anything. Do you have a room free?'

'I will look. Right away, madame. Without delay,' he said encouragingly as he flipped through a big book that was lying on the desk. His eyes danced rapidly up and down the pages. He was short and thin.

'One night, you said?'

'Two,' I answered and looked at Gíó for confirmation. He bobbed his head slowly up and down, which I took to mean he agreed. I couldn't bear the thought of getting back in the car tomorrow, the possibility of another silent drive.

'One moment… Yes, yes. Room double-o-seven is available. Hehe, that's what I call it, double-o-seven. What luck,' he looked up quickly, clapped his hands together twice and smiled at me, pleased. Then he looked over at Gíó. 'That room should be a perfect nest for you two newlyweds. A corner room. A view of the harbour. It couldn't be better.'

He glanced back down at the book, as if to be absolutely sure his eyes did not deceive him. He placed his index finger at the top of the page and dragged it quickly down to the bottom. Then he looked back up.

He was visibly happy, looking back and forth between us. There was curiosity in his eyes, but the smile didn't leave his lips. He seemed to expect us 'newlyweds', as he'd dubbed us, to give some sign of pleasure or relief, to maybe even clap as he had, but no such thing happened. All that our expressions said, I expect, was that the sooner our dealings with this courteous hotelier ended, the better—we were just waiting for him to point us the way to room double-o-seven. The corner room.

Signor Alfiero stepped deftly around the reception desk. 'Follow me. Right this way,' he said, looking over his shoulder and tittering decorously.

He picked up one of the suitcases at Gíó's feet and bustled swiftly and decisively up the stairs. We weary travellers stumbled stiffly after him. I followed close on Alfiero's heels, but Gíó was slower going. He heaved himself up the stairs with the other heavy suitcase. Now and then, the bag smacked into the handrail with a loud thunk that the hotel owner obviously didn't appreciate. 'Take care, signor,' he called. 'Watch the banister, if you please.'

Room 007 was at the end of the hallway. Alfiero opened the door and gestured us into the room with an open palm and slight nod of the head, before saying mildly: 'You are most welcome. I hope that you rest well. Breakfast will be ready in the dining room at seven. We'll take care of your registration tomorrow when we're all more… uh… in good spirits and well rested. Good night.'

He handed Gíó the key, which hung on a heavy, copper clapper, before turning on his heel. The door to room 007 at Hotel Alfiero closed with a gentle click.

# 47

The night passed and a new day dawned and at the first light of day, all the fishermen of Porto Santo Stefano sailed out of the harbour in search of their daily catch. Such must be the case almost every single morning.

The boats cleaved silently through the mirror-smooth sea on their way past the breakwater and onwards to the fishing grounds not far offshore.

It had stopped raining.

Gíó and I slept in the shade of the thick, floor-length curtains that hung over the window. Gíó was sleeping on the left side of the bed and I the right. We had our backs to one another and although the muted clatter of the fishing boat engines had weaselled its way into the hotel room, Gíó's sleep was undisturbed. But I opened my eyes long before morning, lay there listening to the day awaken.

Gíó slept soundly.

Not long after, the tranquillity of the morning was shattered again when the egg seller drove up in his loud, light-blue Piaggio with the few eggs his hens had laid in the last twenty-four hours. He sold them under an umbrella in a little square by the harbour, not far from where the fishing boats moored.

# 48

I'd slept well, even if I hadn't slept for very long, in spite of the malaise that had accompanied me to bed.

When I twitched back the curtains, I noticed the young egg seller in the square by the harbour.

I'd been lying in bed for a long time, waiting for daybreak. Morning had long since arrived when I finally pulled myself together and got to my feet.

The square was bright, and I watched the egg seller bask in the sun and putter about his stall. I imagined that he'd already sold a dozen eggs to two women he knew well, but there was no way for me to know if anything like this had actually happened. I imagined that these transactions took place while I was still lying under the covers and waiting for the day to begin. He was going to sell another half-dozen this morning—or so I was hypothesizing. But these were just passing fancies to amuse myself with.

The market was just below our window, and I stood there for a long time, watching the lanky farmer smooth out the red-checked tablecloth he'd spread over the table, transfer a couple of eggs from one carton to another, and take great pains in displaying his wares.

I later discovered that the egg seller lived in a little cottage just outside town. He was a young man with a hangdog expression; his eyes expressed a vague sorrow, and he said little. Every morning, he began his day by arranging a white statuette—or more accurately, a white water pitcher—that was shaped like a hen with a yellow beak and a red comb on his table, as though to indicate beyond a shadow of a doubt that chicken eggs were sold at his stall.

I was just about to leave the room and go down to check out what splendid breakfast Alfiero had conjured for us when I noticed that Gió was awake. I was going to leave him to his own devices, but when he started to get up, I shuffled my feet and decided to put off going down to breakfast for a moment. I turned back to the window.

New morning, new day. Every day has its own life.

Gió had slid to the edge of the bed with his eyes still closed. He sat there for a moment, as if to convince himself that he was awake. He yawned. Then he got on with it and dragged himself towards the shower. As he squeezed past me, he held me by the waist and said in a tender voice: 'Good morning, my love.'

The great silence was over.

Every day has its own life.

# 49

I was pleased to hear Gíó's endearments. It appeared he was revoking his biblical vow of silence, the sure-fire torture method of every dejected spouse.

His morning greeting was confirmation that today would be easier than yesterday. But the touch of his hand and gentle words still awoke that familiar feeling of resistance in me. I couldn't seem to tamp down the unpleasant sensation that was welling up in me like pus in a wound and nearly overpowering the relief I'd felt only moments before.

I wished I'd never come on this trip with Gíó. I'd overestimated my patience. He felt a constant need to show me what misery our relationship caused him and how much he suffered for love. I could barely stand it. I missed the Gíó I knew at the beginning of our trip: cautious, considerate and calm. That man was gone. Now he needed me so badly that he sapped all my energy. He was going to have to snap out of this mode, and soon.

I shook off my irritation and decided to head down to breakfast.

The hotel dining room was much too bright. It was tiled in white marble, and the sun was shining mercilessly through large windows that faced the harbour.

Three old women were sitting around a circular table. They all had poofy grey hair that made them look like three little dandelions. They moved their heads so much when they spoke that I was almost worried their dandelion fluff would shake loose and blow around the room. A used coffee cup and saucer had been left on another one of the tables, alongside a small plate dusted with cake crumbs.

I thought about putting on my sunglasses but, after looking around, elected to sit over in the corner where the glare wasn't so intense. I looked out the window of Hotel Alfiero onto the same sunny square that I'd observed from the window of room 007. The egg seller, I thought. I was pleased that I could keep watching him ply his trade.

He was in basically the same place he had been, still standing in front of his stall with his arms crossed over his chest, hardly moving a muscle as he waited for his next customer.

Alfiero had not, truth be told, conjured forth anything close to delectable for his guests. At a long table up against one wall, a few cake trays had been arranged with different kinds of crumbly cake. A raffia basket contained a few slices of bright white bread. A silver tray on the corner offered up pots of yogurt arranged in three tidy rows.

I looked over at the three old women just as one of them dropped a slice of bread on the floor. It was a light, airy bread, and for a moment it looked like it would never land. It swung in a small, slow parabola before landing softly on the marble floor at the women's feet. She bent down to pick it up, but not before glancing hesitantly at her dandelion-headed friends. But they clearly hadn't noticed and just kept chatting away as though nothing had happened. The old woman sneaked the bread back onto her plate. She'd most likely eat it later, after its time on the floor had been forgotten.

'How would you like to be an egg seller?' I asked Gió once he'd taken a seat across from me. He set his coffee cup on the table next to a slice of cake he'd chosen for himself. I hadn't noticed him come in, get his breakfast, pour himself a coffee. The old women had captured my attention and I'd been distracted.

I looked back out at the square by the harbour. I wasn't sure why I'd decided to put that question to Gíó. I probably just wanted to have a nice conversation in which both of us could say something true.

Gíó glanced at me and then out the window, where he saw what I'd been looking at. His black hair was still damp and shiny from his morning shower. He watched the man at the egg stall for a moment and then said: 'I'd like to be an egg seller, I think. I'd like to trade places with that man. I've got nothing against having such a simple job, just showing up in the morning with some eggs, selling them, and having a friendly chat with the young women from town,' he said quietly. He smiled at me.

'So, you'd like to take over for him,' I said, nodding towards the egg seller, who, at that very moment, looked up towards the hotel as if he knew that someone was talking about him.

'Yes, sometimes I dream about that kind of life. Because it's not really the job itself that's the point, but rather the life—the simple life that goes hand in hand with a simple job,' he said thoughtfully. 'I don't know anything about raising chickens, but a calm existence in an Italian village couldn't be anything other than good. It's a good life. I'd need to learn about chickens before I took over… but I'd be up for it. Maybe I'll be an egg seller when I grow up.' Gíó smiled and I was glad to see happiness in his eyes again.

We were quiet as we went back to watching the lanky egg seller who'd looked away and now had his hands clasped behind his back as he walked out onto the pavement in front of his stall.

'I met an egg seller once,' said Gíó, and I knew right away what he was going to tell me. I'd heard the story before. It was one of Gíó's go-to anecdotes and I was always surprised that he forgot having told me this story so many times before. Or maybe he hadn't forgotten. Maybe he just wanted to tell it again and again.

# 50

Gió was on a ski trip high in the French Alps. He was a young man. Mont Blanc loomed over the landscape, its peak a glowing white.

There'd been unusually heavy snowfall that week. The whole place was literally buried in snow. The branches of the conifers lining the ski slopes sagged under heavy powder and large drifts reached halfway up the wall of the ski lift's motor room.

Gió had noticed that one of the mountainsides, visible between the trees, was dotted with numerous chalets of varying size. He examined the rustic log cabins as he rode the lift to the top. Most of them appeared to be vacant and a few were in a state of disrepair, their timber walls rotting, windows broken and roofs damaged.

But one of the cabins particularly caught his interest. It was a long way from the ski trails, high on the mountain just below the treeline and far from any human traffic. But despite its remote location, the cabin appeared to be some sort of café. Red umbrellas, which popped against the white snow, had been arranged around it as though refreshments were sold outside. But Gió couldn't make out any road or trail leading to the cabin. He spent a fair amount of time wondering about this mountain café peeking through the treetops from his vantage point high above.

One day, he decided to split off from his ski buddies, rent some snowshoes and trudge into the forest to see what exactly went on at the cabin with the red umbrellas. He hadn't gone very far into the dim conifer forest when he started to worry he'd lost his bearings. The forest was dense and dark, and there was no path for him to follow.

Gíó considered turning back around but gathered his courage and continued wading through the trees, sweaty and hot. He was, to be quite honest, enjoying the solitude and tranquillity of the forest. The snow muffled all sounds, and the silence was soft and woollen. It was like he had slipped through to another world. Now and then he paused in his exertions, caught his breath, listened and tried to figure out where the cabin could be.

It was dead calm deep within the forest.

Gíó hadn't seen any sign of other people and there were no footprints anywhere in the snow. But then suddenly, without any warning, he entered a large glade and the cabin was right there in the middle. Grey smoke curled placidly from a stone chimney and at least ten rough-hewn wooden tables, each under a red umbrella bearing the logo HAWAIIAN TROPIC, had been meticulously arranged in front. There were four chairs around every table, and each one had been spread with the same type of red-checked tablecloth the egg seller in the Italian square would later use to adorn his stall.

It boggled the mind. To think that two thousand metres above sea level, deep in the middle of a forest, there was a café that could seat more than twenty people at a time. He took in the astonishing sight. The sun was shining from a blue sky. The glare was sharp, and the trees crackled in the silence of the forest. There was no one here—not a soul to be seen. All these tables, all these chairs, all these umbrellas, but not a single customer.

Gíó decided to knock on the door. The proprietor must be inside.

He walked towards the cabin and much to his surprise, spotted a man by one of the gables, binoculars up to his eyes and trained on the mountain peaks. Gíó went and stood beside him, but the man didn't move a muscle, just kept his vigil with the binoculars. Gíó squinted up at the mountaintop, trying to see what was holding the man's attention.

'What are you looking at?' he finally asked, shyly.

'Birds,' answered the man.

Nothing seemed to faze this Alpine restaurateur. Gíó looked up but couldn't see any birds, no matter how hard he peered at the sky.

After a brief wait, he asked cautiously: 'Is it possible to buy a beer here?'

'No, I don't sell beer. But you can buy a Fanta, Pepsi or tonic.' The tone of his voice was neither friendly nor unfriendly, simply businesslike.

'Oh, great. Then I'll take a Pepsi, thanks,' answered Gíó.

There was a sweet smell in the air.

'The special of the day is quiche,' said the man out of nowhere, still staring up at the sky with his binoculars.

'Thanks very much, no. I'd just like something to drink. I worked up a sweat getting up here,' Gíó answered.

The proprietor took the binoculars from his eyes, turned to Gíó and gave him a bland look. He was the spitting image of Bob Marley, this man: the same hair colour, the same Rasta clothing, the same goatee, the same dark-brown eyes. He extended a hand to Gíó and introduced himself.

'Marley.'

Gíó couldn't help but smile.

'Marley?'

'Yep. Marley. What's your name?'

'Gíó.'

'Listen. I don't serve anything but quiche and I only have enough eggs left for three quiches.'

'Thanks, but no. Just a Pepsi.'

'Have a seat, buddy.' Marley pointed towards the tables.

Gió took a couple of steps towards the sitting area but then called out: 'Do you live here?'

Instead of calling back, Marley walked towards Gió, in no particular hurry.

'I live down in the village, but I come up here every morning with a backpack. It takes an hour to climb the slope if there's been a lot of snow; otherwise, it's only forty-five minutes or so. I carry up everything I sell in my backpack. Always a dozen eggs, onion, cheese, fizzy drinks and bottled water. With a dozen eggs, I can make three quiches. If I don't sell the quiches, I eat the eggs myself when I get home. If I do sell the quiches, then I go to bed on an empty stomach.'

'That's quite the ascetic life.'

Marley smiled, turned away and ambled into the cabin, but returned presently with a can of Pepsi and a glass. He placed the glass on the table and poured the Pepsi like an experienced waiter.

'Would you mind if I took your picture in front of the house?' asked Gió hesitantly. 'This is so unique. A restaurant in the middle of a forest.'

Marley shook his head and started to laugh, his businesslike manner forgotten.

'Forgive me, comrade, but no, you may not. I don't like people taking pictures. Not of me or the café.'

He grinned to himself, looking down as though trying to find the right words.

'I look so much like Bob Marley, you see.' He paused as though to give Gió time to confirm this for himself. 'People might start making up rumours about Mister Marley still being alive. But he's dead. And then there's the fact that I don't want to advertise my café. Almost no one ever comes here and that's just the way I like it.'

Marley took a seat across from Gíó and hummed tunelessly. Gíó drank his Pepsi and tried to hear if his song had a reggae beat.

# 51

But I digress.

I was still sitting in my car, my new sanctuary, in front of my house, feeling the cold that had spread through my body. I'd been sitting there reminiscing about the old days for quite some time.

I started the car and drove off. There was really nothing else but to wait for time to pass.

Traffic was light in Vesturbær. It seemed few people had business on the west side of town at that time of day. As I approached the hotel—a convex, four-storey building lined with windows facing west out over Faxaflói Bay—I was surprised to see that it had a strangely deathly look about it: nearly every one of its windows was dark.

Was it really a hotel? I wondered. The building was known locally as JL House, after Jón Loftsson, the man who built it, and had been home to many entities over the years: an art school, an office for freelance academics, the Alliance Française. And now a hotel—wasn't that what the detective had said? Maybe no one was staying there right now… Maybe there weren't so many tourists in the country after all.

I slowed down to take a better look at the building and noticed that the sign above the entrance was broken. Part of the establishment's name—SSON HOTEL—flickered in backlit, wrought-iron letters.

I gazed up at the sinister-looking building. Someone had tried to decorate it in a hypermodern style by painting different coloured triangles around the windows. Some of the triangles were blue, others pink or green, but otherwise the building was painted white with a dark-red roof. The design scheme was certainly not in step with the latest trends in hotel design.

I pulled up in the car park in front of the main entrance. The heavens had opened and although the wipers were sweeping back and forth across the windscreen at top speed, they could barely keep up. The car was rocked by sharp gusts of wind coming off the sea, and I quailed at the prospect of opening the door and stepping out into such demented weather.

A man in the boiler suit was grappling with something in a white delivery van in front of me, undeterred by the deluge and the gale-force winds. The back door of the van was inscribed in blue letters:

*Pipes Pernickety?*
*Crapper Clogged?*
*We'll flush your problems down the drain.*
HERMANN HERMANNSSON, LICENSED PLUMBER

Maybe it was Hermann himself pulling a long metal pipe out of van and giving me a sidelong glance under his dirty cap. I noticed a raindrop hanging from the brim of his hat just before it dripped onto his nose. I watched him lug the long pipe down the pavement that ran along the hotel wall but once he'd disappeared around the corner of the building, I steeled myself, pushed the car door open, stepped out into the storm and hurried towards the hotel.

# 52

Although the broken hotel marquee was still shining at the entrance, there were no lights on at reception inside. Everything pointed to the decline and fall of this hotel, which previously had been a source of great pride to its owner, I'm sure. But currently, there was nothing to attract guests or give them any reason to choose to spend a night here.

There was no one around.

Had the hotel gone out of business?

I'd little hope of getting into the lifeless building but nevertheless gave the door an experimental push. I didn't expect it to budge, but to my surprise, some hidden mechanism opened it automatically.

I walked hesitantly into the shadowy entrance, which looked like a hotel reception but also a kind of unfinished mock-up of a hotel reception, like in a play, because it was all so bare. Everything had been taken off the walls. The computers and phones were gone. There was an enormous floor-to-ceiling mirror on the wall behind the reception desk. A crack ran across the mirror and warped both my own reflection (I looked like an apparition) and that of the room, making it look all the more unreal. There was a bookshelf in the middle of the reception area, as if someone had suddenly decided not to carry it all the way out. If there had ever been books on the shelves, there weren't any longer.

I crept across the thick carpet and into a palpable, mysterious silence that was made all the more tense by the general disorder.

There was no way this hotel was still in operation and it was even less likely that Gió would have taken shelter here.

But I paused for a moment to survey the fascinating scene.

There were no chairs, or seating of any kind. If you can't even sit down, it's not very likely you're going to stay here for long, I thought.

I could see a faint glow of light from a room deeper in the building and hear the echo of voices. I stood there listening for a moment before walking down a wide hallway towards the sound. The voices were coming from a room that was marked CONFERENCE ROOM II.

The door to the room was ajar. I heard a man's loud laughter, then a moment later a woman giggled and made a jokey remark. The man guffawed even louder. His laughter reminded me of the bark of a frantic dog.

Did I know these people who were so amusing to one another? Did I recognize their voices?

I gave the door a gentle push and looked in.

At first, I saw no one. The conference room was big and completely empty. No conference table, no décor on the walls, and there were no seats in here either, only a grey office carpet under giant light fixtures that hung from silver chains and illuminated the room.

The voices fell silent when I walked in.

A man and woman were sitting in a corner on the left side of the room with their backs up against a wall.

They both looked up.

They didn't belong here.

They were like deer in the headlights, creatures that had sneaked in where they had no business being. The man pricked up his ears and his jaw dropped open in an exaggerated, theatrical manner that was obviously supposed to convey his surprise at seeing me there. He was holding an oversized white coffee cup—I thought it was a bedpan at first, if I'm honest—while the woman, who was a few years younger than him, was eating a baguette sandwich that was sticking halfway out of its cellophane wrapper.

Gíó?

No, it wasn't Gíó.

The man leapt to his feet when he saw me venturing into the room.

'Sorry for intruding…' I began.

'Come in, yes, do come in, you're not intruding at all. Welcome, welcome…'

'I was told that my husband was here, but there must have been some sort of misunderstanding. I can see the whole place is shut down. It was obviously some other hotel and I got the wrong end of the stick…'

'What's that now? You've lost your husband, you say?' said the man, walking in my direction with a smile. He walked with a strange hitch, pausing with every step, as if he didn't want to frighten me off. He inched forward, the coffee cup in his left hand, his right extended, as if he was preparing to wave in greeting, though there were hardly more than a handful of steps between us. He had black hair cut rather short; his eyes were brown and bulging. And although the room was hot and muggy, he wore a long, black wool coat.

The young woman kept munching on her sandwich and observed our conversation with interest.

'No, no. I haven't lost him. I was just told that he was here,' I said, trying to sound upbeat.

'Shall we take a look? Together, I mean?' said the man encouragingly, taking my hand unexpectedly and leaning forward as if to bow. 'Mosi—my name is Mosi. What's yours?'

'My name's Júlía,' I said, immediately wondering if it was smart of me to tell him my real name.

'Yes. Júlía. Yes, yes, yes… Right, well, c'mon, Júlía. I'll show you around.'

Without letting go of my hand, he led me out the door to the stairs, which were a few metres down the hall. I was uncomfortable holding this man's hand. His grip was firm, but soft.

'This is a hotel, as you know, but it's closed… or… or maybe there are still some guests staying here, lost sheep, you know… but I don't think so.'

'There couldn't still be any guests here,' I said sceptically as we walked up the stairs. The further up we went, the darker it got. There were no windows in the stairwell and all the sconces had been removed so the electrical wiring was sticking out like the antenna of some gigantic insect nested within the walls.

'It's pretty spooky in here,' I said quietly.

'Spooky, yes… yes… yes… Mystical, even…'

I slowed my pace, but he didn't let go of my hand, rather half dragged me up with him until we reached a door.

'Let's just check it out. I'm an artist, you see, and we're preparing for a kind of exhibition here—just over the weekend. A hotel, an abandoned hotel like this, is, well… we're looking at a whole different kettle of fish, really. The word "hotel" has, in some ways, a completely different meaning now. Naturally, when you think about quarantine hotels and such… isolation, things like that…'

I said nothing because I didn't know how I was supposed to respond to these musings.

He opened a door onto a corridor and light streamed in from the windows. The same grey office carpet was on the floor in the hallway, which was lined at regular intervals with at least ten massive, closed, brown doors, all of which had numbered gold plates on them. Clearly, the hotel hadn't spared any expense when it came to doors.

The artist pulled me over to the first door, where he finally dropped my hand and knocked for a long time, gently and tentatively. Many knocks.

'Room service,' he said in a muffled voice, his mouth right up against the door, his tone servile. 'I have the coffee and caraway buns you ordered…'

He grinned at me.

I gave him a sidelong glance.

Then he knocked again, this time hard, fast and aggressively, shouting so loud I nearly jumped out of my skin.

'Police! Open the door in the name of the law!'

Again, he grinned at me. There was an impish look in his eyes.

'Wha—?'

'The knock, yes—it's sort of… yes, how do you say… sort of a sound picture… and… a kind of portrait of a person… or… yes, something to that effect, something we all know and connect with… different kinds of knocks say so much about the people knocking…'

'Umm,' I said, looking around. I half expected someone to open the door, peek out into the hall to see what all the noise was. But nothing happened. Everything was silent and none of the doors opened, no heads popped into the hallway. The artist stood there smiling and rubbing his hands together. He was solemn, his eyes boring holes into me as though he was expecting some sort of reaction.

'This is… completely… ever since I was a child… you know, uh… the knock, it's just one of those sounds that immediately… *immediately*… has, just like, this profound effect on me… I felt just so *aware* of something… yes… yes, ever since I was a child, you know… just aware of this, this *hand* that was… was…'

'Knocking? Impelling?' I said to contribute something and help him say what he was trying to say so we could bring this peculiar conversation to an end.

'Impelling, yes… yes, yes, yes, exactly, impelling, yes… and, you know…'

'Sure,' I said, walking slowly towards the stairwell. I wasn't all that interested in his art—impossible under the circumstances—although I genuinely liked this man and appreciated his attempts to help me. But there wasn't a single thing to suggest that Gíó was here, and I didn't feel like I had any further reason to be this place. Best thing would be to hurry back home.

'Yes… really and truly… yes… yes… yes… exactly, I've really… I've long been interested, just… in observing our true nature is… our nature, or what do you call it, this, uh… you know, the part of us that comes out in how we move or… or… or… or… uh… or the sounds we make.'

'Or things we do, perhaps?' I added.

'Yes… yes… yes… exactly.'

He took my hand again and made as though to lead me back down the stairs. This artist wanted to guide me, hold my hand. It wasn't uncomfortable this time. I could tell he didn't mean anything by it but to ensure my safety and show me the best way back down.

'We haven't found your husband… yes… we have to find him… but, so… before he… he… got into mischief… or… wait, what's his name?'

'Gíó.'

'Yes, Gíó, yes… yes, yes… yes… of course. Shall we try upstairs?'

'No. He's not here. I'm sure of it. I must have misunderstood the message. He'd never stay here. It's just a ruin.'

'Yes, exactly. Yes… yes, yes a ruin… it's sort of beautiful, a hotel like this, a hotel that's being nibbled away, things taken or removed from it bit by bit… so that… so that it becomes a kind of, a kind of blend of… this strange blend of ruin and also… some kind of, some kind of crime scene or evidence…'

'Thanks for your help,' I said hurriedly to stem this speech, which was about to drive me insane.

'You let me know, Júlía… yes… when you… uh… when you find your husband,' said the artist, giving me a sincere smile. 'I'm happy to help…'

'Don't worry—he's not that kind of lost, you know,' I said and tried to give a carefree laugh. In spite of everything, I liked this solicitous artist. I found him rather adorable—funny, even.

'Worry, no… no, no, no… I'm not worried. Here's my phone number… look… you give me a call, okay?'

He handed me a business card that was white on both sides. On one side was his name, phone number, email address and the URL for his website. On the other, it read *Rarely Never Ltd.* in tiny letters.

'Rarely Never Limited… that's my company, okay?' He tapped his chest with his index finger. 'D'ya get it? Always… often… sometimes… rarely… never…'

'Got it,' I answered.

'Could I… maybe… have your phone number, so if I get lost, too… hmm?… if I vanish… then I could… like, call… and you could come find me?'

'You're not going to get lost.'

'Your number… you know, I could look you up if I… if I strayed off the path, you know?'

I hesitated.

'Do you have a pen and paper? I'll write it down for you.'

# 53

I was on my way out of the hotel ruins when my phone rang. I was standing in what used to be the reception area and observed the disarray once more before taking out my phone. The artist had hit the nail on the head when he said that the place was being nibbled away.

I recognized the detective's phone number immediately.

'Hi, Haraldur,' I said. 'Is there any news?'

'Hi… hi… listen. Where are you?'

'At the hotel in JL House. I came to see if I could find Gíó here, but—'

'Listen now,' the detective interrupted me. 'Can you be back at your house in fifteen minutes? I need to show you something.'

'Yes, I'll drive straight over. What is it that you want to talk to me about?'

'It's better that I show you. Actually, that's the only way. You'll need to see it with your own eyes, you understand. I just need to show you. I'll see you soon, Júlía. I'll be at your house in fifteen minutes.'

He hung up.

I jogged through the pouring rain to my car and drove towards home.

What now?

When I turned onto my street, I saw the same white police car Haraldur had used the last time waiting outside my house. I parked behind it and got out.

I looked over at the house across the street where the new tenant had supposedly taken up residence. All of a sudden, I had a strong sensation that someone was at the window, that someone was watching me park the car and waiting for me to get out. All the lights in the apartment were still off, but a blue glow from some electrical gadget deep within the apartment got me thinking about flowers in greenhouses, cold storage in a mortuary. I don't mean to suggest that those things ever occur in one and the same place—the cultivation of flowers and the storage of the deceased, I mean—but those were the two things that simultaneously popped into my mind. Mortuary. Greenhouse.

The lights may have all been off, but that blue glow proved that there was life in there. Either someone was sitting and watching TV, or they'd turned on a computer and the blue glow of the screen was visible through the window. I squinted through the rain, but couldn't make out anyone standing at the window watching me. I turned back to the detectives, both of whom had stepped out of their car and were walking casually towards me, paying no mind to the rain.

Sigurður Jón was carrying a flat black parcel in one hand. He was holding it rather high in the air and approached me like a waiter with a tray.

Haraldur, on the other hand, was walking as slowly as possible and seemed to be distracted. He lit a cigarette, hunched over and greedily inhaled the smoke. He stared at the ground. I briefly considered bumming a cigarette to keep him company while he smoked, but I didn't manage to because Sigurður Jón elbowed past him, lifting the parcel above his head as he stiffly slid by, insisting: 'It's important for you to focus now, Júlía. Let's go upstairs.'

He was worked up about something. On a mission. He turned decisively and marched up the front steps.

'Hold on a moment, Siggi, lad,' said Haraldur, holding up a hand to indicate that his colleague should stop. 'Let me finish my cigarette. I'm just going to chat a moment with Júlía here while I smoke. It does a body good to be rained on now and then.'

I walked over to him and looked at Sigurður Jón, standing halfway up the steps and still holding the parcel aloft.

'How'd it go at JL House?' Haraldur asked. 'Did you find anyone?'

'Yes. Some artists.'

'The hotel's been closed for a long time, as you could no doubt tell. Nothing going on there now.'

'No, Gíó was nowhere to be seen and was probably never there. But I did go in.'

'It's an inauspicious place. One of Reykjavík's cursed spots, where everything declines and dies, if you know what I mean. It's an ill wind that blows around that building. As if it's under some elfin spell. Something's disturbed the peace there. An ice cream shop opens in JL House and Bob's your uncle, the ice cream's sour, clumpy and maybe not even all that cold. Someone opens a hotel in JL House and from the very first day, everything about it is sloppy and off-putting—the walls are greasy, the windows dirty...' He thought for a moment. 'No guests, just tradesmen fixing drippy taps, flickering lights, clogged toilets and whatever other headaches.'

'Mmm.'

'Sorry, just thinking out loud. Just rambling.' Haraldur waved his hand as though he regretted everything he'd said and wanted to take it back.

'But I agree with you.'

'No, no, I'm getting off track. But I did have something to say to you, and it's important. Júlía: you are not to follow up on every tip you get. We get lots of tips every day about your husband's possible whereabouts and most are misunderstandings, misconceptions or the result of the need, on the part of the person calling, to get the attention of the police or even relatives. So, what I'm saying is: you're not to go running every which way, it will do you no good. It isn't good for you. We will weigh each of the leads we receive and see to it that nothing important gets past us.'

He laid his thick hand on my shoulder, and I felt a real affection for the detective in that moment. He was a good man.

'All right. I just find it hard to sit around waiting at home. All I do is wait and…' I tried to find the words to describe my state of mind, but my head was blocked. *Crapper clogged? We'll flush your problems down the drain,* I thought, picturing the plumber at JL House. I couldn't think of another way to describe what I was doing—other than waiting. Thinking? No, it wasn't thoughts that were darting chaotically around my mind. It was disorder, a hodgepodge, a vague stream of images and words and I couldn't seem to impose any order on the wayward torrent.

'I understand, I do,' said Haraldur with sympathy in his voice. 'You also need to be aware that sometimes strangers may take it upon themselves to be in touch directly—directly with you, to call you on your phone, you understand? And they may not always be nice messages. They may even pretend to be your husband, to draw you in—it happens sometimes. There are people in this world who just call up relatives to torment them. So you're not to go chasing everything down—just pass it along to us. You understand?'

'Umm,' I said, thinking.

'Is there no one who can stay with you? Don't you have any good friends or your sister—no, you can't call your sister. Right? That would be out of the question?'

'My sister? No. Are you crazy? My husband's mistress? Never. On top of which, we aren't even that close. We look alike and maybe have similar temperaments, but no. I can't trust her. And she's not really… the caring type. That I can tell you flat-out: I'm not looking to have a sleepover with my sister.'

'No, no. There's that, of course,' said the detective. 'And, of course, you know her better than most.'

'I'll put it like this: she is remarkably driven but affection is not in her DNA. Like, not even a single gene,' I said. 'She can be rather cold, and she can't be bothered with sentimentality. I'm just saying it like it is, it's fine. I'm so mad at her, I obviously can't stop thinking about her and Gíó. I somehow got it into my head that she could be helping him to hide from me. I even got the idea that I'd unexpectedly burst into her house and find Gíó there. But no, that's obviously just nonsense. Gíó would never do anything like that. But there's no way I can even think of having her with me.'

Haraldur gave me a thoughtful look, as if he was going to say something but stopped himself. Then he sucked deeply on his cigarette, so the glowing tip illuminated his face. He held it up between his thumb and index finger, considering the half-smoked length of it for a moment before he took one last, deep drag, and flicked the butt so it flew in a gentle arc into the street.

Then the detective squared his shoulders and lumbered towards the house, following Sigurður Jón up the steps.

# 54

The instant I'd let them into the house, Sigurður Jón pressed me: 'Where can I put this down? Where's a good place for us lay this all out?' He waggled the parcel at me, which I noticed was wrapped in black plastic. He was as excited as a little kid.

'Give me a moment, I'll show you in just a sec.'

Haraldur was standing in the hall in his wool socks, waiting to be ushered in. I hurried to step out of my shoes and then walked into the living room where everything was just as it had been.

'Come on in.'

I took in the four chairs that were arranged around the table. Each on its own side. There were four chairs, but there was easily room for six. The plant was still lying in a heap of dirt on the floor. Forensics still hadn't come by to take a look and it didn't seem like anyone had any interest in a possible break-in. Haraldur had probably sidelined any talk of that. Maybe he found the proposition of a break-in and a disappearance occurring in the same place at the same time too absurd. He was probably right that such things rarely if ever happened simultaneously unless the incidents were related, which he probably didn't find very likely in this case.

I'd have to vacuum up all that dirt.

It was as if Haraldur read my thoughts. 'I thought about sending forensics over but then decided it wasn't necessary. They're not scheduled to come by are they, Siggi?'

'I don't think so,' answered Sigurður Jón.

'Okay,' Haraldur said to me. 'Just leave everything as it is, like I asked you, and I'll look into it. I'm still of two minds, still unsure about what to do, what the best and most fitting course of action is.'

'I haven't touched anything in the living room here.'

I led Sigurður Jón and his parcel to the dining room table so he could put down his precious cargo. He immediately began to unwrap the packaging and it slowly became clear that it contained dark-coloured clothing. I anxiously watched his fumbling, clumsy hands. Haraldur came and stood next to me.

'This was found on a beach. We wanted to know if you recognized it.'

I looked at Haraldur in disbelief. I was shocked and felt apprehension taking hold of me like a steel fist. Sigurður Jón was still struggling with the parcel. I was almost unbearable waiting for him to remove the plastic bag, which in his ineptitude, he'd somehow managed to tangle around his right hand.

I stood there, as though paralysed, watching his clumsiness and sensing Haraldur's impatience growing until all of sudden, he snapped to and reached for the piece of clothing, which he pulled out of the plastic while gently pushing Sigurður Jón aside.

'It's a trench coat, as you can see,' said Haraldur. 'Wet, of course. Soaked through. It was lying in the rain for some time, down on the beach. I don't know if it had been in the sea. But as best I can tell, this is what you'd call olive green. Would you agree, Júlía? An olive-green trench coat?' He looked questioningly at me.

I easily recognized Gíó's coat. An olive-green trench coat, the same one he'd been wearing on Geirshólmur when I sailed off and left him there. I wasn't in the slightest doubt.

'Where did you find this trench coat?'

'Trench coat, yes, of course. This garment was found in a place called… Blue-something. Just south of the whaling station in Hvalfjörður.'

'In Hvalfjörður? Near the whaling station? It's Gíó's,' I said with a gasp.

'The coat was on the beach there. Soaked. Someone had laid it there. It was carefully folded and left on the foreshore. It was, I must say, as though someone had taken great pains with it.'

'Folded? I don't understand anything you're telling me. In Hvalfjörður,' I said, still short of breath. I felt like something was tightening around me. Like someone had their hands around my throat. I could barely breathe.

'The two of you made a trip to Hvalfjörður the day before yesterday, you told me, or us. Did you stop anywhere around the whaling station? Could it be that Gíó maybe set down his coat while you were out and forgot it on the beach?'

'No, we didn't stop. We just drove around the fjord. He came home in the trench coat, I'm certain of that, and went out that night in the same one. That one.' I poked the coat in Haraldur's hands. 'He was wearing that exact coat when I watched him walk out the door of our home and told me that he was going to María's. I think you ought to ask María if he showed up wearing an olive-green trench coat.'

'Interesting,' said Sigurður Jón, nodding thoughtfully and resting his chin in his hand.

'Don't you have anything else to say? *Interesting?* How bloody clichéd can you get?' I hissed at the officer, who shrunk away from me.

'Take a good, close look and make sure this is really your husband's coat. We must be absolutely sure. Do you recognize the brand?' Haraldur pointed at an embroidered tag with the logo for Massimo Dutti. He didn't seem to be troubled by my outburst.

'Yes, that's Gíó's brand,' I said shortly.

'If you're absolutely sure, we're going to send Search and Rescue out to Hvalfjörður immediately. Siggi, get in touch with the duty officer and apprise him of the situation. Make sure we get both divers and searchers on land, okay?'

'Right away,' said Sigurður Jón, taking out his phone. We both watched him walk out of the kitchen and into the living room. I heard him start speaking, urgency in his voice.

'In the breast pocket, there was a folded piece of paper,' said Haraldur after a short pause. 'A note, a scrap.' He pulled a plastic sleeve out of his own coat. It seemed like he'd stuck it there to protect it from the rain. A crumpled, lined piece of paper that had been torn out of a little, spiral-bound notebook was pressed inside the plastic.

'The note was pretty worse for wear, but not entirely sodden, so either the coat wasn't in the sea for a very long time, or the pocket was relatively waterproof. Do you think this is something that your husband might have had in his pocket?' He laid the plastic sleeve on the table in front of me so I could take a closer look at the note.

It was a Post-it. In the top-left corner, there was a string of seven numbers, most likely a phone number, the dates 12 October–14 October, and the name Jósep. The name was underlined twice, and the phone number had been circled. Everything had been written with the same pen: a thick blue marker. I clearly recognized Gíó's handwriting. The note was wet, a little ripped and waterlogged, but the marker writing was still quite clear.

I thought for a moment.

I didn't know any Jósep and had never heard Gíó mention anyone by that name. The number sequence was almost illegible because the paper was soggy and had been torn in that very spot. I took out my phone and took a picture of the note.

The 12th of October. That was tomorrow. What was supposed to happen on the 12th of October? It was probably something to do with Gíó's job. That strange job I never felt suited him.

'I don't know if the note was Gíó's. It's just some scrap that anyone could have scribbled on. It could be Gíó's handwriting, I think. I'm not sure. But I don't know of anyone he knows called Jósep. If this was in the pocket, then it's more than likely something Gíó wrote. But at the very least, that's his trench coat.'

'We called the phone number on the note. No one's picked up today,' said Haraldur.

'Oh?'

'And neither could we find any connection between Gíó and the owner of the number. According to the National Registry, he's an elderly widower who lives in a remote part of the country. He's no longer working and doesn't seem to be connected to Gíó in any way. But we'll keep trying to get hold of him.'

'I'm not aware that Gíó knows any elderly man named Jósep.'

'Fine, fine. But now to another important matter. Earlier today, I received a call from a farmer in Hvalfjörður,' began Haraldur. He spoke slowly, as though he was weighing each word and had to think about what he was going to say.

'Yes?' I said, waiting for him to continue.

He said that your husband, the very same man who the papers have declared missing, borrowed a boat from him. A small, rubber boat. He said he'd spoken to Gíó, your husband, on the phone on Sunday morning about the boat, but that Gíó had told him to talk to you,' Haraldur said in puzzlement.

I nodded and waited for whatever he was going to say next.

'The farmer said he knew you both, he mentioned you by name, and said that he'd also talked to you about the boat on Sunday and promised to loan it to the two of you for a short sail. He said the boat was returned to the beach just north of the Miðsandur oil pier in the evening that same day. This was all done by arrangement with you. Do you know anything about this?'

I thought for a moment. Had I been led into a trap?

'Yes, we'd planned on taking the boat out, we're acquainted with the farmer and arranged to borrow his boat, but then we didn't feel like it, so we didn't go out, we didn't use the boat.'

Haraldur gave me a searching look.

'The two of you requested to borrow a dinghy and drove out to Hvalfjörður, but then decided not to make use of the boat that you had, with a fair amount of forethought, arranged to borrow,' said Haraldur evenly. 'It sounds like you had a specific reason for being in Hvalfjörður. What was it exactly? Where were you planning to sail? Can you tell me that?'

'We were just going to… look around a little.' I said, hearing as I did just how terribly unconvincing that sounded.

'Look at what?'

'Nothing special, just the fjord.'

'Were you going to go fishing, perhaps? Did this maybe have something to do with the whaling station? Some sort of anti-whaling protest?'

'No, no, nothing like that.'

'I'm sure you can see yourself how unconvincing it all sounds. You got in touch with an acquaintance in Hvalfjörður to ask him to lend you a boat. He takes the time to drag the boat down to the shoreline for you. You and your husband drive to Hvalfjörður on Sunday afternoon. The next day, you report your husband missing, say you have no idea where he is, he's not been in touch and no one but you has seen him since the two of you went to Hvalfjörður together. Then today, we find an olive-green, Massimo Dutti trench coat. In the same place the farmer's boat was left for you. You tell me there's no doubt in your mind that the trench coat is your husband's.' He gave me another questioning look. I didn't answer and tried to think of something sensible to say. But no matter how hard I puzzled over it, I had nothing to offer, nothing that would be any help to me in these circumstances. So I kept my mouth shut.

'Is there anything you'd like to tell us, Júlía?' Haraldur gave me a mild look.

'Tell you? I've told you what I know. My husband is missing, no one knows where he is, and I—I just don't know—I have no idea what I'm supposed to do,' I stammered, fighting to hold back the sobs that were trying to burst free of my attempts to stifle them, squeezing up my throat. My face was hot and probably bright red, too. I had to think of something to say, I thought. Breaking into tears was out of the question.

'I want you to think hard, Júlía. You're not hiding anything from us, are you? That you can't do,' Haraldur added in the same mild voice.

# 55

I stood in the hall for a long time after I closed the front door behind the detectives. I still felt like I was on the verge of tears. A hot feeling was welling up in my body, my throat, travelling up my nasal passage and out my eyes.

Was I totally losing my grip on this?

I breathed deeply, inhaled for a count of five through my nose, let the air fill my lungs and then swallowed the hot feeling, the fear and sorrow rising like a wave deep within my body.

Was I now suspected of a crime? I hadn't been at all convincing. Was Haraldur hinting that he knew something about Gió's disappearance that he wasn't saying? Was he waiting for me to confess, or did he intend to paint me into a corner, so I had no choice but to admit my horrible mistake?

I moved over to the living room window and looked out into the garden. I could hear the cawing of a raven, which reminded me of a child's cries, but I couldn't see the bird anywhere. I was sure he was fluttering around and raging against the wind, wheeling in circles overhead like a vulture.

The scribbled scrap of paper that I'd found on the windowsill the day before was still there. 'Together they went to sow the same field,' I read, but I no longer found the same comfort in the words that I had before. I crumpled the paper in my fist and threw it back on the sill, only to pick it right back up and smooth it out again. I decided to put it in the jar where I collected notes with words and phrases I'd jotted down.

The sky was heavy. Dark clouds rolled across the city, wind gusted and rain spattered against the windowpanes.

## Icelandic National Broadcasting Service (RÚV) | ruv.is | 11.10.22 – 15:22

Police are still seeking information regarding the whereabouts of Reykjavík resident Gíó Ísaksson, who disappeared from his home just before midnight on Sunday.

In their latest bulletin, police indicate that Gíó is known to have been in Hvalfjörður in the vicinity of the whaling station after he left his home. Anyone who was travelling around the fjord and has information about Gíó's movements after midnight on 10 October is asked to contact police by calling 112.

Gíó is thirty-four years old and 187 centimetres tall with a muscular build. He has dark, medium-length hair and blue eyes.

When last seen, he was wearing a green trench coat, black trousers and black leather ankle boots.

Gíó's last-known location was around the Óseyri harbour at 1 a.m. on Monday morning.

# 56

I'd been standing at the window for a long time. I wandered out of the kitchen and back into the living room, where I took up residence at the window once more.

It was completely silent. Silence is like cheese. When it gets old, it begins to smell. Is it then the rotting smell of silence that the ravens have caught a whiff of, I thought. Is that why they're gliding overhead?

I jumped when a shrill beeping issued from my phone, clanging like a hammer pounding on an anvil. I pulled my phone out of my pocket, even though everything in me resisted looking at it.

I didn't recognize the phone number, but I opened the text anyway.

It was a picture of a man standing in a dark room. There was no caption of any kind. Just a photograph. I squinted at it and of course, immediately thought it was Gíó. Gíó was appearing to me all over the place, in all dark-haired men, in all tall men… I brought the phone closer to my face. It looked like a picture of Gíó standing up against a concrete wall. I checked his hair, his eyes, his chin, his nose. The image wasn't sharp and the lack of light wherever it had been taken only made it more unclear. It could be a picture of Gíó, but it could also be someone else entirely.

Maybe I *was* just seeing Gíó everywhere.

The image was grainy, but I thought I could just make out the wall Gíó was leaning against. It looked rough somehow, like the building he was in was either unfinished or old and dilapidated.

It seemed like he was in an unfinished building or a house on the verge of collapse. I peered at the photo some more. Was it Gíó? No, it wasn't Gíó. Or was it?… It was impossible to tell.

The man's expression was neutral. He was gazing solemnly at the camera, neither smiling nor angry, frightened nor sad. His expression gave nothing away. The image reminded me of the photographs that are sometimes published of people who've been taken hostage by terrorists. The man was wearing some kind of tracksuit jacket—a grey cotton tracksuit jacket with a zipper and ribbed cuffs. He looked like he was from Serbia or Macedonia or one of those countries. In my mind, young men from that corner of the world often wore that kind of tracksuit. And Gíó, dark-browed and thick-lashed, had Balkan ancestry.

I enlarged the image on the screen, but it didn't help. It was so dark and of such poor quality that zooming in only made things worse. There was no way to tell if it was an old picture or a new one.

I found it strange that there wasn't any explanation to go along with the picture because I definitely didn't recognize the sender's number. I thought about calling it and simply asking why I'd been sent this picture and who it was of. But then I remembered what the detective had said about how people might start sending me unpleasant messages. How there were people who took to frightening, deceiving and harassing individuals who'd been in the news or their loved ones.

I looked at the picture again.

Maybe I shouldn't let the sender know how uncomfortable it made me. That might provoke them, encourage them to keep going, possibly take it even further.

But in the end, call I did; I couldn't help myself. Someone picked up on the first ring. A mild female voice: 'You have reached the number…' I hung up.

What was someone trying to tell me with this photo? Why was I being sent a picture of a man in a tracksuit standing in front of a wall? I had to have been the intended recipient. Was this some kind of threat?

Was Gíó sending me this picture of himself to tell me he was alive? Maybe, though very unlikely. But if that *was* the case, what was it supposed to mean? Instead of coming forward, he sent this strange self-portrait from an unknown phone number? Did that bode well? No.

I thought for a moment and imagined Gíó, hiding out alone in some rough, unfinished building. No. There was no way Gíó sent this text.

But what did it mean if someone else was sending me a picture of Gíó without identifying themselves? Who could it be and why would they waste the time and effort sending me a picture like this? Did *that* bode well?

No.

It could also just be some idiot, some fool playing a prank. I'd done things like that when I was a kid. There was a time, for instance, when I used to call and order taxis for my neighbours and then leave the poor driver waiting outside for ages until they realized they'd been had.

I probably shouldn't give it another thought. I wasn't going to reach any conclusions.

The man in the photo could be almost anyone. A dark-haired, serious young man.

Until then, I probably hadn't really believed what the detective had told me about people sending such horrible things. I sighed and looked again at the photo, poring over all the details in the picture yet again, hoping I could glean some useful information about when and where it had been taken.

I opened my laptop and googled the phone number, but none of the search results were helpful. I was absorbed in this new project of mine when another text clanged its arrival on my phone. The same number.

I AM NOT FAR AWAY

I am not far away? That was obviously supposed to scare me. The sender wanted me to be scared. Was someone really on their way here? Who? And what did they want?

I walked to the kitchen window and looked up and down the street. Although I'd been calm when I first read the text, now, standing at the window, I felt afraid. I was suddenly terrified that I was about to lay eyes on a menacing figure striding down the pavement towards my house. I pictured a shadowy character in a long trench coat, the coat-tail rippling like the hem of a robe, moving at a supernatural speed.

I sincerely regretted having never got an unlisted phone number. I'd often considered it, because of the articles that I wrote. I was strident and provocative, took things as far from political correctness as I could, so my articles often inspired aggressive reactions. Up until now, however, it hadn't really mattered that my number was listed. It was easy for people to find me. But now, anyone could look up Gíó Ísaksson in the phone directory, find his address and then see my own name and number connected to that same address.

The rain pounded on the windows. Everything was draped in a dense mist, making it almost impossible to see if there was anyone out on the street. The droplets trickled down the panes and the world seemed to be dissolving in this endless deluge.

I'd got myself pretty worked up. My heart was pounding in my chest and my only thought was to flee. To run and hide as fast as

I could. There was something diabolical about those texts, wasn't there? Something malevolent and spiteful. I couldn't stay here. I had to get away.

Again, my phone clanged.

Get thee behind me, Satan. Leave me alone.

I hesitated, hardly daring to read the text, but I forced myself to open it.

Another picture. This time of some old sheds, and under the picture, it read:

> You hurled me into the depths,
> into the very heart of the seas,
> and the currents swirled about me;
> all your waves and breakers
> swept over me.

It took me a long time to get my bearings, but I was sure I recognized the quote, even though I couldn't immediately place it. It seemed all too horribly fitting.

# 57

I'd had enough. I leapt into action, as if the Devil himself were on my heels. I threw on my shoes and jacket and ran down the front steps to the car. There was no way I could stay at home. I had to find someone to calm me down, I couldn't be alone any longer. I couldn't live my life like this—always on the run, perpetually fleeing.

I got in the driver's seat, locked the door and drove off without knowing where I was going. For a while, I just drove aimlessly while my thoughts swirled in my head. I drove west along the coast and had made it all the way to Seltjarnarnes when I decided to stop and take a walk. I pulled over to the side of the road and turned off the engine.

I got out and walked down to the shoreline. It had stopped raining. A giant cargo ship was sailing not far offshore, packed to the gills with shipping containers. The ship slowly glided along the surface of the water, heading out to sea. Its progress was so slow that for a moment, I wasn't sure if it was in motion or at anchor. Even though I was standing on the shore with waves rolling in and the ship was a good distance away, I could still hear the heavy, low rumbling of an engine.

A wind was blowing in from the sea.

I quickly grew bored of my gaping and turned around. Across the street, two young gardeners were smoking in the shelter of a building wall. They had long hair and grass stains on their knees, and each one was holding an electric strimmer. I suspected that they, too, were watching the freighter while they smoked; they were both looking towards the ocean, at the very least. Between us, on the pavement, a woman in a pink baseball cap was out for a jog.

I noticed that the gardeners were just about finished with their cigarettes, and I figured it wouldn't be long before they flicked away their butts and took up their scythes. Their electric scythes.

I wasn't thinking about death or the time that was racing by. No, I wasn't thinking about death, but rather whether the texts were proof that Gíó was alive.

*All your waves and breakers swept over me.*

Should I take seriously an anonymous text from a phone number I didn't know? It wasn't Gíó. Would he send texts like that?

No, he wouldn't. But where was the quote from? *Your waves and breakers*? I knew the poem, or whatever it was, but I couldn't recall where the verse came from.

Was I afraid of Gíó?

Yes.

I was afraid. Perhaps Gíó wasn't a man who would take revenge or resort to violence. He didn't have anything like that in him. But maybe I'd awoken such a fury in him that he'd do whatever it took to get even with me.

Of course, he was livid with me.

He would never be able to forgive me.

Should I call the police? Tell them about the texts?

What good would that do?

Maybe the police would look after me, protect me from harm?

I got back in my car, took out my phone and looked up the picture of the scrap of paper the police had found in the pocket of the olive-green trench coat. I looked at the date that was written on the note and checked it against my diary calendar.

Starting on 12 October, I was scheduled to take a two-day class at the university. One of those so-called 'masterclasses' in creative writing, taught by foreign lecturers. My flirtation with literature. Nothing that had anything to do with Gíó.

I punched the number from the paper into my phone. It didn't correspond to any of the numbers in my contacts.

I decided to call it.

The phone had been ringing for a long time and I was about to hang up when someone answered. It seemed like the man on the other end of the line had sprinted to the phone, because he was short of breath.

'Jósep,' he said before he took a heavy, deep breath.

His voice was old and tired.

I thought about hanging up, but instead said cheerily: 'Is this Jósep?'

'Yes, this is Jósep.' Deep breath in and out.

'Sorry to disturb you, but I'm calling on behalf of my husband…' I trailed off while I thought for a moment.

'Yes?' The response was dry and didn't betray the slightest bit of interest.

'You know him. Gíó Ísaksson.'

'Gíó Ísaksson?'

'Yes. He's been in touch with you.'

'Yes.'

I waited for the man to say something. He waited for me to explain the reason for my call.

'Are the two of you supposed to meet on 12 October? That is, tomorrow?'

'Meet?'

'Yes, it says here in his diary that he's meeting you.'

'Yes, meeting—he's coming here.'

'Sorry… I… Well, he's so absent-minded… and he's got so much on his plate that he forgets… so much depends on him… Can you maybe tell me what the goal of your meeting was… if I…'

'Goal?' His voice was still entirely absent of curiosity, and I was afraid that he was going to hang up on me if I couldn't say something that would illuminate this conversation.

'No, not the goal… Sorry, do you remember why you were going to meet?'

'Yes, I remember well.'

'Ummm… That's great… Could you maybe tell me…?'

'He's going to rent from me.'

'Rent? Rent what?'

'My holiday cottage.'

'Your holiday cottage? Sorry, I'm being slow… but it's my job, if I can put it that way, to sort out my husband's diary. You have a holiday cottage you rent out?'

'Yes.'

'And where is it, if I may ask?'

'It's just a holiday cottage that I rent, a very out-of-the-way holiday cottage. Gíó's rented it before, and he ought to know very well where it is. What kind of conversation is this?'

The line went dead.

Why did the man hang up on me like that? I called back, but this time, Jósep was in no mood to take part in any further conversation. He didn't pick up.

Gíó had rented from Jósep before? I'd never heard him mention the holiday cottage or spending time in any such out-of-the-way place. He'd sometimes gone away for a few days, but that was always in connection with work: team building, conferences, working groups—whatever else white-collar men invent to justify their absence from the home.

# 58

I knew there was no point in calling this tedious man back right away. He obviously didn't intend to waste any more time on me. I decided to try to get hold of him again later when I had all my facts straight and knew exactly what I was going to say to breach his defences.

I looked up from my phone and out through the windscreen. The freighter was gone. It had sailed out beyond the horizon. The gardeners were also gone, and there were two young women standing and smoking in their place. I looked at the building they were standing in front of and wondered why all the people huddled in the shelter of its wall were cigarette smokers. At the other end of the building was some sort of coffee kiosk. I noticed a cardboard coffee box at the women's feet. They were cold, judging from the way they hunched over their cigarettes and wrapped their arms around themselves, stomping their feet now and again to keep their blood moving. They paid me no mind.

I gave some thought to my best course of action. Dusted off the dash, pushed back the driver's seat and stretched. I couldn't even think about going home. I turned on the car, cranked up the heater and switched on the radio, where some author was reading from their book and seemed to be directing all his energy into enunciating all his Rs and R-words as crisply as possible.

I turned the radio off.

'Rrrridiculous wrrriter,' I chided, though I didn't know the man from Adam.

Perhaps because I didn't have any better ideas, I decided to call

Detective Haraldur and tell him about the photos I'd been sent. I felt less confident that any good would come of telling him about the poem: *You hurled me into the depths, into the very heart of the seas.* That could only serve to draw his attention in an uncomfortable direction. I suspected he wouldn't take the photos very seriously but would comfort me and calm me down. He seemed very generous with his compassion.

Haraldur was apparently waiting for my call because he answered on the first ring, as always. He always picked up immediately.

'Hello, there. I was just about to call you.'

'Oh? How come?'

'No, tell me first why you called.'

'Something's happened. I got some strange texts, on my phone. Threatening, actually. Pictures, one of a man who could be Gíó... At first, I thought that maybe it was him who sent them to me and then...'

'Why do you think that it was your husband who sent the photos?' asked Haraldur.

'I didn't say it was.'

'Yes, but you suggested that it *could have* been him. That's how I understood you. Why should he want to threaten you like that? There's no ill will between you two, is there?'

'There's no ill will between us, and I didn't say he was threatening me. I just said that the texts were threatening and that they scared me. There's someone out there texting me, someone who knows who I am and what's happening to me...'

'Let's calm down, now, calm down. I told you that you could expect these kinds of things. It happens all the time in cases like this. We see it more and more. You're not to trouble yourself about such things—not for the moment, at least. But if it keeps happening, we'll check it out. Send me the pictures. I'll take a look.

Don't worry. We won't do anything for the time being; we can't be chasing down this kind of thing at the moment. There are always some sick people out there who get the bright idea of trying to scare you, shake you up. We've seen this exact pattern many times before. I can't imagine that anyone really wishes you harm. But there's something else I need to talk to you about.'

He paused, as though planning out his next sentence.

'I just found out that your husband's last phone call was to your sister. That is to say, María. He even texted her, said he was on the way to her house. The phone pinged the tower by the Óseyrarbraut pier.'

I didn't say anything, just waited for Haraldur to carry on. But he seemed to be giving me time to process this information. The silence stretched out longer than was comfortable. I heard him sigh and then clear his throat as though preparing to continue. I wondered if I should say something about this new discovery but decided to let the detective keep talking.

'This seems a bit odd to us, given that your sister swears up and down that she hasn't heard a single word from your husband. María, who we spoke to again just a moment ago, said—after some waffling—that she did receive both the text and the phone call. But she swears she didn't talk to your husband because he hung up immediately—the moment she answered.'

'He called and hung up? And then what?' I asked, feigning eagerness.

'Yes. And then nothing, except a text that said he was on his way to her place.'

'That he was on the way?'

To my great surprise, I felt intense anger welling up inside me. I knew, of course, that Gíó hadn't sent María that text. And yet, I seethed—bitterly.

'Yes, the text said he was on the way to hers. There's no question of that. He sent it from his phone—said he was coming to her house and then his phone went offline.' Haraldur fell silent.

'Did you go to her house?'

'Yes, we went over. She was very accommodating.'

'Did you search it?'

'Search the premises? No, there was no reason for us to do that. She said she'd been very confused about both the phone call and the text. She picked up right away to say he was welcome to come over, but to question whether that was really the right time for a visit and ask if something was wrong. But he didn't answer. And he never showed up, either.'

'She's lying,' I hissed. 'She insisted she hadn't heard from him when I spoke to her. She never tells the truth. You can't trust a single word she says.' That last sentence was tinged with an irritating whine. I cleared my throat and stretched my back.

'The messages made her uncomfortable and she said she didn't want to get mixed up in a matter that was obviously between you and your husband. She didn't think there was any reason to draw attention to her phone contact with Gió because in reality, there hadn't been any. They hadn't even spoken to one another. Gió didn't respond to her text, and he never came to her house, as he'd suggested he would. The whole thing was strangely pointless, according to your sister.' Haraldur sighed again, as though he was capitulating in some fashion.

The whole thing was strangely pointless.

I closed my eyes.

'What happens now?'

'Well,' he said, seeming to weigh what the next steps would be. 'We keep searching.'

## Icelandic National Broadcasting Service (RÚV) | ruv.is | 12.10.22 – 00:55

Icelandic Search and Rescue (ICE-SAR) has paused its operations and is awaiting further instruction from the police regarding the search for Gíó Ísaksson, who has been missing since Sunday. This was confirmed by ICE-SAR's media representative in an interview on state radio.

Gíó is thirty-four years old, of muscular build, and 187 centimetres tall. He has dark, medium-length hair and blue eyes.

According to the police bulletin, he is wearing an olive-green trench coat, black trousers, and black leather boots.

Gíó left his home just before midnight on Sunday and his last known whereabouts were in Hafnarfjörður around 1 on Monday morning. New information received by police today may indicate that he was in the Hvalfjörður area yesterday.

Anyone who can provide information about Gíó's movements is asked to contact police immediately on 112.

# 59

I woke early the next morning but was late getting up. I just lay there for a long time under the blankets, letting time pass. The curtains were drawn, and no light came into the bedroom. I watched the red numbers on the digital alarm clock on the nightstand count the minutes with one eye. It was morning, but it would be a long time before the sun rose.

Before I went to bed the night before, I'd found Gíó's laptop and tried to get into it. I'd tried one password after another, but nothing worked. Júlía, I typed. María, I typed. I tried Gíó's birthday, my birthday, María's birthday. I had Gíó and María's relationship on the brain, that much was clear.

I rooted through his desk drawer in the hope of discovering something that might help me get into his laptop. The drawer was full of stuff: papers, books, stationery, old leads and chargers, dry cigars, a figurine of an eyeless alien creature… I pulled out notes and pieces of paper filled with doodles trying to get an idea of what Gíó's password might be, but to no avail. His laptop was completely inaccessible to me. I clearly didn't know him well enough.

I went through the pockets of all his trousers and jackets. I found change, receipts and also a yellow Post-it that particularly caught my interest because it had the name Jósep jotted on it, as well as some squiggle that looked like it might be an address, but I couldn't make it out for the life of me. The address had clearly been written in some haste; the letters were either half-written, clumsy smudges or random lines. The word that was presumably the street name was hardly more than one long line with two apostrophes above it. I could, however, discern the letter S and the number 371.

I stared at the scribbles for a little longer, but there was no decoding this chicken scratch. It wasn't until I'd been at this fruitless task for quite some time that it occurred to me that I could type the phone number I had into the online phone directory. My computer hardly needed more than a fraction of a second to spit out a result:

JÓSEP JÓSEPSSON
Former Headmaster
Sjónarhóll
371 Búðardalur

I stared at the result of my search and shook my head that it had taken me so long to think to seek my computer's assistance. Have my pipes become that pernickety? I looked up a map and found Sjónarhóll in Búðardalur, a small village in a remote corner of north-west Iceland. I decided that I was going to pay a visit to that tedious old man as soon as I'd properly woken up.

# 60

While I lay in bed, reviewing the previous day, my phone rang on the nightstand. I glanced at the clock; it was time for me to finally get up.

I saw on the phone screen that it was Haraldur calling.

'Hello,' I answered wretchedly.

'Hi, again. I'm sorry I always seem to be calling you. Apologies for disturbing you.'

'You're not disturbing me. Something new?'

'Yes… actually, I have to ask you to come down to the police station.'

'What? I have to come to the station? Why?'

'You know where it is?'

'Yes, I think so. I've just woken up.'

'On Hverfisgata.'

'So, I should come down there? Has something happened?'

'No, nothing has happened, per se. But it would be best if you came in now, Júlía.'

'Can't you come to mine?'

'We need to comply with the formalities, so it would be best if we chat at the station, it makes the questioning easier.'

'Questi— why?'

'It's just routine; everything needs to be documented. We've got to do everything by the book. So I'll be expecting you.'

'Listen, wait a minute, just wait a minute. Is there something new? Have you found something?'

'We haven't found any clues as to your husband's movements, though the search's grown rather extensive. And we haven't found him. Either he doesn't want to be found or…' Haraldur hesitated. This seemed to be something he did—pause mid-conversation to think about what he should say, find the right words. 'We've investigated all the tips we've got, a large team of people has been searching Hvalfjörður, we've sent divers out to Óseyri Harbour, we've run pictures in the papers, our beat cops are keeping their eyes peeled when they're out on patrol, we've scanned all the airline passenger lists, and there's been no movement on his bank accounts. All of which is to say: no clues as to where your husband could be. Unfortunately.'

'It's all I think about…'

'Of course. I understand.'

'Haraldur, why do I have to come to the station? Is that really necessary?'

'There's something I need to show you, and we're going to do things by the book this time. Tick all the boxes.'

# 61

There was nothing to please the eye in the room, or cubicle, that Haraldur led me into. Just one ugly table and two chairs.

One for me, one for Haraldur, and a table between us.

The walls were bare and white as bed sheets. I'd expected there to be a mirror on the wall. A one-way glass mirror that was actually a window for the officers who were sitting in the room next door, listening and watching as the suspect sweated through the detective's aggressive line of questioning. But there was no mirror in here and no window—just bare, white walls. Four white walls.

'Sit, please… Take a seat, Júlía. Let's not drag this out.'

'No,' I said miserably. I could tell that Haraldur had something important to tell me and I feared the worst.

'Now, you must answer me with complete honesty. That will be, by far, the best thing for you. Tell the truth, tell the whole truth. I'm such an old hand at this. So when I tell you this, I'm giving you good advice. The best advice I have. Believe me. Be completely honest. I am, of course, not implying that you're lying to me. But it is difficult to tell the truth. You know how falsehoods and fact have a way of getting mixed up.'

I didn't say anything but tried to understand what Haraldur was getting at and what he wanted to tell me. I could indeed imagine how falsehoods and facts could, in some instances, blend together and become one and the same thing.

'Before we begin, I want to remind you of an article in the penal code which dictates that those under questioning must always tell authorities the full and unedited truth.'

'What are you talking about? The penal code? Have I committed a crime?'

'Be calm. I want you to be calm and answer me to the best of your ability. We've received some information that quite puzzled me. I was rather surprised.'

'Oh?'

'Yes.' Haraldur sighed and stroked his forehead as though wiping away sweat. 'I received a tip—all right, this isn't particularly easy, but I received a tip about things that you've done and then deliberately concealed from us. There's no other way for me to see it. At the very least, it seems that you haven't felt the need to tell me about these doings, which are patently relevant to the case. As you well know. And I have to be able to trust what you say.'

'What?'

'First, I find out about the drive you and Gió took to Hvalfjörður and the arrangement you made with a farmer to borrow his boat so you could sail out into the fjord. That's important information, and if you're keeping mum about that kind of thing, the only way I can interpret that is to your disadvantage. Now I've been informed that you were driving around Óseyri Harbour late Sunday night, early Monday morning. Which is to say—as I know you're capable of working out for yourself—not long after you said your husband left home and basically the exact time that he made that last call from his phone.'

'I was seen driving around Óseyri Harbour?' I wasn't sure what I should do. I wanted to get out of there, flee that two-chair room, but I might just as easily hope for Gió to reach down from the heavens and pull me up to him. I wouldn't be getting out of this bomb-proof vault until I'd answered the old detective's questions.

'Yes, so I'm told. Is that not correct?'

I thought in silence for a moment, picturing the gap between the motorcycle cop's front teeth. His red, ice-cold cheeks, little blue eyes, the raindrops on his white helmet.

'I have this from a reliable source, as they say,' added Haraldur when he felt he'd waited long enough for my answer.

'Yes, it's true.'

'Yes, it's true? That is to say: you were in Hafnarfjörður, near Óseyri Harbour, at the aforementioned time?'

'Yes...'

'Júlía, why on earth didn't you tell me that before?' The disappointment in Haraldur's voice was almost palpable. I was ashamed to have disappointed this benevolent man. 'Is there anything else you've been hiding from me... from the police?'

I couldn't answer. I tried to think clearly but my mind was too much of a jumble to be logical and systematic.

'Do you know something? Something that could shed some light on what happened to your husband that you haven't told me?'

I said nothing.

Haraldur said nothing.

'Am I right that there's something you don't want to tell me or can't tell me... or...?'

I said nothing.

Haraldur said nothing.

'All right,' I finally said. 'When Gió left, I got so scared all of a sudden that I just got in the car and started driving and when I looked up, I'd gone all the way to the Óseyri wharf. And then that policeman stopped me.'

'Did you know that Gió was somewhere in the area?'

'No. I just drove.'

'Ugh, I don't want to hear any more nonsense,' said Haraldur sharply, so sharply that I was genuinely taken aback. 'You must be able to hear how unconvincing that sounds: it's pure nonsense. You don't think I'm so stupid that I'm just going to nod along, *yes ma'am* and *righto* to this utter rubbish? I don't buy this story. You need to tell me the truth.' His voice was growing sharper by the second and there was a note of impatience in it.

'Yes, but that's…'

Haraldur gave me another disappointed look.

'No more. Stop this nonsense. You are hiding something from me. Whatever it is that's weighing on you… just tell me what it is. I want to help you.'

'I don't know what I'm supposed to say. This whole thing is so unreal.'

'Yes, it's all so unreal. I know that's what you're claiming. But tell me what happened the night Gíó went missing.'

'I suspected that Gíó might go out to Óseyri. He was always talking about it… by which I mean when he threatened… when we were at loggerheads… he'd always tell me he was going to jump into the harbour there. Drive out to Óseyri wharf, the most desolate spot in the country—that's what he said—not on Sunday, but he'd said it before…'

'And then what?'

'I went out when I started getting worried. But that cop stopped me. He showed up out of nowhere and stopped me and told me to turn around. That I had no business wandering around there at night.'

'Is that right?'

'So I turned around. The cop can confirm that.'

Haraldur looked at me thoughtfully.

'I might know where Gíó is,' I hurried to say. 'The note that was in his pocket… the pocket of his trench coat. The note you found. I found another note with the same phone number in his desk drawer yesterday and I called it and spoke to an old man who said that Gíó had made arrangements to rent his holiday cottage… this would have been before he went missing… so I'm going to go up to the holiday cottage later…'

'Yes?'

I could see that none of this was coming as a revelation to him. 'Is this the holiday cottage belonging to the ex-headmaster, the old widower?' he said wearily.

I told him about my phone call with the old man and gave him Jósep's address.

'Sure, you can go up there, why not? But what I'm hearing is that you think your husband is in hiding. And if the man's just hiding, there's little or nothing that we can do about it. He is allowed to hide if he wants to. It would, of course, be best if you were to find him… a good idea for you to try and track him down. If I'm understanding you correctly, that is, you think it's most likely that he's hiding?'

'I'm just holding on to the hope that he'll be found, that he's come to no harm.'

'Maybe the two of you just need to talk. I hope he'll come forward so that you and he can work things out. But I'm telling you now, Júlía…' He paused and looked at me soberly. 'Your position is going to be a lot more tenuous if it comes to light that something serious has befallen your husband. I'm not threatening you, but I am telling you that you cannot properly account for your actions and your movements in the hours around Gíó's disappearance. Your explanations are not particularly believable. We still don't know if any crime has been committed, there's no evidence of that, and as such, there is currently no reason to take the measures the police are obliged to take if they suspect that a criminal act has been committed. I expect you're familiar with the criminal code and I remind you, again, of your obligation to tell the full and unedited truth to the authorities. Anything less is punishable by law. You keep that in mind. But at any rate, now I need to ask you to…' He paused, organizing his thoughts. 'You stay in the country, where we can reach you. Do you understand? We have got to be able to call you in for questioning at a moment's notice.'

'Yes, I understand.'

'If you try to sneak off, I will consider that the act of a criminal attempting to flee.'

'How dare you call me a criminal! If you think I've committed some kind of crime, then you should lock me up here and now, rather than threatening me. Do *you* understand?'

'Listen to what I am saying.' Haraldur didn't seem perturbed by this sudden attack of mine. He was calm and spoke slowly and clearly. But I could detect an anger trembling within him that he was trying to cover.

'I didn't call you a criminal. All I said was that your explanations of your movements are not believable and that you should make truth your watchword. Otherwise, this is going to go badly for you.'

# Icelandic National Broadcasting Service (RÚV) | ruv.is | 12.10.22 – 12:21

ICE-SAR resumed its search for Gíó Ísaksson just before noon today. Between twenty and thirty people are taking part in the search of Hvalfjörður, around the whaling station and its environs, with the help of dogs and drones. This has been confirmed by ICE-SAR's media representative.

The police have received no new information since yesterday.

Over a hundred ICE-SAR volunteers took part in the search for Gíó yesterday, in addition to which the Coast Guard's helicopter was also brought in to offer assistance. No decision has been made regarding how long the search will continue today, nor whether the helicopter will be called out again.

# 62

And off I drove again. I was like a one-woman search team. I had neither drones nor dogs at my disposal, but I did have a little gym bag, in which I'd thrown together what I'd need for one or two nights away from home. After leaving the station, I'd gone back home to pack, and from there I'd zoomed out of the city.

It was still raining. The streets were wet, black and glistening, the headlights reflecting off the puddles in the asphalt.

I felt numb. I was simmering in a porridge of my own thoughts and avoiding other people. All phone calls, texts and warm wishes that I'd received—all of them I'd left unanswered.

I didn't talk to anyone.

I knew it was wrong of me, but I couldn't bear the thought of nattering away on the phone.

I wasn't sure how good an idea it was for me to go find the holiday cottage in the middle of nowhere. Maybe it was the refuge that Gíó had sought while they were looking for him. If he wanted to hide out, the holiday cottage seemed an ideal place for it. It wouldn't occur to anyone to look in the uplands outside Búðardalur.

I couldn't shake off the thought that the note in the trench coat pocket was actually a message from Gíó telling me he could be found at that isolated holiday cottage. That he wanted to be found, even though I couldn't picture Gíó hunkering down in a secret hideaway in a remote part of the country while half the nation was out looking for him. I didn't believe it was coincidence that the coat was found where it was found or that the note was found in its breast pocket. But to be honest, I didn't have much of a choice but to follow the clues. I couldn't just sit at home and wait.

The afternoon traffic was light and there weren't many people making their way out of the city. I'd never been to Búðardalur or to that desolate corner of Iceland more generally, and I didn't know what to expect. The area wasn't known for its holiday cottages. As far as I knew, there was little there other than run-down, out-of-the-way, wind-battered and long-since-abandoned farms tucked under towering mountains.

I pictured the holiday cottage as an old country farmhouse that had been converted into a seasonal rental. I was imagining cows grazing. Plump sheep perched on cliff sides. Moors and tussocky meadows. Stark and barren mountains, screes and boulders.

Although I'd got in the car with the best of intentions—namely, that I wouldn't stop before I'd reached my destination—the disquiet that had been simmering within me grew as the trip progressed, to the point that I could no longer focus on driving. I was forced to turn into the nearest service station and park my car in the shadow of a big pink lorry bearing the logo *Buena Strada—Lady Truck Driver Team*. The text wasn't in Icelandic, but the lorry did have an Icelandic number plate.

The moment I turned off the engine, a wave of emotions crashed over me. I started gasping for breath and suddenly, a half-stifled cry burst up out of me, up from the depths of my soul. I burst into tears and cried with my whole body. I couldn't stop.

My own personal volcano had erupted.

I thought about misfortunes—small misfortunes and great ones alike.

I thought about my own misfortunes. I thought about recent misfortunes and old ones that had had time to fix themselves in my mind. If you stop recalling memories, they just switch off, like lights in a theatre.

I thought about death.

I cried over death and myself in the shadow of that pink lorry owned by a collective of women truck drivers. I cried over Gíó and over the two of us.

I leant forward on the steering wheel and let the tears explode in all directions, like my own crystalline ash and tephra. I let the thick lava of my emotions well up from the deepest caverns of my body.

I let the tears convulse and shake me for a few minutes. Emotional vibrations that would measure at least 1,000 on the Richter scale. I was an earthquake zone, a disaster area, and I gave myself over completely to the power of this genuine and unpolluted surge of feeling.

And then it was over.

I stretched, blew my nose, dried my face and steeled my mind before the steely women truckers discovered me, tear-stained and snot-nosed in the driver's seat of a tiny car. Neither I nor my little car was going to inspire any sort of admiration in them. I'd never be able to explain my grief if they found me whimpering over my steering wheel. I looked in the rear-view mirror, dried my tears and blew my nose again.

I thought about my dad. If he'd been looking down on me from heaven, he would have nodded approvingly. Not at the situation, but at my tears.

When I was a child, I had a tendency to cry over the unhappy fates of people on TV, but I always tried to hide my tears. But my dad knew I was crying, of course, and he'd always whisper to me: *Júlía, sweetheart, don't hide your tears. The fact that you're crying just shows what a good and beautiful heart you have.* And I think he was right—in spite of everything, I do have a good and beautiful heart.

The good, which I want, I never do, while the bad, which I don't want, I do all the time.

I looked once again in the rear-view mirror to examine my puffy, tearful face.

What a sight.

I started the car and pulled out before the women from the Lady Truck Driver team returned.

# 63

It went as I feared it would; I got lost. How was that even possible? It was more or less a straight shot all the way there. But I still managed to take a wrong turn and drove in the opposite direction. Most likely the emotional earthquake had turned the world on its head for me. But at any rate, I ended up driving east when I was sure I was driving west.

It probably wasn't that big a deal if I arrived a bit late to the meeting with the old widower.

When I realized my mistake, I stopped to call Jósep, who was still expecting to meet with Gíó. Just to be on the safe side.

I was relieved that he picked up the phone this time. There was no doubt, however, that there was some annoyance in his voice when I said I'd taken a wrong turn and would be there slightly later than planned. I was coming to pick up the key for Gíó, as he'd been held up at work. Jósep may have been starting to doubt the wisdom of giving me access to his holiday cottage—this woman who got lost so easily and drove in the opposite direction to where she wanted to go. At the very least, he did not sound happy on the phone. Maybe he was just a curmudgeon.

That could also be the case.

He was a curmudgeon.

A crusty old curmudgeon.

It was dark by the time I parked the car outside an ugly little house in a small residential area that seemed to have sprouted up for no conceivable reason in the moors just off Route 1, like a toadstool on a dung heap. It was the ugliest place I'd ever laid eyes on, the buildings dumb and cloddish, everything around the houses bearing witness to the fact that an entire community of imbeciles lived here.

Was I being too uncharitable?

There were no lights in Jósep's windows and, for a moment, I was sure I'd stopped at the wrong house. It seemed to me the place had been abandoned for many years, and in some respects I was right. Everything had abandoned this house except for loneliness, lassitude and sorrow.

I knocked hesitantly at the worn door and waited in the dark. After a good long while, I heard some movement inside and then the door opened. At first, just the slightest crack, a single grey and suspicious eye appearing in the gap.

'Good evening, are you Jósep?' I asked uncertainly, leaning towards the eye.

The door opened all the way, revealing an aged, stooping, grey man. He didn't answer, but rather stepped aside to signal that I should enter the murky world awaiting behind him.

I stalled for a moment, wondering if I should repeat the question, but then squared my shoulders and walked in.

I watched the bent back of the man vanish through the living room; he hadn't asked me to take off my shoes. He dragged his feet when he walked so there was a scraping sound every time his felt slippers scuffed the rough stone floor.

He hadn't said a word. Maybe language had also abandoned him, like everything else that seemed to be absent from this house: occupants, souls, joy.

I hurried to follow the gloomy old man through the doorway that I could make out at the end of the hall. Jósep waited for me to enter what I supposed might most accurately be termed the parlour. There were bookshelves on the wall and framed photographs of elderly people and old photos of children. He'd taken a seat on a hard wooden chair; another identical chair was positioned across from it with a desk in between, a table lamp with a metal shade atop it. A narrow beam of light fell on a sheet of paper and set of keys on the desk.

The rental contract, I thought, and the keys to the holiday cottage.

'Sit down,' said the man finally, after I'd stopped in the middle of the room and peered curiously around the woeful room. Jósep pointed an old, crooked finger at the seat facing him.

His voice was weak and hoarse.

'Sit down,' he repeated a little louder when he decided I wasn't reacting to his command quickly enough.

I gingerly sat on the vacant chair and continued looking around the room, which was just as gloomy as the man. The dim table lamp was the only light. There was a thick brown rug on the floor under the desk. There were stains on it, and in some spots, it was so threadbare that I could make out the canvas underside.

I fumbled for my wallet and placed it on my lap so I'd have something to hold on to. I also wanted to be able to quickly produce the money when it came time to settle accounts and then get out of here quick. I couldn't imagine spending any more time than absolutely necessary with this old codger.

'Yes, uh, I'm here because of the holiday cottage… the rental. You and Gíó agreed on the time and price, is that right? I was the one who called—'

'I worked that out,' he interrupted in his scratchy voice. 'I wasn't expecting anyone else, just you.'

He didn't say it in an unfriendly way, but then fell silent, tapped on the rental agreement, stared blankly ahead, and breathed heavily through his nose, as though stringing those two sentences together in the same breath had completely taken it out of him. The spirit was almost certainly leaving him.

I couldn't bear the silence; it was driving me mad. Isn't that precisely what people say when a silence becomes oppressive? 'It's driving me mad?' I hurried to pull out the money. Cash.

'So yes, I'm Lára von Dunk.'

I have no idea where I got that name. For some reason, I didn't want to give my real name when introducing myself as Gíó's wife. That was just the first name that had occurred to me when I called ahead of my arrival. Von Dunk... It made me sound like a character out of the *Donald Duck* comics I'd read as a child. Scrooge McDuck... Ludwig Von Drake. Lára von Dunk.

Truth be told, even I found this pseudonym of mine unbelievable. Laughable. But I hadn't had the foresight to settle on a normal name before I called. So I just chose the first thing that popped into my head. That was so like me. Constantly tripping over my own feet. So Lára von Dunk is the name I'd be stuck with for as long as I was a guest at this old man's holiday cottage.

It could be worse.

'I brought cash with me. You and Gíó agreed on two days, correct?' I looked inquiringly at him, but it seemed like he had no intention of answering. Now he looked down at the floor and I started to suspect that he was going to back out. The best thing would probably be for me to go back to Reykjavík. This was a harebrained scheme, plain and simple.

'Yes,' he said finally. 'I've prepared the rental agreement.' Again, he used his crooked finger—the same one that had directed me to sit down—to tap on the paper on the desk.

'Everything in the holiday cottage ought to be self-explanatory. I've prepared a book—"The House Book", as it says on it, on its title page, I mean. It contains instructions. Everything is explained in detail: the heating, how to use the oven, hot and cold water and everything else. As you might expect, I mostly rent the holiday cottage in the summer. There aren't many people who come out this way in the autumn and winter. I made up the name—the name of the book: "The House Book".'

'Yes. Nice name,' I said, feigning enthusiasm. 'Short and sweet and to the point.'

He wasn't listening to my affirmations, however—he didn't even look up. He didn't understand what I was talking about any more than I understood why he was telling me that he made up the name. There was nothing novel or nice about it. Maybe it was because he knew I'd made up my own name. But at least that was original.

'Is it okay to smoke… I mean, is smoking permitted inside the holiday cottage?' The words tumbled out of my mouth. I had no idea what I was saying—I didn't smoke. At the very least, not indoors.

'No. There is no smoking inside the house,' he said, his tone stricter. The same heavy, woolly silence settled over us again. Then he cleared his throat.

'You can take a hike up the mountain if you get bored. There's a small path that ends at a grave I dug fourteen years ago. My dog is buried there. He's dead.'

'Yes,' I said lamely. It came out a high-pitched bleat. Extraordinary stuff. So the dog he'd buried was dead, eh?

'He's dead?' I asked.

'Yes, he's dead,' said Jósep. 'He died fourteen years ago. Otherwise, I wouldn't have buried him.'

Maybe Gíó is dead, too, I almost said, but I stopped myself. I couldn't think of anything else now. Truth be told, death was just about all I could think of in that house. It had even briefly occurred to me that Jósep himself was dead. But the poor man had no way of knowing that I had the question of death on the brain, or more accurately, the question of *presumed* death. Impending death, slow death.

He opened a drawer in his desk and took out another piece of paper.

'Here's the route, the directions to the house. It's in a remote place and the road there is not much travelled. But here's how to get there, so you won't get lost again.'

'Thanks,' I said, taking the directions.

I had nothing else to add or ask so I drew the rental agreement to me, bent over the page and scanned for the line where I should sign.

'Remember to sign on behalf of Gíó Ísaksson. It's his name on the contract, as you know.'

That gravelly, ancient voice.

'Is that really his name? Gíó? What kind of name is that? Is it a nickname? For Guðjón, perhaps?'

'Ummm, I'm not sure what you mean. His name is Gíó.' Although I was trying to sound convincing, I found myself in two minds because all of a sudden, I wasn't entirely sure that his name *wasn't* Guðjón. Maybe he'd just got stuck with the nickname Gíó.

'But yes, while I'm thinking about it,' I said after a short pause, trying appear cheerful. 'I want to surprise him—Gíó. He doesn't know that I've come ahead of him. If he should come here, may I ask you not to mention that I've been here? Or that I'm going to be at the holiday cottage when he arrives? Would you be so kind?'

Jósep looked at me open-mouthed, as if he didn't understand what I was asking. 'You want to surprise him?'

'Yes.'

The old man snorted. I took that as an assent.

There was no line on the contract to sign, so I just scribbled my new name beside his: Jósep Jósepsson.

I penned my new signature for the first time. I wrote: On behalf of Gíó Ísaksson, Laura von Dunk.

L-A-U Laura, not L-Á-R-A, as you'd write it in Icelandic.

Why?

I didn't know what was going on in my own head.

# 64

I followed my short-term landlord's instructions to the house. The tedious man's directions led me into a deep valley. I would never voluntarily follow any other instructions this man wrote. I could somehow just tell that he wasn't qualified to direct anyone anywhere but the shortest route between two houses. But he obviously had a talent for making the route plan itself because he'd managed to fill a whole, densely written page with instructions and the place was only twenty-five kilometres away.

I knew the holiday cottage was remote—he'd told me that from the start and that was probably one of the reasons that Gíó had chosen it. A hideout far from everyone and everything. I suspected that this was where he'd played out his sexual games, the ones he'd written down. But why did it have to be so far from Reykjavík?

It might sound as though I had a plan. I didn't. Or yes, maybe I did. My plan was to see if I'd find my husband and if I did, what would happen. I wasn't sure of anything; I was just muddling along.

I immediately regretted having not set out much earlier. I was leagues from civilization, and I wouldn't get to the house until long after sunset. It was unlikely that anyone would see me arrive at the holiday cottage, but I hadn't thought about how afraid I'd be all by myself in the dark in such an isolated place. It was so very far from anyone else, and the idea that I'd be lolling about in a strange house in the gloom sparked considerable fear in me.

Nature reveals its soul at night. During the day, it sleeps and allows itself to be observed, but in the dark, it becomes a living thing, unsparing and unpredictable.

# 65

After leaving Jósep's house, I'd taken a right, just as he'd written in the directions. Then I took the first turn off Route 1 to the left and drove up a narrow gravel road. Here ended anything reminiscent of human habitation; the wilderness took over. No houses, no people. Just stones, cliffs and a long, potholed road leading into a valley, with tall mountains looming overhead and all around.

The road was so narrow that for a moment I thought about turning around because I could hardly believe that this was the right way.

Was I driving on a hiking trail or maybe a sheep track?

How were you supposed to get a car up this path? Of course, there were no street lamps to light up the way and the night darkness in the countryside was as black as thick tar.

I really hoped I wouldn't encounter another car because the one-lane road was also on a sheer mountainside.

The precipice on the left-hand side should have been included in the instructions. I drove skyward, up a mountainside along a road that twisted and turned like a worm, like a serpent. Up and up and up.

I felt like I'd been driving up that endless gravel road for an eternity. I repeatedly found myself on the point of stopping. But how was I supposed to turn the car around on a road this narrow on the side of a mountain?

I could only drive in one direction. And that was up and into the valley.

I was afraid I was going the wrong way and also terrified to be travelling alone in the pitch-dark middle of nowhere. What if the road just ended without reaching a destination, just came to a stop at a cliff wall? I'd have to walk back.

I was so stressed that I had the steering wheel in a death grip and was sitting stiff as a board in the driver's seat. What on earth had I got myself into? Shouldn't I just go home, reverse down the hillside, give up? No, there was no turning back. There's no way but forward, Laura von Dunk.

I pressed my face up to the windscreen. Still rigid with fear. Until finally, I came to the driveway I'd been looking for.

> Gravel drive on the left. A black gate (it should be open, otherwise, the keys to the lock are on the key ring). Drive through the gate and straight on for roughly seventy-two metres along the gravel road. Then you'll see the house.

It was exactly as Jósep described. I drove along the gravel road until a white house appeared ahead of me, illuminated by faint moonlight. It was situated on top of a hill, with wide stone steps leading up to it. I stopped after turning onto the driveway at the gate, parked the car on the roadside and got out. For a moment, I stood in front of the car, just staring at the holiday cottage seventy-two metres away.

It didn't look like anyone else had arrived ahead of me, unless they were on foot, because there was no car in the parking spot at the base of the steps, and there were no signs of life in the windows. Nevertheless, I tried not to be conspicuous.

I opened the car door and took my small gym bag out of the back seat. The silence was so complete that I was almost afraid my breathing could be heard all the way up at the house. I focused on breathing soundlessly.

I closed the back door of the car as quietly as I could.

Not a sound.

Then I crept stealthily towards the house, inched up the steps and stopped at the top to look around. An endless expanse, as far as the eye could see, illuminated by the faint glow of the moon. I stood still and listened. In the distance, I thought I could make out the bleating of sheep. So pure was the evening silence that I felt like I could hear the watchworks of the heavens ticking away. I closed my eyes and cleared my mind and discovered a new sound, at a higher frequency, a hum, a vibrating hum, and I imagined it was coming from the gears that were propelling the moon. My father the watchmaker could have explained what caused that unbroken tone. Maybe the mainspring was too taut and that was what was causing those odd vibrations. Maybe it was falling apart and the watchworks of the heavens would soon grind to a halt.

I opened my eyes again and tiptoed towards the house. The front door was sturdy and seemed solid and strong, and I was relieved that this formidable barrier would stand between me and the world while I slept. I placed my ear up to the door and waited to hear any rustling inside. I waited patiently in this position. Focused. There was no movement whatsoever.

Either there was no one inside or, if there was, the person was either sleeping, sitting completely still and holding their breath, or dead. No, no, I'd just stopped thinking about death.

I didn't have much of a choice but to risk opening the door and seeing what was on the other side. The keys that Jósep had given me were big and blunt. I stuck one of them into the lock as gently as I could, turned it slowly and gingerly pushed the door open. The hinges squeaked.

# 66

I hesitated in the doorway, hardly daring to enter this temporary abode of mine. I nearly expected someone to be waiting for me there, sitting inside with a smirk: 'So you've come at last, have you? At last.'

I stood still and listened.

Dead silence.

The watchworks of the heavens were still quietly ticking away.

I was met by a faint, musty odour. The only living thing in there was undoubtedly the mould on the walls.

No one was waiting for me.

I was there and you were where you were.

The holiday cottage was plain. Some might say spartan. Right as you walked in, there was a small living room. A table with two chairs. In a corner, next to a large fireplace, there was a worn, bright-red easy chair and a small circular table next to that.

Otherwise, the room was empty.

To the right was a door into a confined, sparely appointed kitchen and on the left a bedroom. The bed was big.

Big enough for two.

Big enough for both of us or both of them.

I stood there clutching my gym bag in an unfamiliar house. I walked into the bedroom and laid my bag on the floor before going into the kitchen. There was a caramel wrapped in old-fashioned foil on the table. Under it, a note on a small scrap of white paper: 'For the next guest. For enjoyment on the porch.'

‘How terribly worded… *for enjoyment,*’ I snorted, the sound of my own voice taking me by surprise.

What was I supposed to do with a single caramel?

I stuck the sweet in my pocket and glanced around.

I hadn’t noticed any porch door, come to think of it, so I went back into the living room. I found the door hidden behind some long, thick curtains, opened it, and stepped out onto a wooden deck. The moon appeared above me like an X-ray as I looked out over the frozen world.

Truth be told, it was beautiful. I could allow myself to admit that much. The sky was awash with stars. I peered into the darkness, watched my breath cloud in the frosty night air.

# 67

Sleep was out of the question, there wasn't a wink of slumber in me. My head was filled with a low moaning after the long day and I felt the same confounded uneasiness.

The tides of fear.

I opened a bottle of red wine I'd brought with me, poured a little into a blue plastic cup I found in the kitchen cupboard—there were no other glasses to choose from—and settled into the red easy chair in the corner by the fireplace.

I didn't feel like labouring away to light a fire now, even though I was trembling from the cold. Rather, I'd sit and let the chills shake me until I was ready to sleep. I longed to sleep. I longed to forget. I longed for a reprieve from this constant fear.

I knew just sitting here would give me no peace and so I emptied my glass of wine in one gulp. I double-checked that the front door was locked before lying down on the big bed fully clothed, spreading both duvets on top of me. The cold had buried its claws deep in my bones, my marrow—my very core. The temperature of my heart hovered around freezing. Zero degrees. I'd like to say negative zero, but, of course, that's not a real thing.

I'll not describe all the fears that assailed me over the course of that night. I don't know how to be alone. Or at least, I don't know how to be alone in the dark in the middle of nowhere. The longer I lay there in the inky blackness, the more fearful I became, and I tossed and turned under the blankets, stuck in that strange purgatory between sleep and waking.

I was a coward. A spineless wretch.

I'd noticed that I had no phone service. Out in the sticks, there was no connection with the city or even nearby villages. I couldn't call for help.

I began to imagine that I was being ambushed, that someone was lying in wait for me in the darkness. Could someone break down the front door? Were there any windows someone could crawl through?

Again and again, I heard a knock at the door.

Again and again, I got up to make sure the door was locked, the windows securely fastened. I didn't dare open the door to check outside, rather pressed my ear against it to try and hear whether someone was moving outside, whether there'd actually been a knock at the door.

I waited, my forehead resting on the door and my eyes closed. I waited like that for a long time. I don't know how long, but in my head, I stood there for at least two hours. And no one knocked.

I crept to the window and peeped out into the darkness, trying to catch a glimpse of anyone who might be creeping around the house. Nothing stirred.

Eventually, I screwed up my courage and opened the door. I was prepared to slam it shut again immediately should someone step out of the darkness. I had the key in the lock and made ready to fling the door open, look around and then lock it right after.

I took a few deep breaths, like a high jumper before beginning the run-up, making one final attempt to get over the crossbar. Then I swung the door open in a flash, stuck out my head, and scanned in all directions. There was no one there.

But then, just as I was about to close the door, I saw something that made my blood freeze in my veins, my heart stop beating, my eyes fade to black. I slammed the door and locked it.

What was that?

I stood behind the door, frozen in fear, and it took me several minutes to muster the courage to open the door again.

Outside, right on the threshold, was a white flower. A single white flower. It was lying on the top step. A white flower with three petals on a green stem. It practically glowed in the darkness.

I hesitated and then shot one hand out to grab it before slamming the door. I sat with my back against that massive door, twirling the flower in my fingers to examine it. Somehow, I'd expected there to be a message attached. But there was no note of any kind.

A white flower.

I knew that purple was the colour of regret; I should really be shrouding myself in nothing but these days. Didn't white symbolize death? I stifled that thought immediately, cursing my constant catastrophizing. White was the colour of purity.

But someone was out there, that much was certain.

I twisted the knob once more to assure myself the door was locked. At least it was thick—you'd need a bulldozer to break it down.

I placed the flower on the coffee table and got back into bed.

Who had put the flower on my doorstep?

One flower.

What kind of greeting was that?

After I'd lain there, agonizing over my thoughts, my isolation, the cold, for what seemed like ages, I began whispering a strange prayer in my head: Oh, you, Lamb of God… Have mercy upon me.

I'd no idea where the refrain had come from, but shortly after, I took up another supplication:

I am here and you are where you are.

Come to me.

Come back to me.

# Icelandic National Broadcasting Service (RÚV) | ruv.is | 13.10.22 – 07:49

The search for Gíó Ísaksson has been put on hold while authorities review leads and decide how the investigation will proceed and where it will be focused.

This per DS Sigurður Jón Kælk of the Reykjavík and Capital-Area Police, in an interview with RÚV this morning.

'We'll be speaking with the man's relations and reviewing evidence and leads before deciding where Search and Rescue teams should be deployed. The search will resume once we've concluded these inquiries.'

Sigurður Jón says the police have received numerous reports from the public but would not comment on whether any definitive evidence has surfaced regarding Gíó's movements. The investigation is extensive, however, and the disappearance is being treated as a serious incident. Nothing has been seen or heard of the missing man since Sunday.

Search and Rescue teams are standing at the ready, says ICE-SAR's operations director. 'We're just awaiting orders from the police. It's hard to search when we've got nothing to go on.'

It's anticipated that over 100 people will take part in the search today; nearly as many volunteers participated yesterday as well, scouring a wide area. The search was paused shortly after midnight.

# 68

When I woke the next morning, I made the decision not to dwell on the terrors of the previous night. Another night would follow, and I had decided to survive.

The sun drove away the monsters lurking in my mind. They live at night, in solitude and darkness.

It's strange how nature—living, breathing creature that it is—can ill-treat a person when they're alone.

I opened the porch door and let the light into the holiday cottage. And though the sun didn't manage to deliver its warmth to me so early in the day, I was thankful for its brightness.

# 69

One night down.

My hypothesis that Gíó was en route to the holiday cottage or that I'd find him here seemed to be both wrong and nonsensical. The hope that I'd so welcomed yesterday was gone and had been replaced by a new, unsettling feeling.

The white flower from the night before was lying on the coffee table, wilting and awaiting its slow demise.

While I made my morning coffee and puttered in the kitchen, I tried to bat away my grief. My mind drifted to thoughts of a man I often saw when I went out for my morning walk around the neighbourhood. It was a pleasant association.

The man owned a dog, although he wasn't a 'dog guy' by any means. But walk his dog he did—every morning. Every morning of the year, the man and his dog went out for their stroll, often long before anyone else woke up. He wasn't particularly fond of his dog—he'd adopted it as an indulgence for his daughter who'd rather quickly outgrown her interest in man's best friend—but they still walked around the neighbourhood every morning, he with his thermos of coffee and the dog on a leash.

The dog was black and stocky—can you call a dog fat? There seemed to be a fair amount of adipose tissue on its thickset trunk, let's put it that way. The animal walked on long, stick-like legs, legs that didn't look at all likely to support such a heavy hound, and yet they did. And so every morning, the dog wobbled along on stilts behind its owner.

I was always happy to see the man—I had no opinion on the dog—and I think he was also glad to greet me. I saw him often, although we didn't always stop to chat. Sometimes, we just waved at one another and continued on our way. But more often than not, we stopped, tarried for a brief chat.

It was always as though I was jumping directly into the man's train of thought because he generally launched in without ever warming up for the exchange by introducing whatever it was that was on his mind. He just started talking, mid-thought. Often, the topic was religious in nature—or at least existential. I don't know why he was so preoccupied with the sublime.

Maybe it was because of the man's ongoing existential crisis and my newfound angst that I found myself thinking about him and his dog. It was, at the very least, not the norm for me to say my prayers at night or for my late-night woes to compel me to beseech the Lamb of God.

'Listen…' the man once said to me on the street corner, standing right in the middle of the cone of light cast by the street lamp. This was at the crack of dawn one winter morning and frost crystals were glittering on the pavement. '…when I was a kid, I was horribly bullied.'

'Bullied, you say?' I asked cheerfully. 'Good morning to you, too.'

'Yes, sure. Good morning,' he said with a grin. 'I was thinking… I was so terribly bullied and made to endure every imaginable insult and humiliation.'

I had trouble imagining this polite and lovely man having to suffer such treatment in his youth. I considered his solemn face. There was calm in his expression, remote though it was.

'I never stood up for myself or tried to protect my head. But I often cried when I walked home from school; never so anyone else saw, and my parents knew nothing about it. They had no idea how bad things were for me. They thought I was a cheerful schoolboy, a happy child.'

'That's awful,' I said. This information took me aback, and I couldn't picture this healthy and wholesome man in front of me contending with such difficulties.

'Yes, and I also wept in secret in my bedroom,' he continued. He turned thoughtful and inward-looking, as if he were going back in time and replaying those years for himself. 'But the worst part was that I had these terrible revenge fantasies.'

'Revenge?' I asked. I was so surprised by this unexpected confession that I just parroted back what he said. I couldn't think of anything else to say. He was always catching me off guard.

'Revenge, yes, and I'll tell you straight out: I still walk around with these fantasies in my head. There's so much anger and ill will and violence accumulated within me, violence that has never found an outlet. And revenge is still very much on my mind. That's the God's honest truth.'

'I find that hard to believe. It sounds awful. Should I be afraid of you?'

He laughed and gave my arm a friendly rub.

'No, it's never occurred to me to carry out all these acts of vengeance that I've schemed up; all the violence that goes on in my head, it stays there.' He fell silent once more and then added, after brief consideration: 'But there's one man in particular who I still think about. I'll never do anything to him, but I don't think I'd be especially polite if I ran into him. I despise him.' He delivered the last sentence angrily. Hissed like a snake.

I remembered how that conversation stuck with me. I couldn't forget the look on his face when he hissed like that. Now, I was recalling the conversation once again, though it had been a very long time since we'd had it.

The thought of revenge had kept me warm at night.

I've never considered myself to be vengeful, and yet I tried—and was still trying—to understand what had come over me when I made the decision to sail away and leave Gíó behind, helpless.

That wasn't revenge. Was it?

# 70

It was still raining, and the weather had grown colder. So I couldn't sit outside, even though what I wanted more than anything was to just sit and look out over the valley, listen for animals and try and spot sheep.

I needed something to read. Not having any reading material isn't something I'm accustomed to, but here in Jósep's sparse holiday cottage, there wasn't a single volume—not even an old newspaper to peruse. Everything was so stark, so soulless and shabby. There was nothing to gladden the eyes, nothing that existed solely to beautify or delight. Nothing but two hard chairs to sit in next to the coffee table, an ugly, uncomfortable easy chair, a bed on which to sleep and a stove on which to heat food.

I had to get out of there. I immediately thought of Jósep's dead dog, which you could go visit if you got bored. Why not? I'd go and see his grave.

I put on a wool sweater and a thick jacket. The sky was veiled in grey clouds. It was still raining.

I'd noticed a narrow footpath up the hillside behind the holiday cottage and concluded this must be the way to the canine burial site. Although the path was rarely used, it was still relatively distinct. Yellowed grass and long straw had been trodden into the soil, and every few steps there were bald patches of ground.

Jósep hadn't been lying when he said the path ended at the dog's grave, at the top of the hill. It literally did, as if no one could have any other reason to be up there except to visit a long-gone four-legged friend.

The animal's final resting place was a small, grassy mound. Above it stood a tidy, square headstone bearing the inscription:

JÓSEP JÓSEPSSON, DOG
1996–2008
Rest in Peace

So, the dog had been named Jósep, just like his owner. But could you really say he was the man's son? Son of Man. Jósepsson, son of Joseph, like the Christ child himself, if such a comparison could be permitted. Not Fidosson. The relationship between man and beast must have been a special one. Close.

Fresh white flowers lay on top of the mound. Someone had visited, either earlier that morning or the day before. They were the same kind of flowers as the one that had been left on my doorstep.

Why had Jósep left a flower at my door? That is, if it was even Jósep Dogspapa who'd left flowers on the grave of his dog, his son. But who else would have brought flowers to a dog's grave?

Had Jósep left a white flower on my doorstep to cheer me up? He wouldn't have meant to scare me half to death.

The dog's grave was high on the hillside, and from there I could see across the whole valley, down to the house and all the way out to the road. Tall mountains towered in the distance. There was no sign of life. No house or anything that bore any indication of human habitation. I needed to buck up and get back to the city. There was nothing for me at this grave and maybe nothing for me at the holiday cottage, either. Waiting any longer would just be a waste of time.

Was I so quick to abandon the idea that Gíó was coming here? No, I couldn't let myself do that. I'd wait until tomorrow, which meant enduring another day and night. Disbelief is darkness, faith is light, as I'd heard a priest say once.

I picked my way back down the path and towards the house. The valley must look beautiful from up here when the sun is shining, but now, beneath these heavy, grey clouds, there was little to please the eye. I stopped every so often on my way down to look over the countryside and get my bearings.

The dirt road that ran past the house was little-travelled and I doubted there were any other holiday cottages in the valley. Or at the very least, they weren't visible.

I was all alone in the world.

And the clouds were getting darker.

# 71

I decided to make some coffee and wait until after lunch to hike up to the heath. Not so much happened here in the back of beyond. I'd have to resign myself to my own company.

I turned on the radio to listen to some music, but the reception was poor. The station crackled and hissed, and I soon found the interference unbearable. I switched it off. In the sink was the dirty blue plastic cup.

After I poured myself some coffee, I took my mug outside and sat on a bench there. The sun had risen over the peak of the mountain to the east and, when its rays managed to break through the thick cloud bank, it shone right on me.

I sat contentedly with my back against the wall, letting the sun warm me.

I'd not been sitting there for very long when I heard an indistinct noise, like metal being scraped along metal. For a moment, I thought a spanner had been thrown into the watchworks of heaven. I looked up.

The sun was still in its place, though, as were the sky and the clouds.

I closed my eyes and focused on the unexpected sound breaking the country stillness.

The racket seemed to be coming from down the road, so I stood and went to the corner of the holiday cottage, trying to see if I could make out anyone on the road below.

A few moments later, I saw a young cyclist labouring up the

hill and slowly making his way along the rocky road in my direction. He looked exhausted. His face was red from exertion and his expression was one of pure fatigue as he pedalled the last few metres towards the holiday cottage.

His bike was old and yellow, and everything on it seemed to be lopsided and hanging by a thread: the front mudguard, the back mudguard, the handlebars, the carrier, the saddle. Every scrape and screech it made sliced through the silence like a knife.

The young man had long hair and was shockingly ill-dressed for a cycling trip this far out in the country at this time of year. He was wearing red tennis shoes, white trousers and a white T-shirt.

I put my mug of coffee on the bench, walked down the steps and out onto the gravel road, facing the man. To my astonishment, he didn't slow down as he approached me, rather biked right past. I was so surprised that I could think of nothing to say. He'd ridden about five metres past me when he braked hard, the back wheel skidding across the dirt road and spitting pebbles in all directions. Then he turned around and cycled back towards me at full speed. I watched, agape, as he rode two circles around me without so much as a word.

I said nothing, just looked at the man.

Finally, he put an end to the odd display and stopped the bike, though he didn't dismount.

On the front of the man's shirt was an inscription in thick, black lettering:

STRAIGHT
FROM
HELL

—

# I AM ONLY TWO HANDSHAKES FROM SATAN

'*Góðan daginn,*' he said after a beat, and there was a breathlessness in his voice.

I could hear that he was foreign.

'Hello,' I said, indicating with my tone that I expected an explanation for his business here.

'I've come all the way from Italy,' he said without preamble.

'Indeed… On a bike?'

He laughed. I didn't know what was so funny.

'No, I didn't cycle all the way from Italy.'

'Of course not. What could I be thinking? You've come straight from hell.'

He looked down at his shirt and laughed again.

'Well, now I'm here with you. Here we are, in the blissful countryside.' He smiled obsequiously. His lips were thin and his mouth lopsided. There was something malicious in his expression. 'Ha ha,' he then added, no doubt to indicate that he was joking.

Then he looked around—up the hillside, over the valley. He considered the holiday cottage, gave himself a good, long time to get the lay of the land. While he did, he acted as though I wasn't standing right there, and I was nettled by this lack of courtesy. But just as I was about to ask what he wanted he blurted out: 'Do you live here by yourself?'

It was as if he didn't care about the answer, though, because he turned his attention to dismounting, pushing the bike aside so carelessly that it clattered to the ground at my feet.

On this evidence, I wasn't at all surprised that it was so dilapidated. That was no way to treat a bike.

'D'ya have some coffee or something... Could you give me a drink?'

There was an aggressiveness in his tone, an insolence in his voice, and yet he was still smiling that repellent, lopsided smile. His pencil-thin lips were blue, as if they were entirely bloodless.

'No,' I said. I couldn't take my eyes off that unsightly mouth of his.

He gaped in surprise at the unexpected refusal. And he didn't try to hide his gaping, either. It was like he was an actor in a highly melodramatic play and was now miming shock and stupefaction with his whole body. He stood there for a long time with his mouth open, letting his head fall forward as he widened his eyes.

'No?!' he nearly yelled, jutting his chin out. 'No?!' he repeated. He'd arranged his feet in a grotesque position, as though he was suffering from some nerve disorder. He was practically doubled over.

I looked down and gazed at the sad wreck of a bike at my feet because I couldn't bring myself to watch the bizarre histrionics of its rider. I bent down, picked up the bike, held it a moment, and then pushed it towards him, so he'd take it. But he just watched me without moving, still holding the same weird pose, as though the bike had nothing to do with him.

'No?...' he said once again. 'Do you know how long I've been riding?'

I didn't answer, just pushed the bike closer to him.

'Do you?' He leant back, practically yelling.

'No. I don't know how far it is to hell, but what I do know is that this place is in the entirely opposite direction,' I said, looking at him blankly.

'I have been cycling for hours without anything to drink. And you can't give me a glass of water?'

'No,' I answered coldly.

'Is there no running water in the house?'

'There may well be. But I don't want to give any of my water to you.'

'Don't want to give me water? You're so stingy you won't give a thirsty man one measly glass of water?'

'No. I will not.'

'No?' he barked. There was a vicious glint in his eyes.

I didn't let that get to me.

We stood and stared each other down in silence. I wasn't afraid of this snotty foreigner. I didn't care for him. I didn't care for the slogans on his T-shirt. He was a loathsome man with an ugly mouth and an ugly mug. He could die of thirst for all I cared. He could die at my feet. Waste away. I couldn't care less about the life or death of this man. He could desiccate and shrivel. Wither like the white flower on the coffee table. But he would not slake his thirst at my door.

He cast around for words that he knew might convince me to give him something to drink. Or maybe he was just looking for a better explanation of my strange obstinacy.

'I... have... ridden... very... far...' He hurled out the words, one after the other. And then he added: 'I mean, *really* far. And I'm really thirsty.'

'Sorry. Go somewhere else.'

Something snapped in him, and he leapt towards me. I thought he was going to attack me, but instead, he grabbed the handlebars of the bike. He wrenched it towards him and gave me a hard shove, so I toppled backwards. He gave me a look of utter contempt before getting on his bike and riding off. He'd only gone a short distance when he stopped, jumped off the bike, and shouted: '*Norn!* Witch! You're a witch! *Fokk* you, you *fokking* witch hag! I'm gonna come back and *fokking* kill you!'

Now, I've already explained how much I dislike this *fokk* coinage, so I won't get into that again. But suffice to say the young cyclist didn't grow any in my estimation.

He was flustered when he got back on his bike, and his feet kept slipping off the pedals. He swore. It was like he couldn't control his movements. He was furious as he zigzagged down the road without looking back. I heard the screeching metal fading in the distance.

I couldn't figure out what he'd been doing here. Why was he all the way out here? He didn't come this far to ask for a glass of water. I wanted to go back into the holiday cottage, but instead, I decided to keep watch and wait.

# 72

My vigil on the bench outside Jósep's holiday cottage came to nothing. I sat with my back against the wall, wearing all the warm clothes I'd brought with me. I was cold, but I made myself endure it and stayed outside until I started to shake. Then I went back inside, locked the door behind me, and paced around the holiday cottage without knowing what to do next. I flung myself into the red easy chair.

I got out my notebook and recorded the episode with the young cyclist. Nothing he'd said was particularly nice, so at the top of the page I wrote: Ugly Dialogue with an Ugly-Mouthed Man.

I closed my notebook and stared vacantly into the air, resisting the urge to pay another visit to the bygone canine, in spite of the aged owner's insistence that it was the best way to lift one's spirits when staying at the holiday cottage.

It seemed clear that Gíó was not going to appear in search of shelter or a place to hide.

Rather than going back out into the cold, I continued my vacant staring and dozed a little. My phone was stone dead; I'd no connection with the outside world. No one could call me, and I couldn't call anyone. Maybe someone was trying to call and console me.

But I was inconsolable.

It was late afternoon when I woke up to the sound of someone knocking at the door. It was a polite knock, as though the person wanted to apologize for bothering me.

The first thing that occurred to me was that the cyclist from hell was back. I sat still and waited. I had no intention of opening the door for that dreadful man.

Again came the knock. Now harder and more impatient.

I hesitated for a few moments, considering my options. Who could it be?

I got up, walked to the door, and called: 'Who's there?'

'Open up. It's me,' said a fractious voice on the other side of the door.

# 73

I recognized the voice immediately. I knew that impatient tone. It ran in the family. That uncompromising voice that never did anything to make itself amiable, friendly or affectionate.

I opened the door to see my sister standing on the front step. Irritation was etched across her face.

'What… What are you doing here?' I asked.

'Checking on you. Since you can't be bothered to answer your goddamn phone. You're driving me crazy, worrying about you. This is totally irrational behaviour.'

'There's no service here. Come in… How did you know I was here?'

She walked in and glanced around. 'I got in touch with that pot-bellied policeman. He told me you were here.'

'How'd he know that?'

'I don't know… I didn't ask him.'

'How'd you find the place? Have you been here before?'

'Have I been here before? No.' She shook her head and frowned, like my question was absurd.

'No?'

'Why in the hell would you think I've been all the way out here, in the arse crack of nowhere, before now? What possible reason could I have had for coming out here? Of course I haven't been here before. And since we're asking, why the hell are *you* here?'

She seemed sincere in her denial, sincere in her annoyance with her big sister and my choice of refuge.

'Are you all right?' she said after a short silence, now with just a hint more concern in her voice.

'I'm waiting for Gíó. Maybe the detective told you, but he was supposed to be coming here.'

'What do you mean "supposed to be coming here"?' She cast around a dismayed look. 'Who owns this place?'

'I'll start by telling you—if you honestly don't know already—that this is where Gíó sometimes comes to stage his sexual fantasies. He meets his girlfriends here and they play all sorts of amusing games: Mummy games, "Little Red Riding Hood and the Big Bad Wolf" games… Has he never invited you here to play?'

'Júlía… You're not well. Please, come back to the city with me. You can't be out here all alone. There's absolutely no reason for you to be here while half of Iceland is out searching for that man of yours. You can't just hide here. It won't do. Now, c'mon. Let's go.'

'I'm going home. I've had it up to here with this place. You can relax, I haven't lost my mind. I'm perfectly well. I just need to tidy up, and then I'll head back to the city.'

'Would you like me to help and then follow you back?'

I looked at my sister in surprise. I wasn't accustomed to such generosity from her.

'No, you go on ahead. I'm fine. I just had to prove to myself that Gíó wasn't here. I wanted to be here if he turned up, but he's not coming. I'm going to go home.'

María let herself be cajoled. Her hug goodbye was both longer and more warm-hearted than I've ever known her to be.

# 74

My sister wasn't so far from the truth when she said I was sick. I wasn't so far gone that you could say I was having a breakdown, but I was aware that it wouldn't be good for my sanity if I continued to passively sit out here in the back of beyond, allowing myself to be hypnotized by my circumstances.

But in spite of everything, I was having trouble tearing myself away from the place, as though I was afraid of missing Gió, lest he appear all of a sudden.

Instead of getting started on the cottage clean-up and setting off for civilization, I stood up and put on my shoes. A hike up the mountain would be a balm for my soul. The weather was, perhaps, not particularly suited for a long hike. The rain was still coming down and it was cold out. Grey, leaden clouds were concealing the mountain peaks and unfurling down the slopes.

It wasn't walking weather but what was I supposed to do? I cursed myself yet again for not having brought anything to read. I was too restless to stay in this dreary abode with nothing to do. I wasn't doing anything useful. Search and rescue teams were combing the better part of south-west Iceland, and yet here I was, loafing around and pretending to be helpful. I couldn't wait around doing nothing any longer. There was nothing for it but to go outside and get my blood pumping.

I hadn't brought much of a selection of outdoor gear, so I put on two sweaters under my jacket before trudging out. Of course, I took the trail up to the dog's grave. The white flowers were still on top of it, a little scraggly by now but still gracing the plot nonetheless. It was a pretty place to bury your dog.

I thought about sitting down by the grave and enjoying the opportunity to be alone in nature, but I decided to continue my walk instead and go further up the slope. It was a windless day, though a fine, dense rain was falling from the sky.

I soon found a trail that ran along the mossy banks of a creek, and I followed it. But little by little, the going got harder. My feet were soon wet, no matter how I tried to avoid marshy ground. The trail was spongy and waterlogged every inch of the way. My feet sunk deep into wet earth with each step I took, and I had a hard time yanking them up out of the mire. All the while the rain was falling harder.

The wisest thing would probably have been to turn around, but I wasn't ready to give up and decided to go a little further. It couldn't hurt to tire myself out before this evening so I'd be more likely to sleep.

I plodded through the muck and struggled uphill. Clambered through a birch thicket where the ground was denser and drier, and hoped that I'd reached more solid ground. I spotted a raven perched on a boulder no more than a few metres away from me. The bird's jet-black body was glossy, and its feathers gave off a blueish tinge, as if it were slicked in oil. My corvine friend didn't look particularly inclined to fly away, just calmly held me in the gaze of one of its eyes, giving me a careful once-over without moving at all. There we stood, facing one another for a long moment, standing absolutely still and gazing into each other's eyes—he with one eye and I with both. Then he had enough of our staring competition, spread his wings, and lifted himself into the air without saying goodbye. The raven was quickly swallowed by the fog, which was biting cold and thick as cream. From a distance, I heard a caw so ear-splitting it could have been the bark of a dog.

I could see that it would be madness to wade further into the creamy cloud rolling towards me. I turned around. I was forced to scurry down the slope, fleeing ahead of the wall of fog. But it was hard going, the earth was spongy, and I stumbled when I stubbed my toe on a stone that I hadn't noticed in my path because I could no longer see my hand in front of my face. I wasn't even sure I was going the right way.

I edged along for ages, step by step in the wilderness. The dense wall of fog encircled me, swallowed me completely, and when I looked around, I couldn't see anything but its white, tightly woven curtain.

Onwards I inched, half-blind. I squinted, peered down in front of me to try and see if I was still on a path and in the hopes of avoiding the deepest quagmires.

I lost all sense of direction; I felt my way forward as slowly as I could. The only thing I had to guide me was the slope itself and I knew I had to struggle my way down and out of the cloudbank. I had no way of knowing where I was or what path I was on. Whether I was walking further into eternity, off a cliff, or whether I was at risk of falling into a crevice or chasm. Maybe the earth would swallow me. I felt overcome by despair and could hardly bear to take another step. Should I just stop where I was, sit down and wait for the fog to clear?

No, I was already frozen through, soaking wet and poorly dressed for the elements. The fog was ice-cold, and I felt like I was standing in a white-painted, walk-in freezer, encircled by frosty air. If I sat down, I'd die of exposure. I'd freeze solid as soon as the night-time chill really started to bite.

Maybe it wouldn't be so bad to die.

Maybe I should lie down and let eternity take me. In that moment, standing on a mountainside in a remote corner of the country, completely lost and surrounded by a thick wall of fog, I found myself recalling a story I'd heard about an old man lying on his deathbed and waiting to take his last breath.

The man's family had gathered around his bed where he was lying with his eyes closed, the last drops of life seeping out of his body. Some of his loved ones were crying and the atmosphere was thick with sadness, loss and melancholy. Suddenly, the old man sat up, fixed his mild old eyes on his nearest and dearest and said hoarsely: 'Don't cry. Don't be sad or downhearted. To be honest, dying is quite the unique experience.' And then he laid his head back on the pillow and died.

The old gentleman's blandishments notwithstanding, however, I wasn't ready to die. No, I did not want to die, in spite of everything. I was not going to lie down on the ground and rest my head on a pillow of moss and wait for death to get its claws into me. I was going to make it out of this ordeal in one piece. I steeled my mind, continued to inch my way forward and resumed making my way downhill.

It was like being completely sightless. I squinted into the fog and waved around my hands like a blind person. There was a kind of uneasiness in the air, and I perceived an indistinct movement in the fog.

I felt like I wasn't alone on the heath any more, but I couldn't see anything. Everything was grey, no matter where I looked. I couldn't see more than one step to either side. It was soon going to be even darker and colder, I realized. Then I'd be done for. I couldn't just wander aimlessly staring out into the middle distance.

But what was I to do? I had to keep going and make it down this mountain. And I could clearly feel a presence near me.

I decided to shout.

'Hello? Is someone there?'

I stopped and waited for a response.

'Hello! Is someone there?' I repeated. No answer.

'Gíó! Is that you? I'm here. It's me, Júlía.'

I took one step forward and then another. Ever so cautiously and slowly. I paused again, and this time, I heard something. A rustling. Footsteps. Heavy breathing.

I stood absolutely still until I felt anxiety overtaking me and shouted once more: 'Is someone… there?'

'Gíó?'

I closed my eyes and listened. I knew that your hearing sharpened when your eyes were closed. And even though I couldn't see anything, I could still make out a disturbance in the air. Someone was clearly moving around. I waited for someone to answer my call. No response, no crow's caw, no tittering birds, not even the howling of the wind. But someone was moving as silently as a bat through the night.

The moment passed and then another and then I heard it again, that rustling sound. Someone was walking on the heath. I was no longer alone in this wilderness. There was no doubt about it. The susurration was getting clearer all the time. Though I might be wrapped in a fog blanket that seemed to be dampening all sounds, I was sure I could hear something and someone moving ahead of me.

I looked down at my feet and saw that my shoes had sunk into the sopping ground.

I was stuck fast in a muddy sinkhole.

And I'd completely lost my way, too. Hadn't I? I had, at any rate, no idea what direction I'd come from or in which one I was headed. I couldn't tell you where north or south was. Cardinal directions no longer existed—just up and down. I psyched myself up, yanked my feet out of the muck and crept forward a few more steps until I stopped in my tracks. Again, I heard this peculiar echo, as if someone with a deep voice was calling out from a distance. At the same time, I realized that the movement in front of me was slowing.

A black mass appeared, like a shadow gliding ever so slowly towards me. I only barely managed to stifle a cry on my lips. I stood like a statue, thought about throwing myself to the ground and crawling away, slinking silently like a snake through the stillness, but I couldn't budge.

Everyone was in hiding on that hazy heath. There was absolute silence—no sound but for the pounding of my heart.

The creature came up close and bumped heavily into me. There was a familiar smell. It took me a moment to realize it was the smell of a horse, after which I figured out that I'd wandered into a paddock that, for some reason, was teetering on the edge of a mountain.

Wild horses?

Were these animals dangerous?

Did wild horses bite?

Were their hearts driven by viciousness?

I took a step towards the mass and was able to make out a few horses clustered together. I could feel the warmth of the animals cutting through the cold, foggy air; I had so much of their horsey scent in my nostrils that I felt like I recognized their breathing, heavy and unhurried.

I reached out towards the horse that was standing nearest to me, stroked its flank and gently petted its mane. I rested my cheek against the animal's neck and felt its heartbeat. The fog was so thick that all I could see was the outline of the horses that were keeping their distance. They huddled together as though keeping an eye on one another in the dim fog. They hardly moved. Just stood there, waiting for the fog to lift.

That was the reality.

Horses are just horses.

And a pasture is just a pasture.

I spoke gently to the horses, commended them for looking after their friends, praised their beauty and courage. I gave them pats and caresses. They were gentle animals, mild. There was no vengeance or anger in their hearts. What drove the hearts of horses? What drove my own?

Before I took my leave, I gave one of them the caramel I'd put in my trouser pocket and then continued on my way down the mountainside as fast as I dared to go.

# 75

Gradually, the dirt path became firmer and I was distinctly relieved not to have encountered a ghost, troll or—worst of all—a person up on the heath. After I'd been walking down the mountainside for a while, the fog began to dissipate and I could finally see the trail ahead of me.

I looked at my watch and figured out that I'd been on that hopeless hike for over three hours. I walked slowly along the gravel road, exhausted. The going was easier now, even though it was getting dark, and I had the road entirely to myself. I felt an unexpected relief, verging on delight, walking along the road, unconfronted by anyone. No cars driving, no horses or livestock that I could see, though I did occasionally come across sheep tracks on the trail.

When the holiday cottage finally appeared, looming on a hill among the mountains, I felt a rush of joy, as though I'd finally escaped an imminent threat to my life. I trudged through the open gate, weary and muddy up to my knees. Big mud puddles had formed on the potholed drive leading up to the holiday cottage. I could see my woeful old rust bucket, parked at the edge of the drive right by the gate. The vehicle bore visible signs of its advanced years and the fact that its days were numbered—its carcass was crooked and sunk, its paintwork matte and rusty on the doors and bumpers. It was a car you'd easily recognize. If Gíó were to arrive on foot, my car would be the first thing he'd see on his way down the drive. He'd know it right away and it's possible he'd turn around and go somewhere else. What, did I think he was going to just park his car next to mine, get out and knock on the front door?

No.

Maybe?

What would he do if he were on the way to the holiday cottage and saw my car outside?

Would he consider anything beyond just going back the way he came?

If he was still alive, it was obvious he wasn't going to come to me smiling and happy. 'Hi, honey, good to see you again. I don't know if you realize, but you forgot me out on that little islet of yours. Maybe you didn't notice that you left me behind? But hey, no harm, no foul. I just swam back to shore, no biggie. And now, I've thankfully found you once again, my love.'

I shook my head at my foolishness. There was no question that it would have been better to hide the car somewhere and thereby lure him all the way to the holiday cottage door. I just don't think sometimes. How incredibly dumb of me to park it right at the gate. Not smart if I wanted to take Gíó by surprise—it was ill-conceived and careless.

I stood next to the car, deep in thought, until I shook myself out of my reverie. Out of the corner of my eye, I noticed that something had been written in the dust on the car, which hadn't been washed in years. The trip out here had been along dusty dirt roads, which hadn't helped, either. The paint was crusted over with a thick layer of grime.

Though it had started to get dark, I could easily make out what had been written across the driver's-side door in capital letters.

REFSIGLEÐI

GLEÐIN VIÐ AÐ REFSA

I was taken aback. Someone had come all the way out here to scribble on my car. As rattled and astonished as I was, however, I couldn't but wonder at the choice of words. *Refsigleði*. Vengefulness. But more literally: Punishment-joy. Or as the person had taken pains to write out: *The joy of punishing*. It was an unusual word, formal—ceremonial, even. I didn't think I myself had ever used it. How odd to write such a long and uncommon word in the dust on my car. Truth be told, it didn't occur to me that Gíó was behind the message, although that was maybe the most obvious explanation. But this kind of thing wasn't like him at all. On top of which, I thought it very unlikely that he'd choose that peculiar word. *Refsigleði*. Or maybe he would? Did I know him well enough to know what he might do in these unusual circumstances? What other business did he have here? If it wasn't Gíó, who would have come all the way out here—far, far away from the nearest village or town, way out here where no one came by chance—just to write threats on my car?

My sister María had, of course, been here, but I could rule her out. She'd never think to use her fine finger to scrawl on a grimy car. She wasn't so brutish as to be jotting missives in road dirt. If she wanted to send me a message, she'd do so in a more refined manner.

My mind turned to the young vulgarian on the bicycle whom I'd refused a glass of water. The thirsty foreigner. Foreigners are sometimes more likely to use words that no one else does. *Refsigleði* could be a word that he'd stumbled upon in a dictionary. Was the man trying to say that he intended to punish me for not giving him anything to drink?

I glanced around to see if anyone was waiting for me by the house. Everything was calm in the twilight; besides the writing, there were no other signs of life. I looked down but didn't see any new tracks from a bike or tyre tracks from another car. But the best thing would probably be to take cover and sneak up to the house, just to make sure that no one was waiting at the door with thoughts of revenge or punishment. Although the message was unsettling, I wasn't filled with the same overwhelming fear as before. I was uncomfortable, but not terrified like I'd been the other night.

Maybe I'd had my fill of scares for the day. Maybe I'd depleted all the fear-producing chemicals in my brain.

The thought of that unmitigated moron on a bike returning had, perhaps, put me in a foolhardy state of mind. Or at least, I couldn't properly work myself up to being afraid of him. But I did walk silently up along the side of the holiday cottage and creep with my back to the wall into a nook beside the front steps. Standing there at the corner of the house, I decided to wait, to be patient and see what would happen. Maybe he'd come walking around the corner and down the steps if he got tired of waiting for me.

Although I waited a long time, I didn't pick up on anything to suggest that anyone other than me was here at this holiday cottage in the middle of nowhere. But nevertheless, I waited patiently and stayed put a good, long while.

While I was huddled alongside the house, I found myself wondering if anything had been written on the other side of the car. Had the man only written on one side? I hunched over and sneaked back to the passenger side of the car.

Another long word had been scrawled on the passenger door. It wasn't as easy to read in the dim evening light so I decided to use the torch on my phone.

HEFNDARÞORSTI

ÞORSTI Í HEFND

Vindictiveness, or literally: vengeance-thirst. Or, as the author clarified yet again: *a thirst for vengeance*. Not precisely the thirst that had plagued the cyclist earlier. Maybe he'd slaked his thirst for water while simultaneously thirsting for revenge. Would he slake this new thirst for vengeance here?

The message on the passenger side disturbed me more than the one on the driver's side. There's so much violence in the word vengeance. Revenge. I felt my heart pounding in my chest and my body screamed for me to flee. I shouldn't stay here any longer.

I couldn't imagine where that arrogant foreigner, that lunatic cyclist, could be holed up. He'd cycled all the way out here; if he'd come back, it could hardly just be to scrawl threats in the dirt on my car. Had he brought friends back with him? We hadn't parted amicably, he had a mind to avenge himself for my effrontery and he wasn't likely to go easy on me should he get anyone else to help him. He would slake his thirst for vengeance.

Which brought me to the conclusion that I had no choice but to gather my things and leave. I could forget about Gíó. He was hardly going to appear at this point, but if the threats on the car were not just empty words, I could assume that the Italian cyclist wasn't far away and might even be lying in wait for me.

After brief consideration, I got the bright idea not to take the steps from the parking spot and approach the house head-on, but rather go around the holiday cottage and come at it from an unexpected direction. That way, I'd be able to see if anyone was waiting for me. If everything looked safe and sound, I could creep to the front door from the opposite direction and throw my stuff together quick as a wink.

As I'd anticipated, the path behind the house was easily passable because Jósep obviously made use of the back door and the shaded side of the house, using it as a storage area for all manner of old stuff. There were old flowerpots, most of which were broken, an old concrete mixer, shovels, sacks of potting soil, scrap wood and much more besides. I scrambled through the junk heaps as quietly as I could.

I looked up and out over the valley, saw the silhouette of the mountains in the distance and all the vast emptiness unfurling itself into eternity. Heavy clouds still hung in the sky. Darkness had settled over the valley, and I was a long way from help. What had gone on in my head, that I'd thought I'd have the slightest chance of saving myself from the clutches of a punishment-happy, revenge-thirsty man if he'd been waiting for me in the shadows? I was alone. How stupid it had been to try and make it unseen past the man—or men—and into the holiday cottage by sneaking up from another direction.

Gíó had often told me that I overestimated my own strength, that I miscalculated situations, and here I'd done just that. I was standing wet and bedraggled in the middle of a rubbish tip, all by myself out in the back of beyond, and darkness was falling.

All I wanted to do was to turn around and drive away in my car without taking any of my things with me.

I clambered back the same way I'd come. I managed to slip silently between all the rubbish, or almost, until I ran into a tin bucket that flipped over and rolled off an old garden table and onto the ground with a huge crash. I froze in my tracks and waited for what would come next.

# 76

I closed my eyes and pricked up my ears. Although I could only make out faint sounds, I felt like something was lurking in the shadows and watching me pick my way through the rubbish. It was difficult to stand still and wait for the other shoe to drop, and so I leapt into action and paid no mind to anything in my path, though it meant overturning all sorts of things and making a fantastic amount of noise.

When I reached the corner of the house, I caught sight of someone going down the long flight of steps to the parking area. I broke into a sprint, ran as fast as I could to the car and grabbed the door handle. But as was so often the case, the door stuck and wouldn't open.

Then, cutting through all the racket with the car door, I heard someone calling out to me in a hoarse voice: '*Halló! Halló!*'

In a state of pure desperation, I used all my strength to pull on the door, used my whole body to pump and jiggle the handle until I finally managed to yank it open. I was about to leap into the car when I heard the same voice call out: '*Halló!* Frú von Dunk! Miss Laura von Dunk! Is that you?'

I stopped mid-leap because I realized that no one in this world called me Laura von Dunk except for Jósep Jósepsson, holiday cottage owner. And who else was going to call me *Frú*? Such an old-fashioned form of address: Frú von Dunk. Little Miss Muffet.

When I looked up, I saw the stooped old man making his way slowly and cautiously down the steps. He had a black flat cap on his head and was wearing a black trench coat. So instead of jumping in my car and driving away, I turned and walked slowly towards the old man.

'I was scared when I saw someone lurking around the house. I was literally about to run away,' I jabbered, realizing how tense I was.

'I was visiting my dog. He's dead and is buried up on the hillside.'

'You've told me that.'

'Yes, I did tell you that.'

'Listen,' I said, pointing to the car door. 'Someone's been here and wrote on my car. They're rather menacing messages when you're so far away from anyone else. They scared me.'

Jósep looked at the door. He laughed. His laughter sounded like someone banging on an empty barrel. Hollow and dry. He gave no other response. Maybe he couldn't read it in the dim light.

'Did you see anyone here when you came?' I asked, talking just as quickly as before.

'No.'

'How'd you get here?'

'I drove.'

'But then where's your car?'

'My car is where I parked it, out on the road. I walked the last stretch.'

'Oh? Why did you park out on the road?'

'That's what I always do. But I was delayed by the fog. I'm later getting back than usual.'

'Well, I'm actually about to leave. I should take the opportunity to return the key to you, since you're here. Could you wait a moment while I gather my things?'

'Yes.'

I thought about how I might find out if Gíó had come to pick up the key for the holiday cottage. I couldn't just ask him straight out.

'Thank you for not telling my husband that I was here when he came to pick up the key. I was able to surprise him,' I said innocently.

'He never came to pick up the key. No one ever showed up.'

# 77

I gathered my things in a rush and tidied up the holiday cottage, Gíó's alleged sex palace. Then I handed the key over to Jósep, said goodbye, and drove away from that deserted valley and its horses on the heath. Headed back to civilization.

The journey back to the city went smoothly. It was a strange drive. My stay at the holiday cottage hadn't been particularly pleasant, well considered, or sufficiently prepared for. I was grasping at thin air, not knowing what I was doing.

After I'd been driving for a while, I saw that my phone had revived. I was in signal range of the universe. Texts started to pop up on the screen. I pulled over and watched them pour in, but I didn't open any because I had no desire to talk to anyone.

A lot of people had tried to call me. I scrolled through the numbers but didn't call them back. Most of the calls had been from people who considered themselves my friends, but I also noticed that I'd missed calls from María and Detective Haraldur. He seemed to have something he needed to talk to me about because he'd called a number of times. I didn't have the courage or the desire to talk with him at that moment. I was afraid to hear what he had to say. I felt sure that he was in the process of cornering me with all his vague suspicions and uncomfortable questions.

I knew that sooner or later I'd have to talk to him, but decided to put off that phone call until I got back to the city, provided it wasn't too late. I felt sure he didn't have any good news for me. So I'd probably just wait until the next day to call.

Barrelling down country roads in the darkness, I suddenly found myself singing one of the old hymns my father would sometimes hum. 'May thy mercy come softly unto me,' I crooned.

I was off-key, my voice cracked and I rarely hit a clear note, but I sang with my whole heart. I was both the singer and the sole listener of this plaintive but earnest song, and both singer and listener appeared to be deeply touched by the performance because tears were coursing down both their cheeks.

When I turned onto my street in Reykjavík where everything was so familiar and serene, I stopped singing and dried my cheeks. It seemed like most people had turned in for the night because most of the windows in the houses along the street were dark. Here and there, however, the flickering glow of TV screens could be seen from the street, so a few people must still be awake.

When I parked the car in front of my house, I looked across the street and into the windows of the apartment where, according to my old neighbour woman, a new tenant had taken up residence. The interior was still illuminated by the same blueish glow that seemed to be coming from a room deep within the apartment.

No other lights were on.

I wondered anew what was going on in there—again, my thoughts turned to mortuaries and greenhouses—and whether there was actually a grain of truth in what Finna had told me. I had trouble brushing aside the absurd thought that had been germinating in my mind in recent days—namely that it was Gíó who'd moved in there.

# 78

Maybe I was feeling emboldened by the night or maybe it was just the fog of exhaustion after a long journey, I don't know, but when I got back home, I made the audacious and headlong decision to march across the street, stride up the steps of my neighbour's house and ring the doorbell.

I had to free my mind of the stupid, nagging suspicion that Gió had camped out there, that he was observing my comings and goings from the shadows.

There was no name on the doorbell.

I heard the deep, dignified, drawn-out peal of the bell echoing inside the apartment.

Squaring myself in front of the door, I noticed it was slightly ajar. From my vantage point, I could see shoes in the boot room. My mind was strangely calm, placid as a mirror-smooth lake. Perhaps the hymn had done me some good. I could also see a rusty lamp hanging down in the darkness. The front door had three long narrow panes of glass in it, all of which had been laminated with plastic film so you couldn't see through them.

I saw myself reflected in the matte glass. The face that appeared to me in the half-light was a sorry sight. The shadows cast by the overhead light emphasized the bags under my eyes, my sunken cheeks. My eyes were glazed, looked like crumbling ruins in a skull.

It was a shocking sight, and I quickly closed my eyes. But although my reflection indicated otherwise, I felt entirely calm.

As so often before, I had no idea what was driving my actions. I hadn't prepared what I'd say if someone opened the door.

So I just stood there. What exactly *was* I doing? Did I mean to find out if this new neighbour of mine had a body hidden away in his apartment, or was I just going to ask what kind of herbs he was cultivating under that blue light? I was interested in flowers, myself.

But no, what compelled me, first and foremost, was my need to exclude the possibility that the man renting the apartment was Gíó.

After waiting for a few minutes, I grew restless and rang the bell again. Once again, I heard the deep, dignified and drawn-out peal.

I looked back at the street. There was no one around, just the night, some houses and a few flickering street lights.

I gave the door a little push to see if maybe I'd hear any rustling inside to indicate someone was home. I listened for a long time, stuck my head a tiny bit through the crack. No sign of life.

I hesitated before pushing the door hard, so it swung all the way open. I stepped inside.

The first thing I noticed was the oppressive silence and the next was the strange smell, pungent and rotten. There were umpteen outdoor shoes in a messy heap in the boot room, and it occurred to me that they might be the source of the horrible stench. If you could draw any conclusions from the number of shoes, it seemed like a large number of men were living together under the same roof. But no children. And none of the shoes seemed to have been designed for a woman's feet.

A men's choir? A men's jail? Impoverished migrant workers?

All this ran through my mind, but I didn't stop in the entrance, rather continued silently into the apartment where I found a large living room. No furniture. The living room was completely bare—no table, no chairs, nothing decorating any of the walls.

I considered whether I should call out to see if anyone was at home, but the air was saturated with some kind of horror, a dread that was magnified by the fact that the mysterious blue glow was the only source of light. I hardly dared make a sound.

I tried to remember the name of the man who'd accosted me on my doorstep. 'Jed?' I called in a muted voice.

I listened for a moment and called out again: 'Gíó?'

To the right, there was a half-open door into the room with the blue light that you could see from the street.

I tiptoed towards the door. The stench was so awful that my vision blurred. I covered my nose and stuck my head into the room.

I saw a giant fish tank, as tall as a man, half full of something I couldn't totally make out in the strange light. A viscous, greenish or blueish substance that seemed almost alive, writhing. There were little oily puddles on top of the sludge. A tube-shaped metal lamp hung over the wriggling heap in the tank, bathed the room in blue light. The reek was vile, suffocating. I couldn't bear to be in there any longer. I hurried through the room and out into the hall.

To the right was another door, this time to a small bedroom.

There was a narrow mattress on the floor and, on top of it, a heap of clothes. Someone had slept here.

Next to the mattress on the floor was a single pair of black socks, a black T-shirt, and an open book. The cover was black and grey. *Night Work.*

I walked out of the bedroom and found a door to another room. There was no furniture in this one either, but there was a pair of binoculars on the windowsill. I slipped into the room without a sound. I looked out the window and there was my apartment.

I walked over and picked up the binoculars. These weren't the kind of gadget you used for stargazing, you didn't use them to scan the heavens in search of Pluto or Saturn. But you could use them to look straight into my living room window. There it was, the fat little ceramic angel on my windowsill, though I myself was not at home.

I cried out. An involuntary yelp escaped my lips, shrill and solitary. I turned away from the window. Did someone use these to watch my home? I had to get out of here before someone discovered me in this den of terror.

But where was the front door? I'd lost my bearings in this labyrinth and no longer knew which way to go, which way was the quickest way out. I spun in a circle and just then, as I was doing my solo dance in the middle of the room, I thought I heard something move. Had I roused someone with my strangled cry? Everything swam before my eyes until finally, I took off, ran to the nearest door and wrenched it open, was met by that wall of blue light. I was back in the terrible room with the fish tank. But at least from there, I could find my way out.

I was no longer convinced I was alone in the apartment; maybe someone had come through the front door or was lurking in a room I'd yet to find.

I ran into the boot room with all the shoes, yanked on the handle of the front door, and then the thing happened that always happens in every horror movie ever: I couldn't get it open. For some reason, it was stuck, it wouldn't open, no matter how I tugged or pushed. It was probably just locked, but in my frenzy, I didn't have the sense to turn the right knob, so I just beat on the door, pulled on it like a maniac, waiting with my heart in my mouth for the owner of the blue light to come and grab me.

Did he keep bodies in the fish tank? Those weren't flowers.

I don't know what handle I turned or what I yanked, but suddenly, the door flew open, and I shot out like a cork from a champagne bottle.

I didn't look behind me, just darted across the street like a terrified animal and didn't stop until I was back in the safety of my own home.

# 79

As soon as I'd run through the front door and slammed it behind me, my phone rang. I was convinced it was the new tenant who was now trying to get hold of me. I stood frozen in the vestibule and hardly dared move. The ringtone from my phone was shrill in the silence and it didn't stop ringing. I stood there for what felt like an eternity, my phone reverberating as though it would never stop ringing.

Finally, though, it did, and I breathed a sigh of relief.

I had to gather my courage to take out my phone and see who called. Somehow, I was sure it couldn't be anyone but the new tenant, who was after me and trying to get me on the phone. It was a preposterous idea, of course.

I looked at the screen and saw that it was Haraldur who'd called once again.

What on earth did the man want? It was almost eleven at night. Was he always on his phone? I stared at the screen and tried to make up my mind about whether I should call him back or let it wait until morning. Did he have some news about Gíó? No, he was just setting his trap and trying to snare me in it. But I didn't think I'd be able to settle down if I had the call hanging over me. It wasn't a good idea to try to sleep knowing that that phone-fixated detective would call back before long.

Instead of turning on the light, I walked into the dark apartment and over to the kitchen window. I knew there was no danger of anyone seeing me there; I was cloaked in darkness. The kitchen was safe, everything as it should be.

I looked across the street at the new tenant's apartment. Nothing had changed. I could still make out the blue glow and the place still appeared to be deserted. No one had come running out the door behind me. Whoever lived there now didn't seem to have any intention of staying. That wasn't someone's home. What about that Jed guy, the guy who'd come over to introduce himself? Hadn't he said lived there? Or had he been pointing at another house? That couldn't be Gió's home base, could it? He couldn't mean to start his new life here. Could he?

# 80

A new day had dawned. I hadn't had the courage to call Haraldur after I got home from the countryside. I was too much of a coward.

But I was ready now.

I stood at the kitchen window and looked out at the street. Finna and her old broom were early risers and tottering down the pavement in my direction. She walked out into the road and then stopped right there in the middle. Then she turned around and looked at the house on the other side of the street.

Water was dripping from the tap at regular intervals, the sound echoing hollowly in the kitchen.

I pulled up the detective's number, and as per usual, he answered practically before I'd finished dialling.

'Hello,' he said eagerly. 'Júlía? Is that you?'

'This is Júlía. I see that you've been trying to get hold of me… I've—'

I didn't manage to finish my sentence because Haraldur interrupted.

'Júlía! Listen up now.'

'Okay,' I said, shaken. There was such an unusual intensity in his voice that I knew he must have important news for me.

'I've been trying to get in touch with you since yesterday afternoon. Has your phone been off? You have to answer when I call. Do you understand?'

'Uh, yes, but I didn't have a signal.'

'Things have gone in a new direction in the investigation into your husband's disappearance. A completely new direction. But I need you come down here and confirm some things. Can you come now? I can pick you up… No, no, actually, wait a minute. Don't come just yet.'

'What's happened?'

'We've got a new lead.'

'A lead? Something to do with Gíó?'

'That's precisely what we're unsure about. So we need your help to move forward. It's very important. It's all very strange.' Haraldur sighed.

'I don't understand. Did you get word about Gíó's movements?'

'No, it's not entirely clear. I recommend we meet in an hour. Can you be here at the station then? I can explain everything then. Forensics needs to do their part but they're just about finished. Or… Yes, it'll just be best for us to take a look at this together. But don't worry.'

'What kind of lead?'

'A lead, yes. Yes, it's really unusual, let me tell you… But we're taking care of the forensics, as I said. We'll need your help to confirm some details. Come on down and we'll take a look.'

'But just tell me what new evidence you have. What kind of lead? I've got to know.'

'I understand, Júlía. But I'm telling you straight out that it'll be best if you come in and we go over it together. We need to talk face to face. That will be the best thing by far.'

'Okay. I'm on my way.'

'Hold off a moment. Be here at nine, not before. See you then.' He hung up.

# Icelandic National Broadcasting Service (RÚV) | ruv.is | 14.10.22 – 08:30

ICE-SAR dispatched teams this morning and will now concentrate its search for Gíó Ísaksson on the area around Hvalfjörður. The shores on both sides of the fjord will be searched. Up to this point, search efforts have been fruitless, but new evidence has warranted shifting the focus of the manhunt. This was confirmed by the ICE-SAR's media representative.

DS Sigurður Jón Kælk was not at liberty to disclose what new evidence has led to the refocusing of ICE-SAR's search. 'We're still getting a number leads and it's our job to follow up on them.'

Around fifty people are taking part in today's search and the Coast Guard's helicopter will fly over the Hvalfjörður region at first light.

# 81

I could barely restrain myself. What I wanted more than anything was to speed down to the police station to hear more about whatever new evidence the police had turned up, but at the same time, I was afraid of what awaited me there.

In the predawn light, Finna was still clutching her broom in the middle of the street, apparently deep in thought.

A blue car drove down the street, stopped and waited for the old woman to move out of the roadway. Then it eased into an empty parking spot. After a moment, the driver's-side door opened and to my great surprise, the erotic novelist got out. She looked around and then started towards my house. She had a bag dangling from her shoulder. I watched her come up the front steps and then heard the doorbell.

I realized I was happy to have this unexpected visitor, even though I wasn't sure what business she could have or why she'd suddenly shown up at my home.

The novelist's smiling, cheerful face was waiting for me when I opened the door.

'Hi, Júlía! So you're alive, are you? I'm so glad you're all right. I've called a million times, but couldn't get hold of you. I must have had the wrong number because no one picked up when I called but here you are… I'm so relieved, dear, I just want to hug you.'

'Come in,' I hurried to say, stepping aside.

'Oh, I'm so sorry to come barging in on you like this so early in the morning. I just didn't know how to get hold of you. I have the interview with me... it's so wonderfully written. You made me look so good, so much cleverer and funnier than in reality. Ha ha ha!'

It was clear that the erotic novelist had no idea of my situation. She had no idea that my husband was missing and that half the nation was following the search for him with bated breath. She just carried on talking about her book, perfectly untroubled by anything other than her forthcoming publication day.

'But I'd so love to add just a few things to the interview... I completely forgot, but I'd always meant to talk about lust. I didn't say a single word about that insatiable force...'

'Yes, that's just fine. There's plenty of time to make adjustments. But I have to run. Now, actually. Right now. I'm a bit preoccupied... by something rather important.'

'Oh, I'm so sorry to be bothering you, I'm sorry, I'm sorry. I should have let you know I was coming, of course, but I'd called so many times... May I just say this one thing about lust and then you can add it in? Two seconds. I just really want to make sure it's in the interview... I've thought so much about this, and I think it's really important—the heart of all my writing, to be honest—and it's essential to getting people interested in the book that I address the question of lust. So let me just put it bluntly—and then I'll have said it, and you can add it if you think it fits and then I'll go. Okay, so yes: lust. Oh, shoot, I've lost it now. I'd planned out the right way to say it in my head. Sorry, listen to me jabbering away... I'm atrocious. But the idea is that lust is never satisfied, you see? It's insatiable. And from it, proceeds unending unhappiness.' As soon as she'd said this last sentence, she waved her hands like the conductor of a large orchestra. 'Can you word it better for me in the interview?'

'Yes, I can try...'

'You'll better understand what I mean if you relate it to the notebook I found—you remember? And the scene in the coffee house?'

# 82

It seemed probable that the man at the front desk at the station had been advised that I was on my way because he jumped to his feet as though he'd been sitting on a loaded spring when I presented myself at the Perspex window and asked for Haraldur.

'He's expecting you. You're Júlía, correct?' he said quickly.

'I am.'

'Come with me. I'll show you to his office.' He slipped through a gap in the reception cage and walked ahead of me with quick steps.

He took two stairs at once and then swept down a wood-panelled hallway until he reached an open door. I had trouble keeping up with him.

'Haraldur,' he called through the door. 'I have a guest here to see you.' Then he turned on his heel, smiled by way of goodbye and went back the same way we'd come. I watched him hurry around the corner and down the stairs.

'Júlía,' I heard him call from in the office. 'Come in.'

I walked in cautiously. I could just make out the top of Haraldur's head behind his computer screen. His desk was covered with tall stacks of all kinds of papers, folders, overflowing ashtrays and dirty coffee mugs. On the windowsill next to the desk, there were more stacks of paper. Behind the desk chair that he was sitting in, a folding bed had been pushed up against the wall. I surveyed the chaos in astonishment.

Could the man actually work in this mess?

Did he sleep in his office?

The folding bed might at least explain why Haraldur always seemed to be by the phone.

The detective rolled his desk chair towards me.

'Do you sleep here?' I asked, nodding towards the bed.

'Yes, sleep here I do. Not every night, not at all… but sometimes, sometimes it happens. Or every now and then I'll close my office door and take a siesta in the middle of the day if I'm feeling tired or lazy.'

He grinned, turned around in his chair and considered the set-up. 'My divine divan, hmm.'

The folding bed was an old single, deeply sunken in the middle and covered in a green fabric that was both discoloured and worn. But there was affection in the detective's eyes when he looked at his berth. Then he looked at me, pursed his lips, and rubbed his chin.

'Júlía,' he said with a sigh. His attention was fixed on some unvoiced thought that was taking shape in his mind.

'Yes,' I answered, feeling a knot of anxiety forming in my belly.

'We need to take a short drive, you and I.'

'Take a drive? Why?'

'We'll have Sigurður Jón chauffeur us. He's an excellent driver.'

'Where are we going?' My surprise was genuine. 'Where?' I repeated automatically.

'Yes, where indeed?'

'I have no idea. Has anything new come to light?'

'Yes and no.' He got that look on his face again, the one he got when he was picking his words carefully. 'Júlía, what I want, actually, is to show you the place that Gíó's coat was found.'

'In Hvalfjörður,' I said, trying to sound relaxed.

'Yes, exactly. In Hvalfjörður. We're going to drive out to the fjord. And when we've looked around out there…' He cut himself short, rested his chin on his hand, rubbed the stubble there and looked thoughtfully into the air.

'It's quite a beautiful fjord, Hvalfjörður—totally underappreciated by Icelanders, a real "nature pearl", as we say, but yes, to the matter at hand: we'll go take a look and then come back here and talk things over. I have a number of curious things I want to show you.'

I felt as though Haraldur's demeanour had changed. It was like he was an actor on a stage. The words he chose, the way his voice projected, the energy that streamed off him, the studied casualness of his gestures—none of it was like anything I'd seen or heard from him before. He was pleased. Glad to have me as audience to his performance. He believed he had me in his power. That I was eating out of his hand.

'How does that plan sound to you?'

I didn't know how I felt about Haraldur's itinerary. I had a feeling I'd only been made privy to a portion of what he had in mind. But he jumped to his feet before I was able to answer and said decisively: 'Let's get going, now—we have to hurry. We're not paid to sit around.'

I felt a light pressure on my lower back as he used a hand there to steer me through the office door and out into the hall. Then we walked a few steps until I stepped aside, slipped out of his reach. He doesn't get to be in control, I thought.

Haraldur acted as though he hadn't noticed this evasive manoeuvre of mine, and we walked side by side down the hallway in silence. When we reached an open office near the stairs, he called: 'Siggi. Let's go. Now.'

Sigurður Jón immediately appeared in the doorway, smiling ear to ear and wearing a long black coat, his car keys dangling from his index finger. It was like he'd been hiding behind the door, already dressed to go out and just waiting to be called.

'Hey ho, I'm here. Ready to go,' he said, jumping through the doorway like a naked showgirl leaping out of a cake, expecting us to cheer.

His trousers were too short.

# 83

We stood in front of a white police car waiting for Sigurður Jón. He'd managed, in his unparalleled ham-handedness, to unlock the vehicle, only to drop the keys under it. He was now sprawled on the ground and trying to reach them where they'd fallen, halfway under the chassis.

While we stood around waiting for him to complete his recovery mission, Haraldur repeatedly invited me to sit in the front seat, insisting that he'd sit in the back. But I wasn't in the mood to listen to this misplaced courtesy.

'We'll not treat you like a criminal. You just take the front and I'll make myself comfortable in the back,' said Haraldur firmly, opening the door and pointing.

'Absolutely not. I'd rather sit in the back. It's safer,' I said, smiling as I slipped around his paunch and got into the back seat.

My alacrity seemed to take Haraldur by surprise, and he hesitated for a moment before getting in the front seat.

Keys back in hand, Sigurður Jón got in, started the car, and off we went.

'Do you mind if I smoke? I'll open the window.'

'It's fine by me.'

He pulled out a crumpled pack of Viceroys, extracted a cigarette and lit it. He inhaled deeply and voluptuously before blowing the smoke out the window. Then he turned around and looked at me.

'How are you doing? In light of the circumstances, I mean.'

'I'm not complaining.'

'No. You're made of sterner stuff.'

I didn't respond.

'So, you went to check out the holiday cottage?' he continued, obviously wanting to lighten the mood.

'I went out there, yes.'

'And…'

'And nothing. Gíó wasn't there and I waited for over a day. He didn't come.'

'And you waited over a day?'

I didn't answer so he looked over his shoulder and repeated the question.

'Yes, but all that came of it was some run-of-the-mill psychological torment, as you can perhaps comprehend.'

'Very easily, I can understand that. I can put myself in your shoes with no trouble at all. Were you alone?' He took another drag from his cigarette.

'For the most part. My sister María came out. She was there for all of ten minutes.'

'Oh? She came to see you? That was nice of her… but listen, I wanted to ask you something: how good a swimmer is Gíó?'

'I don't know. I have no idea, actually. We've never gone to the pool together. I think he's probably as poor a swimmer as most men his age,' I answered without hesitation, even though the question threw me. I immediately started wondering what he had up his sleeve to ask such a thing.

'He's not a swimmer, then?'

'I don't know,' I answered, trying to stifle the irritation in my voice. 'I genuinely don't have a clue. Don't all men my age—Gíó's age, that is—have horrible trauma from their swimming class days? I'm always hearing stories about a swimming instructor at the old Sundhöllin pool, a man who was downright abusive with the boys.

He'd push them into the pool with a long stick and make sure they couldn't get back to the side even though they were on the verge of drowning. He wouldn't let them back onto solid ground until they'd swallowed half the pool.'

'Half the pool—no less,' answered Haraldur distractedly.

When it seemed like he wasn't going to ask any more questions, I asked: 'What's got you thinking about my husband's swimming abilities? What does that have to do with anything? Are you thinking about the harbour around the Óseyri wharf?'

'It may have some bearing on things. Like I said, some new evidence has come to light that I need you to take a look at when we get back to the station. Now's not the right time for us to talk about it. First, we're going to take a walk around the area where you two stopped on Sunday.'

# 84

We'd not said much for most of the drive to Hvalfjörður. Sigurður Jón and Haraldur didn't exchange so much as a word. It was clear that Sigurður Jón knew where we were headed because after driving deep into Hvalfjörður, he turned down the same gravel road that Gíó and I had driven a few days before without the slightest hesitation. Nothing surprised these two.

'Jæja,' said Haraldur once Sigurður Jón had switched off the engine. We all sat quietly for a few moments, as though none of us felt equal to the task of leaving the warmth of the car for the cold winter air outside. The wind howled loudly, the sea was choppy and dark. I could feel the car rocking back and forth in the gusts. Finally, Haraldur opened his door and practically tumbled out.

'Damnation,' he said. 'I've got so old and fat that soon, I'll hardly be able to get out of a car.' He sighed. 'Here we are, and here I shall show you, Júlía, where your husband's trench coat was found.'

He started off and Sigurður Jón and I trotted after him like obedient puppies.

I heard a great, heavy droning above us. I looked up and saw a helicopter approaching over the sea. The helicopter followed the coastline in our direction, and I could make out two men in white helmets and dark sunglasses in the cockpit looking down at the ground.

'Can you hear it?' called Haraldur through the din. I looked at him, baffled. Was he deaf, too? I must be going mad.

'The helicopter?'

He looked at me. 'They're conducting a helicopter search of the fjord,' he added.

I could see no reason to waste my breath on this nonsense, and we walked down to the edge of the beach without another word.

Suddenly, Haraldur stopped and looked me straight in the eyes. 'It's Wednesday, right?' he shouted.

'No, I think it's Thursday. And before you ask, it's morning.' Both Haraldur and Sigurður Jón looked at me with surprise. I noticed tyre tracks in the sand on the shore and a throng of footsteps as though someone had been pacing back and forth. I felt like I was going to collapse.

'Argh, what is this claptrap?' I directed my words at Haraldur. 'What is it that you want of me? Or what was it that you wanted?'

I looked towards the towering, majestic mountains at the base of the fjord. The sun had climbed over the peaks, and I could feel its rays on my face. Then I turned and looked in the other direction, out over the fjord. I'd imagined that I'd see the city in the distance, but, of course, that wasn't the case. Sometimes, I get so disoriented, have so little sense of the distance between places, their relative position to one another. The surface of the sea was a dark grey stretching as far as the eye could see. It churned like a pot of leaden porridge come to boil.

Haraldur waited to answer until the helicopter had flown over and was a good way away from us, the drone of its blades fading gradually until it was possible to have a conversation again. I could tell that Haraldur had something all planned out in his head. He stopped, and Sigurður Jón and I did, too. He held one hand over his mouth and his eyes were distant.

'Júlía, are you familiar with Geirshólmur?'

The question caught me completely unawares.

'Yes, it's a little skerry right out in the fjord here.' I nodded towards the sea.

'Have you been there?'

I was about to answer but he raised his hand to indicate that I shouldn't say anything right away.

'I'll remind you to think carefully about how you answer, Júlía. I don't want you to forget anything, so you don't accidentally answer untruthfully.'

'No, I've never been there,' I answered without hesitation.

'You have never sailed to Geirshólmur. I want you to think hard now.'

Haraldur's face had turned to stone. He was staring daggers into me. I felt my heart pounding in my chest, and I tried to evade his gaze. What did he know? What was he referring to?

'No, I've never been there. You're so serious all of a sudden. What do you have on your mind?'

'Tell me about the drive you took here—the drive you and Gíó took here, to Hvalfjörður, this past Sunday. The day he disappeared.'

'Sure. It's practically all I think about. But nothing much of note happened. Nothing, unfortunately, that can explain his disappearance. We set out late on Sunday. Too late, in my opinion, because it had already started to get dark. I'd nagged him, told him we should get going just after noon, but Gíó was in a strange funk, silent and moody. That doesn't happen very often. He's usually in good spirits, cheerful and even-tempered. But there was something weighing on him that day that he didn't want to talk to me about, no matter how I pressed him. He said he had some work to do and then sat there, glued to his computer until the late afternoon.'

'But the two of you had planned to sail out in the boat you'd made arrangements to borrow. Why didn't you?'

'First and foremost because Gíó was so down and negative. He also said he had no interest in sailing out into the fjord in "that old tub".'

'What did he mean, "old tub"?'

'That's just what he called it. He didn't think the farmer's rubber dinghy particularly seaworthy. Gíó was afraid the boat was going to sink with us in it if we sailed out into the fjord.'

'So you didn't take it out?'

'No.'

'Did you see the boat? I mean, did you come here?'

I had an inkling it would be best to say that I'd got into the boat. Maybe the police had found a hair or taken a DNA sample from it. It was clear from all the footprints that people had been busy here, walked back and forth all over the area. Maybe the detective squad? Or forensics?

'The boat was here,' I pointed in front of me. 'About two metres from the shore. We drove down the gravel road and parked the car. Got out of the car and walked around the boat. It was pretty cold but there was no wind, so the sea wasn't as ominous as it is now.' I inclined my chin towards the sea. 'Gíó kicked the sides of the boat, I remember, like a lot of men do to tyres when they're looking over a car. He said the rubber tubing was half deflated. But I climbed up into the boat, sat on the inflatable part, whatever you call it, tested the handle on the motor, and told Gíó to take a seat next to me. So he did and we sat there, side by side for a few minutes, and chatted. I said there was plenty of air in the boat, at least enough to take a short sail.

'But I couldn't convince him it was seaworthy or that it would be invigorating to sail out into the fjord for a little bit. I hadn't had Geirshólmur in mind, but we might well have ended up there.'

'So just to be clear: nothing came of your planned sail? The last time we spoke about your trip to Hvalfjörður, you said you hadn't got out of the car.'

I saw out of the corner of my eye that Sigurður Jón, who'd been wandering aimlessly along the shore, had stopped short and was following our conversation closely.

'No, I never said that. Never. You've misunderstood me,' I said at once, trying to sound as unperturbed as I could.

Haraldur furrowed his brow and gave me a severe look.

'I want to show you where Gíó's trench coat was found.' He stalked off.

I stood still because I wasn't sure if he meant for me to follow him but then he stopped by a heap of seaweed by the edge of the shore and motioned for me to come over.

'Here. This is the exact spot on the sand where Gíó's coat was found. Nicely folded, but wet. It rained that day, too.'

I walked over to Haraldur and Sigurður Jón trailed after me. We gathered around the pile of seaweed, and all looked down as though waiting for the olive-green trench coat to suddenly appear.

'Here?' I said, pointing to the heap. I felt like I needed to take an active role in the conversation.

'Yes, right here… Do you remember whether Gíó took off his coat while you were here, while you were walking around here?'

'He didn't take off his coat, no. It was cold and there was no reason to.'

'No, of course not,' said Haraldur. Sigurður Jón looked at me as if waiting for me to add something to this observation.

'How about this? Do you remember if Gíó had a bottle of Coca-Cola with him? Did he drink Coke?'

'A Coke bottle?' I tittered because I was of two minds about how to answer. I remembered the Coke bottle that Gíó had been drinking from on the way to Hvalfjörður because I'd wondered if he was hung-over. And yes, he'd had it with him when he was lying in the grass on Geirshólmur.

'No, he didn't drink Coke,' I answered resolutely.

'He didn't? You're absolutely sure?'

'Yes, of course. I know very well that he didn't drink soft drinks very often—ever, in fact.'

Sigurður Jón, who hadn't said a word since we arrived, now stepped forward. 'Uh, Haraldur, wouldn't it be better to talk about this down at the station where we can take her statement?' he said in his shrill voice.

'Good point, Siggi. We've taken a look at the scene here. Let's drive back to the city. Júlía, we'll head back to the station together. There are some things we want to show you and we can discuss under the right conditions, get everything down on paper, as Sigurður Jón points out, and thereby prevent any more misunderstandings about who said what.'

'Maybe I'm not quick on the uptake, but am I understanding you correctly that I'm suspected of something or under suspicion of having done something wrong? How am I supposed to take that?' I was rambling and knew I should shut up before I said something I shouldn't and got myself into trouble.

'Calm down. You have nothing to fear. Just tell the truth and everything will be fine.'

What bosh, I thought. If I said one true word, a single true sentence, I'd be thrown straight into jail. Charged with involuntary manslaughter or whatever else. Bread and water, a hard cot and a view between iron bars, that would be life for the foreseeable future. That is, if it's a crime to temporarily abandon your deceitful husband on a deserted island.

# 85

I was back in that depressing room again, sitting alone at the table in the middle of the room. There was a chair across from me, but no one was in it yet. A long time had passed since I'd been brought in here. Sigurður Jón had followed me in and pointed me to the chair that I was now seated in.

'Haraldur will be right in. You just wait here,' he'd said as he closed the door behind him. Although I'd thought interrogation rooms like this were soundproofed, I could easily make out the foot traffic outside the door. I heard voices talking, I heard laughter and I heard footsteps approaching and receding. But the door didn't open.

This was probably some psychological tactic, making me wait for a long time so my nerves would start to fray, my courage weaken. But I wasn't anxious, and my breathing was calm. I wasn't scared; I was bored.

I wondered if I should ask for a lawyer. Wasn't that always the way it went on those crime shows on TV? The suspects were at least offered a lawyer when their interrogation began or when they were told that they were suspected of some awful deed.

Time plodded along and I was just about to lose my patience, was about to stand up and walk out when Haraldur came in. Had he intuited that my patience was at its breaking point, or did they have a way of watching me? I glanced around in search of a camera. Was this all a game?

Haraldur was carrying a small white box with a lid.

'My sincere apologies for the wait. I needed to get some things together,' he said, and placed the box on the table in front of me.

'Are you moving?' I asked drily.

'Hmm? No, no.' He looked down at the box and added: 'Oh, the box... These are the boxes we use here at the station for all sorts of things.'

'Should I be asking for a lawyer?'

'You have the right to a lawyer. I just hadn't got so far as to offer you one before we had a chance to talk. But of course... You are absolutely permitted to call a lawyer. That is your right.'

'No, I've no need for a lawyer. I just said that because I feel like I'm in a movie. This is as funny as...' Nothing occurred to me to liken my circumstances to, so I just trailed off. I hid my face in my hands, elbows on the table.

Haraldur didn't say anything and for a moment, we didn't say anything either one of us, until he broke the silence. He reached towards the recorder and turned it on. He then placed the device on the table between us, reeled off the time, date and who was in the room before he looked at me.

I sat motionless, my head still in my hands.

'Júlía, you have been advised of your right to an attorney, but you have waived that right. Are you sure you don't want to have a lawyer present?'

I looked up and nodded.

'Will you be so good as to speak your responses so that your answer can be recorded?' He made a quick gesture at the recorder.

I leant forward and spoke into the machine: 'I do not need a lawyer.'

'Just speak normally and it will pick up your voice. You don't need to talk directly into it.'

'Okay... Am I being interrogated?'

'Júlía... Take a look... I need to show you something... Now, take your time...'

He gently removed the lid from the box that he'd brought in and set on the table between us. From it, he took a plastic Coke bottle. The label had fallen off.

'Look,' he repeated. 'We found this bottle yesterday.'

'Oh?' I said, looking at the detective and the bottle with surprise.

'We found this Coca-Cola bottle in Hvalfjörður.' He paused and looked at me.

I wasn't sure what I should say, so I just repeated what I'd already said: 'Oh?'

'When you two were walking around Hvalfjörður—on Sunday, that is—did Gíó have a bottle of Coke with him?'

'A bottle of Coke? No, I already told you that he doesn't drink soft drinks. I have never seen him drink Coke.'

Haraldur gave me a serious look.

'Are you sure about that?'

'Yes, absolutely,' I said.

Haraldur fell silent and I could tell that he was thinking before he continued.

'So, what's notable about this bottle here is that we found it in practically the same spot that Gíó's coat was found yesterday. The two discovery sites are less than two metres away from one another. It is, of course, quite curious for an officer of the law to find two things that could have considerable significance for this case and how our work on it develops—much less that they be found in almost the same spot with only a couple of days between them.'

Haraldur looked thoughtfully at me as if to give me time to digest what he was saying. 'Two different things connected to the same event, found in the same place, two days apart,' he then repeated, as if to ensure that I understood.

I didn't say anything.

'Is that not strange? Finding two unrelated things in the same place couldn't really be a coincidence or an act of nature—do you understand what I'm getting at?'

'No,' I said curtly. 'I can't see what connection a Coke bottle has with this case or how you're linking it to Gíó.'

'The Coke bottle was also arranged on the foreshore. Which is why I wanted to hear your thoughts about it, because I can tell you that the Coke bottle is indisputably connected to your husband. You should know that before you air any of your hypotheses, which I've no doubt will be fascinating. We may well have two things to support our view that Gíó drank out of this bottle when the two of you were together, but we'll get to that later.'

He stuck his head halfway into the cardboard box and came back up with two plastic sleeves, which he laid on the table in front of me. He looked at me with the eyes of a victor. His eyes were wet and his mouth partially open. He was triumphal. I should give up now, he'd disarmed me. He was certain beyond a shadow of a doubt.

In one of the sleeves there were three pieces of paper that had clearly been torn from a little spiral notebook and arranged side by side. In the other was a photograph of the back of the same pages; there was writing on both sides.

'Take a look, Júlía, at what was in the bottle we found. A letter. A six-page letter.'

'The letter was inside the bottle that was found in Hvalfjörður?'

'I want you to read what was written and take a good look at the handwriting. Maybe you'll recognize it.'

I hunched over the pages. I did indeed recognize the handwriting. It was the exact same lettering that had been in the notebook I found with all the sexual scenarios. The writing was prim and dainty. The letters themselves were tiny and had been beautifully drawn with an unusually fine-tip black fountain pen.

'And you found these pages in Hvalfjörður?' I repeated.

'Yes, or that is to say: a man from Search and Rescue who walked the shores of Hvalfjörður yesterday did. He found the bottle. A genuine message in a bottle. You'll see when you read the letter.'

I pictured Gió on Geirshólmur as he walked ahead of me with one hand in his trouser pocket and the other holding his bottle of Coca-Cola. Then he'd sat down on a little grassy knoll and looked diffidently around him with the bottle between his legs.

I pulled the plastic sleeve with the pages closer and started reading.

# Geirshólmur, Sunday, 9 October 2022

My name is Gíó Ísaksson. I write from a skerry in Hvalfjörður called Geirshólmur.

I am alone and poorly dressed for the outdoors, no warm outerwear, and night will soon fall. It is growing dark, and the wind is cold.

I have been abandoned on this island.

An hour ago, I watched my wife Júlía sail away from this island in the same rubber dinghy that we arrived in together this afternoon.

I have no reason to think she's coming back for me, and so I have no other choice but to try and swim to land. I'm as good as dead if I stay here out in the middle of the fjord overnight. There is a strong wind blowing from the north, there's no shelter here of any kind, I'm soaked from the rain, and it's very cold.

I don't know when or whether I'll be saved. No one knows I'm here except for Júlía, and I don't expect she's going to tell anyone. I don't know what prompted her decision to abandon me on a deserted islet.

I can't tell anyone I'm here—I don't have my phone with me. I haven't seen any ships, and it's got so dark that I can't see anything but shadows and will-o'-the-wisps. Now and then, I feel like I can hear the sound of a motor cutting through the keening of the wind, but I've stopped hoping that anyone is on the way to save me.

Soon, I will set off on my swim, and I will attempt to make it to shore by the Miðsandur oil pier, close to where we sailed from.

I'm putting this letter into a Coke bottle that I happened to bring along with me. I will swim towards the shore with this message in a bottle and won't set it afloat unless I'm about to give up. That's how I'll try to ensure it is delivered. If the worst occurs, I hope that someone will find my message in a bottle so my fate will be known.

Now I swim. I pray that I be given the courage and strength I'll need to survive.

# 86

When I'd finished reading, I sat quietly for a moment. Then I read the letter once more. Finally, I looked at Haraldur, who'd got up and was now looming over me with his arms crossed over his chest.

'What do you have to say to that, Júlía?'

'Nothing. There's nothing I can say.'

'You have nothing to say about that letter?'

I shook my head and stared out in front of me.

'Will you confirm that that is Gíó's handwriting?'

'No.'

'No? Is that not your husband's handwriting?'

'No.'

'So then you aren't familiar with the chain of events described in the letter either?'

'No. I've told you as much before and I think you need to start listening to what I'm saying instead of believing all sorts of absolute twaddle. I will tell you once more: We didn't sail out into Hvalfjörður, Gíó didn't have a Coke bottle with him and this isn't his handwriting. His writing isn't this nice. He went missing from our home. I'm being tangled in a web of lies. I mean, really. Go out and find Gíó and an explanation for this fake letter instead of spending your days and nights dozing on that disgusting cot of yours. I am not going to sit here in this windowless closet and be subjected to Stasi interrogation techniques for a second longer. What is wrong with you? How could you think I could do something like that to my husband? Can't you see how absurd this is? You're barking up the wrong tree…'

'Calm down, Júlía. I've pointed out before that you've contradicted yourself and that never increases a witness or a suspect's credibility.'

'You don't believe me?'

'All I'm saying is that it is always hard to keep believing what a witness or suspect says if they're caught in untruths, inaccuracies or deliberate misrepresentations.'

'So what do you want to do with me? Are Gíó's fingerprints on this letter?'

The detective paused, as though he needed to stall for time. The skin around his mouth twitched oddly, like ripples in still water.

'We have yet to find a full fingerprint on the pages. They're pretty waterlogged, so some water must have got into the bottle and been soaked up by the paper. The bottle has probably been tossed around in the sea and rain for a long time… But I expect we'll have more to talk about today. We're still investigating this as a disappearance, not manslaughter.'

'Manslaughter!'

'Maybe there's something you'd like to tell us to improve your position. It isn't up to me to decide whether charges will be brought against you, but we should know in the next few hours.'

'I'm telling you that I haven't killed anyone and that should be enough to "improve my position". This thing is so obvious that a Sherlock Holmes like you ought to be see right through it. Someone put that bottle in Hvalfjörður where Gíó's coat was found. As you've rightly pointed out, it can't be a coincidence or an act of nature that the bottle was found in the same place as the coat with only a few days in between. Someone put that letter there… Damn it… No, I've had enough. I'm leaving.'

# Icelandic National Broadcasting Service (RÚV) | ruv.is | 14.10.22 – 19:49

An individual has been brought in for questioning in connection with the disappearance of Gíó Ísaksson, sources close to the matter say. Gíó has been missing since Sunday.

According to DS Sigurður Jón Kælk, the investigation has reached a sensitive point and police will be speaking to a number of people in connection with the case. The detective would not comment further on the matter at this time.

Although extensive efforts to find the missing man have been ongoing since Sunday, the search has so far proved fruitless.

# 87

It had snowed. It had snowed all night. The streets were white, roofs were covered in a thick layer of snow that hung over the eaves, and tree branches bent under the weight of the drifts.

It was still snowing.

All was calm.

I stood rapt at the living room window watching the giant flakes drifting slowly and regally to the ground like angel feathers.

The voices on the kitchen radio were murmuring softly, and a car was driving slowly down my street. A hush seemed to be settling over the world.

I'd been released from the police station late at night after a long wait and a long conversation that kept going over and over the same things. I repeated my answers again and again until Haraldur told me I could go home. He'd probably been longing for his office bed. I'd expected that I'd have to come back down to the station in the following days to continue our meaningless conversation, but several days had passed and no one had called me back in. I'd just sat at home.

Haraldur was convinced of my guilt, but he had no real proof.

I knew what the police wanted.

They wanted to compel me to confess. They couldn't charge me unless they had a confession. And I hadn't confessed; I would never confess.

Gíó hadn't been found, he was still missing, and now that all this snow had fallen, I felt like his tracks had been covered. He would never be found.

Old Finna woke me up. Just after eight, she rang the doorbell with such urgency that I jolted awake with a start, sure that a SWAT team was standing outside my door, about to barge in and arrest me.

I hurried downstairs in my robe and swiftly opened the door so the SWAT team wouldn't break it down and toss tear gas and smoke bombs into my house. But there she stood on my steps, the old woman and her broom, up to her ankles in the snow. She started talking the moment the door opened, but I didn't hear what she was saying because I was so relieved that there wasn't a phalanx of policemen waiting for me.

I was distracted by snowflakes that seemed to hang suspended among the clouds in Finna's eyes. Her mouth was moving, but I wasn't taking any of it in.

'Sorry, I just woke up,' I said, interrupting her. 'I didn't hear what you said.'

'I said that I saw the new tenant sneaking out yesterday before it started to snow. So he didn't leave any footprints behind.'

'Oh? You saw the new tenant? Who was it?' I'd actually wiped that mystery man from my mind. Convinced myself it was unthinkable that Gíó would shack up in such a pigsty.

'It's just him in the whole apartment. A man.'

'Is there something odd about him? Something wrong with him?'

'Yes, something odd about him—there's something suspicious and definitely illegal going on in that place.'

'What did he look like?'

'He had a beard. It might have been the same man who was in your garden the other day.'

I looked over at the apartment on the other side of the street, which had given me such a terrible feeling a few nights earlier. As usual, all the lights were off. The blueish glow from deeper within the apartment wasn't perceptible on this snow-white morning. I looked back at the old woman. She was like a character out of a nineteenth-century French novel. All her lights were out, too; her eyes were milky and reminded me of a full moon in a cloudy sky. They didn't give off any glow either.

'Thank you for letting me know,' I said.

'Would you like me to call the police?' she asked.

'No, don't worry. I'll take care of it.'

I walked back inside, closing the door behind me.

# 88

It was as if the same day was dawning again and again. It was always called something different, the day I woke up to—Wednesday, Sunday, the fourteenth, the third, a day in October, a day in November. I tried to break the days up, find a new rhythm. But I rambled around, walked in circles around myself. The search for Gíó had been called off and the papers were no longer publishing news about how the case was progressing—not updates about the search, not further speculation about what might have happened to him, not rumours or articles about new evidence or unconfirmed reports of suspects being questioned.

But I wasn't out of the woods yet.

I could feel it.

It was only a lack of proof that Gíó was dead that was preventing me from being charged with manslaughter or some other crime that would be enough to put me away with other criminals.

Detective Haraldur was conscientious about reminding me of his presence. Although he never said it straight out, he was completely convinced that I was guilty of the crime that had been described in detail in the message in the bottle found on the shores of Hvalfjörður.

Haraldur was circling me like a buzzard. He called at regular intervals, dropped by my house unexpectedly, would suddenly appear beside me in car parks, cross paths with me on my walks as though by coincidence, and I always had the feeling that he was hoping he could pin something on me. He was usually accompanied by Sigurður Jón. Ol' Victory John.

'What's going on with you, Júlía?' he'd ask, his eyes searching mine. In spite of everything, I liked this man. I understood him in my way.

'Nothing, Haraldur. I'm still walking in circles,' I'd answer, again and again.

Sometimes, I asked him to leave me alone. 'Do you think, perhaps, that Gíó is going to come home all of a sudden like a faithful dog that lost his way? He's gone. He's not coming back. I don't know where he is, I don't know whether he's alive or dead. I don't need you always reminding me of that. Couldn't you be so kind as to leave me in peace?'

'I'm just checking in to see how you are. It's important to me that you feel well. I'm fairly attuned to what one might call spiritual health, the health of the soul. I know that there's much that's eating at you.'

'One thing I will tell you, Haraldur. If you're hoping to get to lock me up for some imagined crime, you can just forget about it. I'd rather walk into the sea than rot away in prison, awaiting a miserable death creeping towards me at a snail's pace. If it's up to me, I'm not going to die bit by bit, like some people, but in seconds.'

But though I repeatedly shooed Haraldur away, he kept turning up with his trusty companion, always casting out his line and bait, always hoping that I'd get tangled in his net, be hooked or snared and unable to wriggle free. He was a patient hunter. Hovered over his prey, tiring it out, giving it a long lead and then pulling it slowly to land. But he wouldn't capture me.

He wouldn't give up, either. It was more than likely that Haraldur just couldn't let this case go, couldn't stop thinking about Gíó's fate, and couldn't bear that I wouldn't get my just deserts. Sometimes, I wanted to talk about crime and punishment with Haraldur. Had I broken a specific law by leaving Gíó on that island? Is there something in the legal code that prohibits that kind of thing? And if some article of the law does prohibit that kind of thing, what is the right punishment for the crime?

Whatever that punishment might be, it could never be more severe than the one I was enduring with all this uncertainty. Uncertainty about what became of Gíó, about whether I was responsible for his possible death, about what might be awaiting me if he *had* survived.

Haraldur knew he was throwing me with these constant reminders of himself, the police and impending punishment. Maybe he thought I'd eventually give in, give up, break down and wearily offer up my confession. As if in so doing, I'd finally obtain the long-sought relief of my conscience, the long-sought absolution for my sins.

I think Haraldur probably hoped that Gíó's body would wash ashore so that he'd finally have confirmation of his suspicions. Maybe he walked the shores of Hvalfjörður day after day, just like I wandered in circles around my apartment, from one room to another, from one window to another, from one part of town to another, hanging between hope and fear that he'd get the news that Gíó's body had been found and that the police thus had cause—after all this time—to turn my fate over to the proper authorities so they could decide on a fitting punishment for my actions.

# 89

Weeks passed, and months. Gió was gone and he wasn't coming back. Maybe he'd sunk to the bottom of Hvalfjörður. It's a deep fjord. Eighty-four metres at its deepest point. If someone had sunk to that depth, there'd be no bringing them back to the surface again.

I'd never been able to bring myself to google what became of the bodies of people who drowned at sea. I was afraid the police were monitoring my search history and would use it as yet another reason to call me in for questioning.

Gradually, however, I was waking up to life again. I left my mausoleum and came out under the wide-open sky. I took on new projects and did them well, I was offered a full-time job (though I turned it down), and I'd started talking to other people and even enjoying it. I had to endure Detective Haraldur hovering around me, but I'd almost got used to that and I'd have probably found it strange if he suddenly stopped harassing me.

It probably isn't fair of me to use such negative words as 'endure' and 'harass'. Anyway, 'harass' is at the very least an imprecise word choice, because Haraldur was courteous and discreet, friendly and tactful. This was a man who was led by kindness and affection.

'Don't you have any hobbies, Haraldur? Why are you wasting your time thinking about me? Don't you have anything else to think about?'

'Júlía, you wouldn't say that if you knew how much pleasure I take from listening to the verses of our great poets set to Icelandic compositions. And I listen to jazz, too. I love music.' He was proud of this hobby of his.

February was almost at its end. I'd found my daily rhythm. All my mornings began in a coffee house on the west side of town. I'd walk down Ægisíða, on the path that runs along the coast, and would stop midway and sit on a bench by the ocean and watch the ships go by. Then I'd head for my coffee shop, a few minutes away on the corner of Hofsvallagata and Melhagi.

Every morning looked like every other. I'd walk in and sit in the same seat in the corner by the window. Every morning, on weekends, too, I'd get there right at eight when they opened. My first order of business was to put my bag on my favourite seat, and then I'd slowly make my way up to the till while I read the menu, which was written on a board on the wall above the counter. I'd order a cup of coffee and bread with sliced cheese. The person who took my order wasn't Icelandic.

She didn't smile.

She never smiled.

She'd listen to me recite my order even though it was always the same. Then she'd silently turn to the coffee machine.

'Where are you sitting?' she'd ask every time.

'Over there in the corner,' I'd say and point. Always in the same way, with the index finger on my right hand.

I'd sit at the table in the corner with the window facing Hofsvallagata on my left and wait for the barista to bring me my order. Then I'd start writing. I always brought along a pink notebook and a fine-tipped Japanese fountain pen.

I continued to write down conversations I overheard in the coffee shop in my notebook, but I also wrote about Detective Haraldur. About my sister María. About myself and about Gíó. I wrote down street names, names of foreign cities. Lecce, Florence, Valencia,

Bilbao, Osnabrück, Salgelse, Montpellier, Bergen, Uppsala… I wrote down the names of stars in the Milky Way. I'd pass several hours this way.

It was a February day, and it was unusually quiet in my coffee house.

I'd sat alone for almost half an hour and no other patrons had come in. The French barista who was usually in charge of the music wasn't working and so it was Bob Dylan on the record player, instead of the French punk he liked to play.

Finally, the first patrons of the day, two young, sour-faced women, appeared in the doorway. They walked in hesitantly—both of them in wide-brimmed hats—took the place in, and seemed to be deciding whether or not to sit down. Both were dressed in some kind of workout clothes, although neither of them showed any signs of having worked out. Neither of them had the graceful body of the well-trained athlete. One of them was also holding a long red scarf. They looked at one another peevishly and decided, by means of simple gestures, to sit down. There wasn't much joy about the two young women; they looked quite unhappy. Dylan warbled, 'Baby, Stop Crying.'

When they sat down, I decided it was time for me to get up and go home. There were still piles of snow on the pavements.

It took me half an hour to walk from the coffee house back to my neighbourhood. When I turned down my street, I saw the postboy on his yellow bike. He was walking letters up each house's steps, sticking them through the letterbox, and then going back down the steps, getting back on his bike and cycling to the next house where he repeated the process.

He saw me walking down the street. He waved with his left hand and cycled slowly towards me, smiling from ear to ear so that his big, white, rabbity teeth glinted in the sun. Then he rolled to a stop in front of me.

I noticed that he'd taken a lot of trouble styling his hair. His quiff stood straight up, forming a sheer cliff that extended from his forehead. To keep it in place, he'd slathered it with a greasy cream that reflected the late-morning sun.

'Heylo!' he greeted me sunnily as he stepped off his bike. 'I have a postcard for the lady. It came all the way from abroad. My colleagues and I at the post office sometimes talk about how rare it is for us post-people to deliver postcards. I think postcards are such a nice way to stay in touch, and it makes me proud to have a hand in carrying such greetings from one person to another,' he said, bending over his mail bag and pulling out a card.

I took the postcard from him without really looking at it and put it straight into my bag. I didn't know who it was from, but I didn't intend to read it in front of this smiley boy. It did not escape me, however, that he was disappointed I didn't show him the picture adorning the card, chat with him about its message or my connection to the person who'd sent it all the way across the ocean to me. I saw his cheerful smile fade for a moment and something flickered in his eyes—a feeling I couldn't entirely read.

'Aren't you going to look at it?' he asked, the smile back on his face.

'Yes, later. When I get home. Thank you for delivering it to me. Yours is a noble profession.'

The postcard remained in my bag for much of the day and I forgot all about it until it started getting dark. I was surprised to find that there was nothing on it but my address. The space for a greeting was as white as new-fallen snow. Nothing was written there; no message, no salutation.

I looked at the picture on the card. It showed a hen with a yellow beak and a red comb. Upon closer examination, I saw that it was actually a water pitcher in the shape of a hen. The hen's yellow beak was the spout, while the red comb formed the rim. The pitcher was against a blue background. There was nothing else in the image.

I turned the card over and took a closer look at the postmark. I couldn't make it out, unfortunately, and it was also impossible to read where it had been sent from. And then suddenly, it hit me. I knew where I'd seen that pitcher before.

# 90

Slowly but surely, my plan was coming together. It had many moving parts, and I wasn't entirely sure that it was realistic or right.

But one step at a time.

In one direction.

My relationship with María had been tense since Gíó disappeared. When I really thought about it, though, there had never been any love lost between us. But out of some inborn sense of duty or vague need to cultivate familial connection, we talked on the phone now and then, and I occasionally stopped by her house when I took longer walks out to Seltjarnarnes.

It was mid-March when I knocked on my sister's door. I hadn't called ahead, and I knew she wouldn't open the door unless she was willing to receive me. If not, she'd ignore the bell.

'Hi, is that you?' she called through the kitchen window. I saw her face in the window as she rinsed her hands at the kitchen sink.

'You didn't tell me you were coming. I've just started making dinner,' she said after she opened the door and motioned for me to come in.

'I'm not going to stay long. I was just out for a walk in the area and needed to use the toilet. I thought I'd come here so I could use your immaculate, sweet-smelling powder room instead of the latrine at the shopping centre.'

'Come in, but I'm... well... I'm cooking, so you can just take a seat in the kitchen, and we can talk while I do. How are you?' She pushed her hair back from her pretty, high forehead, the better to accommodate all her lofty thoughts. Her movements were elegant, effortless and so strong that I couldn't but admire her muscular body.

'Good. Everything's good,' I said, stepping into my sister's perfect world and following her into the kitchen where she picked up a knife and started hacking away at what looked to be a head of cabbage, though I couldn't say for sure. I watched her skilfully slice the acid-green mystery vegetable for a moment before saying I was going to use the toilet.

I walked down the hall towards the bathroom but then quietly sidestepped into the living room where a large cabinet stood up against one wall. The cabinet had two doors and it was locked, as expected. There were four drawers at the bottom and the leftmost one contained several lidded boxes. I picked up a red box, opened it, and extracted a gold-plated key resting on a cotton ball. After everything that had happened, I still knew all my sister's hiding places.

I stuck the key into the cabinet lock without a sound and gently opened the doors. I listened for a moment and heard only the clatter of pans in the kitchen.

The cabinet doors concealed four shelves and on the second from the top, I found my sister's passport and other important papers. I opened the passport and examined the picture of María, who was looking at the photographer without a trace of shyness. It wasn't a particularly old passport photo, and I saw, as expected, that it could just as easily be a picture of me. I hurried to tuck the passport up the sleeve of my thick sweater, which I'd deliberately worn for this visit. I'd shown unusual foresight.

Then I walked into the bathroom and closed the door. I inhaled the fresh, citrusy perfume of my sister's bathroom while I peed, a powerful stream of urine that I thought would never end. I pee like an old heifer, I thought to myself. I kid, I kid. The bathroom was so tasteful that one really ought to relieve oneself in absolute silence.

My sister was up to her elbows, stirring matching pots and pans, and barely looked up when I walked back in the kitchen. There was a strong but refined smell of spices in the air. I sniffed and made a sound of pleasure that was meant to acknowledge her cooking prowess. She was good at everything.

'Are you expecting anyone for dinner?' I said, and to my great dismay, I suddenly pictured Gíó and my sister sitting across from one another over a romantic dinner. Candles, cloth napkins and hors d'oeuvres.

I dismissed the thought but was filled with an overpowering urge to run out. I gripped the door frame. The only thing for me to do was to take a seat at the kitchen table and make conversation. I hadn't done everything I'd come to do.

'I have a present for you,' I said.

María looked up and waited for me to show her the gift. I reached into my handbag and took out a copy of *The Laboratory*, which the erotic novelist had sent me. I'd already been given a copy by her publisher, though. That old billy goat had sent me one as a thank you for the interview with the novelist, which came out on the book's pub day in November.

The cover was black and pictured a woman who was clearly in the throes of unrestrained desire. Her head was thrown back, her eyes were closed and her mouth was half open. The title was written on the bottom in white letters: *THE LABORATORY—Erotic Stories*. The author's name was so small as to hardly be visible.

I held the book out towards María and said: 'This is for you.'

'Erotic stories? Did Gíó write that?' she said, before she clammed up and gave me a fearful look. It was obvious she hadn't meant to say that because suddenly, it looked like she wanted to bite off her own tongue.

I felt like I'd been stabbed in the heart.

'Oh, I'm sorry,' she blurted. 'I didn't mean to say that, it just came out.'

'It's all right.'

She hunched over her pot.

'I didn't mean to say that, and I shouldn't, of course, be talking about this... but do you remember when you told me he had written down some sexual fantasies in which the main character was someone named María? I don't know anything about his fantasies... I don't know anything about any fantasies... Maybe he'd imagined that I could give him some sort of outlet, I don't know... I don't always understand men... but it never happened in real life... just... just so you and I are entirely clear on that point.'

I put the book on the table and gave it a little push with my fingertips so that it slid into the centre. 'Okay. Thank you for saying that. We can't just keep mum or avoid talking about it until we die... but right at this moment, I don't have the slightest interest in talking about Gió or his sexual fantasies.'

'Understood. I'll just say this for the last time, then: his are not the hands that have set me on fire, if you will.'

'Set you on fire? Do you burn? Do you carry a torch for anyone? You're like a railroad spike in Siberia...'

María, partially obscured by the steam coming off her cooking pots, kept stirring without looking up.

# 91

*Rarely Never Ltd.*, I read on the front of the card that by some miracle, I'd found again among all the junk in my desk drawer. The card I'd been given months ago by the young artist in the abandoned hotel in JL House.

I pictured the wide-eyed man as he handed me his card, which was white on both sides with velvet-red text. There was a kind of humility to the way he presented the card, as though he was embarrassed to introduce himself with so much ceremony that high-quality paper goods should be changing hands.

The other side of the card had the artist's name, his phone number, email address, and the URL for his website. Everything in tiny, velvet-red letters that suggested both refinement and modesty.

I got butterflies in my stomach as I picked up my phone and dialled the number on the card. The phone rang. Finally, I heard a friendly and mischievous voice on the other end of the line: 'This is Mosi.' I hung up.

The postcard with the hen-shaped water pitcher on it was lying on the coffee table and I picked it up, examined the picture, turned it over and tried, yet again, to read the postmark. I squinted at the black ink smudge and some new kind of stamp that was actually just computer-generated squiggles. Stamps were no longer pictures of placid mountain lakes, birds, fish and heroes of the Icelandic independence movement, but rather, digitally rendered, square patterns. I was no closer to solving the riddle of the postmark.

I stood up and grabbed the suitcase I'd packed earlier in the day and put it by the front door.

Yesterday, I'd started what, in my head, I'd been calling my death cleaning. This basically meant making the house presentable for strangers who came in after I was gone. Everything was clean, both the floors and the furniture. But I'd primarily focused on making sure my bed was nicely made: the quilt smoothed, the pillows in their places and three decorative cushions arranged in a careful heap in the middle. No dirty dishes in the kitchen sink. That kind of thing was always a clear indication of sloth and loneliness. I would not send that kind of sign to the universe when I'd gone on. I noticed that all of the windows could really use a wash, but it was too late to think about that now; I had to get going. I watered the plants. Gave them a good long drink.

I glanced out the kitchen window, looking up and down the street to be sure that Haraldur wasn't lying in wait in his white police car. It was night-time, but thus far, he hadn't let that stop him. He could chance by on one of his informal visits at any time. I didn't want him to catch me leaving with a suitcase.

That wasn't something I'd get away with.

But there was no one out on the street—not even old Finna with her broom.

Around eight, I closed my front door for the last time without thinking about anything special. I wasn't happy or sad. This moment wasn't connected to anything but excitement, butterflies fluttering in my stomach.

I went down the steps and straight to my car. I put my suitcase in the boot, got in, and drove off.

There were no witnesses but the peeping Tom in the blue-lit apartment. He was none of my concern.

Mosi the artist lived in the centre of town. After I'd found his card, I'd snooped around to find out where he lived and what his house looked like. It had bright-red curtains in the windows. I tried to imagine what the man had been thinking, hanging curtains in this unusual, vivid colour, and my guess was that it had something to do with blood and physical membranes, the thin partition between the world and his artist cave. Or maybe he thought of his home as a kind of womb, the red-tinted light corresponding to that which an infant perceives *in utero*.

I parked in front and got out. A reddish glow was filtering through the curtains and into the garden. The artist was clearly at home. I knocked hard on the door instead of ringing the bell.

It opened almost as soon as I knocked and there he stood. He remained fixed in place for a long time, his mouth open and brown eyes wide, not saying anything. There was a smile in his expression and a smile on his lips. From his posture, he wanted me to know that he was surprised to see me. Shocked, even.

I laughed and let him receive me in his own way and time.

'You? You, you're... you're... wait now...' I could see him searching his memory in despair, staring at me and clasping his hands as though in prayer. I said nothing, just kept laughing softly.

'Okay, okay... Am I right that... uh... wait... you lost, uh... you lost your husband! He was lost in the hotel, he'd gone to the wrong room... or... Did you ever find him?'

'No, as it happens,' I said, hurrying to add: 'Could I bother you for a moment? I need to ask you for a small favour.'

'Bother me... favour to ask...? Of course. Come in, it's nice to see you... I don't know what to say, all kinds of feelings, emotions, associations and speculations... ha!' He stared at me, open-mouthed and mischievous.

'Now I need you to let me talk. You just listen.'

'I'm all ears,' he said, touching both of his.

I walked in and closed the door behind me.

# 92

Three hours later, we drove into Hvalfjörður, taking the long way around. For some reason, it felt wrong to drive through the tunnel.

I was taking no risks.

I'd taken the wheel.

Mosi had agreed to come with me on this expedition. He was driving behind me in his own car and maintaining a distance of at least a hundred metres between us. This was probably an unnecessary precaution on my part, but I didn't want any cameras to pick up that I wasn't alone on my journey or that the artist was in any way connected to my trip.

We drove through the evening darkness to the base of the fjord and when we reached the whaling station, Mosi turned into the car park there, while I continued on my way to the Miðsandur pier.

The fjord was still and quiet.

The moon shone in the clear night sky, illuminating the polished surface of the fjord.

I parked my car on the shoreline where Gíó's trench coat had been found five months earlier. I turned the engine off and looked through the windscreen at the incandescent sea. How could someone make themselves swim through that pitch-black, bottomless void, I wondered. How was it possible, even if your life was at stake?

I was about to open my car door and get out when it occurred to me to call Haraldur and say goodbye to him. I'd thought before that it would only be right to say farewell to that likeable and obstinate detective.

I took out my phone and looked up his number. *Detective Foreigner* it still said for his entry.

He answered on the first ring, as per usual.

'Júlía?' he said. There was a question in his voice. He was surprised by my call and on his guard.

'Good evening, Haraldur,' I said, and then added after brief consideration: 'I just wanted talk to you before I went to bed.'

'It is getting late, yes. Are you okay?'

'Yes, thank you. I'm okay. I just wanted to hear your voice. Be well. Good night.'

I could hear that he was nervous. He mumbled something, didn't want to let me go.

'Júlía,' he said gently.

'Yes,' I said, feeling a catch in my throat and my eyes filling with tears. His tenderness took me by surprise. Tears started running down my cheeks, and all of a sudden I was beset by intense feelings I couldn't identify. Longing, regret, affection… love?

'Where are you?' he asked.

'I'm just going to sleep.'

'Are you crying?'

'Yes,' I said, and thought to myself that this was probably the first time that I'd said something true to this benevolent man. One word that could hardly be shorter. One syllable.

I tried to stifle my sobs.

He hesitated again.

'All right, get some rest. Good night, Júlía. Sleep well.'

I hung up.

One true word. My last word.

I pulled a plastic Coke bottle out of my handbag and unscrewed the cap. I also got out a letter I'd written. I'd made many attempts in recent days to find the right words and the right tone. I was still not satisfied.

But before I rolled the letter up and stuck it into the bottle, I read it for the last time.

# Hvalfjörður
# 30 March 2023

My name is Júlía M.

This is my goodbye letter.

It's night in Hvalfjörður and the sea is dark and cold. Or, truth be told, it's smooth as a mirror and beautiful. There's a black streak offshore that looks like a giant shoal of fish finning into the fjord. I haven't seen any ships, and it's got so dark that I can't see anything but shadows and will-o'-the-wisps.

I'm steeling my mind and gathering my courage because soon, I will enter these bottomless, ink-black waters and swim out to sea. I do not hope to reach land. The whales of Whale Fjord can swallow me whole and spit me out on the shores of another world.

I'm putting this letter into a plastic bottle and leaving it in my car. I ask that it be delivered into the hands of Detective Haraldur, who has been overseeing the investigation into the disappearance of my husband, Gíó Ísaksson.

I thank him for his warmth and solicitude.

This is my message in a bottle. I hope that when this letter is found, I will be in another, better place.

Júlía M.

# 93

After I'd thrown my phone as far out into the sea as I could, I walked towards the road in the direction of the whaling station. I was careful to hide if I heard a car approaching. I couldn't let anyone see me on the road, of course. I was on my way to another world.

I heard the din of the waves and the singing of the wind as it blew down from the mountain. I looked out over the fjord and thought I saw a brief glint of light from a ship.

The artist was waiting for me in the whaling station car park, and I hurried over to his car. I lay down in the back seat as though I expected anyone to be interested in who was travelling around Hvalfjörður with this man.

But we'd agreed upon this.

We drove back the same way we came, avoiding the tunnel with all its surveillance cameras. I lay in the back seat of his car and looked up at the dark night sky through the back window. The street lamps resumed once we reached the city. They passed at a steady rhythm, one after the other.

The artist didn't say much. I think it's safe to say that he'd been astonished that a strange woman had asked him to take part in staging her death and helping her get out of the country unseen. He wasn't afraid and he didn't hesitate when I asked him for the favour. I was sure that he looked at this like any other work of art. Everything became art in this young man's mind.

'I sense that this is do or die,' he said.

'Yes, it's do or die,' I answered.

'I'm thinking about what I should say… I am witness to something, maybe I should… how do you say… bear witness. Speak my truth.'

'You won't be mixed up in any of this. No one will connect the two of us…'

'Maybe I'll be called to sit on a jury. Such a good word in Icelandic, jury. *Kviðdómur.* Stomach-judgement. To judge with your stomach. To feel something deep down. A *gut feeling*. Or *mavefornemmelse* in Danish. My mum—she's dead—but she is Danish. Was. Anyway, I'm just telling you my gut feelings.'

Then he fell silent once more and I could see from the back seat, where I was still lying, that his expression, in profile, was that of a driver who was completing a dangerous but important mission. He leant forward, peered through the windscreen and gripped the steering wheel tight. He was onstage. He was playing a part in the death-drama of a woman on the run and his stage was a little old Japanese car. There were two actors. A young artist and a woman, very much alive, who just an hour before had staged her own death.

The sound of the engine in this Japanese car reminded me of a rapid-fire sewing machine but it was calming and lulled me to sleep, carried me into a dream world.

# 94

It's spring. April's just begun and I'm still writing. I'm sitting in a comfy armchair and taking a break. A stack of white pages sits on my knees. I'm holding a pen, and the pen has such a fine tip that every letter I write looks beautiful to me. The lines are sharp, keen as the blade of a knife.

I leaf through my white, loose leaves, where I've been writing about the green leaves I've noticed starting to open on the trees, small as mouse ears. I'll copy what I've written into my notebook with the pink plastic cover when I have it to hand. Right now, I choose to write on loose-leaf paper. I write not only about the spring and everything that's coming alive, but also about the people I encounter, the colour of their hair, the quirks of their faces, their clothes and what they say when we chat.

It is spring.

These pages aren't ruled and so my writing is crooked and erratic. The lines are bent and curve downwards. The more lines there are, the more this writing looks like a wordfall, plunging over the soft edge of a cliff.

It would have been easier to write in a notebook. Then I could have followed the lines. But my notebook is still in my bag. It would have also been more convenient to sit at a table instead of leaving the pages teetering on my knees. But I keep writing and thinking that maybe on the next page—or the one after—I'll finally be able to record the moment I find what I'm looking for.

Maybe he's standing at his stall. Tall, broad-shouldered and handsome.

I imagine catching sight of him when I get up, draw back the curtains and look out over the market square. But the morning's well underway—I've slept too long and so there's no way for me to know if the newly minted egg seller has already sold a dozen eggs in his dealings with two pretty women from town who he's well acquainted with. But I imagine these sales took place while I was sleeping.

Had I been awake, I might have seen the sunlit square, the harbour, the boats, might've looked down from the window of the Hotel Alfiero and watched my egg seller standing as straight-backed as a soldier, letting the morning light bathe his face. Maybe I'd have seen him ambling around his stall, straightening the little pitcher shaped like a hen with a yellow beak and a red comb, and in that very same moment, he'd have looked up at the hotel, as if he could somehow feel someone watching him.

# AVAILABLE AND COMING SOON FROM PUSHKIN VERTIGO

**Jonathan Ames**

*You Were Never Really Here*
*A Man Named Doll*
*The Wheel of Doll*

**Simone Campos**

*Nothing Can Hurt You Now*

**Zijin Chen**

*Bad Kids*

**Maxine Mei-Fung Chung**

*The Eighth Girl*

**Candas Jane Dorsey**

*The Adventures of Isabel*
*What's the Matter with Mary Jane?*

**Margot Douaihy**

*Scorched Grace*

**Joey Hartstone**

*The Local*

**Seraina Kobler**

*Deep Dark Blue*

**Elizabeth Little**

*Pretty as a Picture*

**Jack Lutz**

*London in Black*

**Steven Maxwell**

*All Was Lost*

**Callum McSorley**

*Squeaky Clean*

**Louise Mey**

*The Second Woman*

**John Kåre Raake**

*The Ice*

**RV Raman**

*A Will to Kill*
*Grave Intentions*
*Praying Mantis*

**Paula Rodríguez**

*Urgent Matters*

**Nilanjana Roy**

*Black River*

**John Vercher**

*Three-Fifths*
*After the Lights Go Out*

**Emma Viskic**

*Resurrection Bay*
*And Fire Came Down*
*Darkness for Light*
*Those Who Perish*

**Yulia Yakovleva**

*Punishment of a Hunter*
*Death of the Red Rider*